Mommy, Mommy

A NOVEL BY

HENRY HACK

Copyright © by 2013 Henry Hack
All rights reserved.

ISBN: 1-4912-3949-2
ISBN 13: 978-1-4912-3949-0

Mommy, Mommy

A DANNY BOYLAND NOVEL

BY HENRY HACK

Dedication

For the gang of kids on 134th Street from the good old days of long ago.

Especially for Willy O'Kane and Alfred Kiider.

And most especially for Georgie Stewart.

Have we ever had as much fun, and enjoyed such great friends, as we did when we were ten years old, and the summer days had no end?

Also by Henry Hack

Danny Boyland Novels
Danny Boy (Salvo Press)
Cases Closed (Dog Ear Publishing)

Harry Cassidy Novels
Cassidy's Corner (Salvo Press)

www.henryhack.com

CHAPTER ONE

Frankie

I still remember the night of the *accident* with absolute clarity although it happened over fourteen years ago. Accident was the official, final ruling of what had happened, but that night I suspected, and the police at the scene suspected, my mother had killed my father – bashed him on the back of his head with a granite doorstop and threw him down the basement stairs. Only nobody could ever prove it, and Mommy sure hadn't confessed.

I remember all the people who showed up at our small house in Levittown, Long Island, on that chilly Wednesday night in October – the police, the doctor and the EMTs. And I most certainly remember the next few days – the wake, the funeral, the investigation, the empty glass and, of course, the note. The note written by Mommy, the words written on it seared into my brain, on the day she left me forever.

• • •

I was nine years old and sound asleep when I awoke to the sound of Mommy screaming. Terror flooded my body as I walked to the stairway and began to creep down the carpeted stairs as the awful shrieking continued. I peered around the banister post at the foot of the stairs and saw Mommy holding her head between her hands, crying, screaming and moaning as she looked down the basement stairwell. I rushed over to her and screamed, "Mommy! Mommy! What happened?"

She grabbed me tightly around the waist and said, "Oh, Frankie, Daddy fell down the stairs. I'm afraid he's hurt bad. He doesn't seem to be moving."

I gasped for air and she released her grip on me. I said, "Was he hitting you again, Mommy?"

"No," she said. "We were getting along fine tonight. He was going to get a bottle of wine from the basement and I was in the kitchen looking for the corkscrew when I heard him fall. It was an accident, Frankie. And when the police and others get here it won't do any good for me – or you – to mention your father and I ever quarreled at all. No mention of yelling or hitting, okay?"

"Sure," I said, "but why would the police come here?"

"I have to call an ambulance and the police have to come when there's a serious accident. Now I have to go down and check your dad before I call. Maybe it's not as bad as it looks."

"Mommy, are you sure he wasn't hurting you?"

"No, no, we were going to have a glass of wine and watch the late news before going up to bed. Let me go check him."

I watched Mommy make her way down the thirteen wooden steps to where my Daddy lay sprawled on the cement floor. When she turned on the basement lights I could see a large puddle of blood under his head. He was not moving. Mommy looked up at me and said, "Oh, Frankie, it's bad. I don't think he's breathing. I have to call the ambulance right away. She ran up the stairs and into the kitchen and grabbed the phone off its cradle. She dialed 9-1-1 and told the operator what happened. When she hung up she turned to me and said, "They're sending the ambulance and the police. Remember what I told you before. No talk of arguing or hitting."

"Yes, Mommy," I said now figuring that maybe this was no accident, that maybe she *pushed* Daddy down those stairs. Not that I could blame her for that, I guess.

Mommy poured a glass of milk for me and we both sat at the kitchen table to wait. Two minutes later we heard the sound of sirens and a minute later they were there – a patrol car from the local precinct and an ambulance. Mommy met them at the front door and directed the officer and the two men from the ambulance to the basement stairs.

They were back in three minutes and asked us to come into the kitchen. The policeman said, "I'm afraid it's bad news. Your husband is dead."

"Oh, my God!" she screamed. "Are you certain?"

"Yes, ma'am," said one of the ambulance guys. "I'm sorry for your loss."

The policeman said, "I'm Officer Daniel Boyland and we have to leave things as they are until we photograph everything and process the scene. I'll go out to my radio to make the notifications, and then I'll come back to get some basic information."

Mommy lowered her head onto her crossed arms on the kitchen table and began to sob. For the first time that night I began to cry. My father was dead and that fact began to sink in. Although he was very abusive to my mother he rarely hit me or even yelled at me. As I started to remember going to ballgames, the beach, the city and vacations, his loss hit me harder. I hoped Mommy was telling the truth. I hoped she didn't kill him.

Officer Boyland returned and sat at the kitchen table between me and Mommy. He stroked her back and asked if she was all right. Mommy raised her head – her eyes were bloodshot – and she said, "Yes, but let me get a glass of water."

She got the water and more milk for me and sat down again. "What do you need, Officer?" she asked.

"Just some preliminary information – the detectives will be here soon for more details."

"Detectives?" I asked.

"Yes, son," he said. "All sudden deaths, accidental or otherwise, must be investigated. Now, ma'am, what is your husband's full name?"

"Jim...James R. Chandler. And this is our son, Frankie. My name is Angela."

Officer Boyland smiled at me and said to Mommy, "Please briefly describe what happened to Jim tonight."

Mommy told the officer the same story she had told me about the wine and hearing Daddy fall down the stairs.

"And what about you, Frankie?" he asked. "What can you tell me?"

"I woke up because I heard Mommy screaming. She told me Daddy fell down the stairs."

Officer Boyland looked at me with squinted eyes. He said, "Frankie, I know you are tired, but I'd like you to stay awake so you can talk to the detectives when they get here. Can you do that for me?"

"I think so," I said.

"Good lad," he said with a smile.

The officer got up from the table and went over to the men from the ambulance. When his back was turned, Mommy whispered, "Remember, say nothing of arguing."

I nodded my head. The doorbell rang and Officer Boyland let in two more men. They were dressed in suits and ties.

Officer Boyland introduced Detectives Wallace Mason and Joseph Giano to Mommy and me. Mason was a big guy with a stern look on his face and seemed to be in charge. He said, "Let's go have a look, Joe. Danny, you come down with us."

The three policemen went downstairs and came back after about five minutes. Mason said, "After the medical examiner and crime scene photographers arrive and check out the scene we'll be able to remove your husband's body. He has to be autopsied tomorrow – all accidental deaths have to."

"I understand," Mommy said, while I was wondering what that word *autopsied* meant.

"You should be able to have the funeral parlor pick him up in the afternoon," Detective Giano said with a sympathetic smile. "Now we know you already told Officer Boyland what happened, but please repeat it for us."

Mommy told the detectives the same story she told me and the officer. When she finished Mason said, "Did he cry out before he fell? Or during his fall?"

"No," Mommy said, "not a sound."

"Did you hear anything, Frankie?" Giano asked.

"I heard my Mommy screaming. That's what woke me up," I said.

"Mrs. Chandler," Mason said, "were you and your husband arguing prior to him heading for the basement?"

"No," she said. "Why do you ask?"

Mommy gave me a glance and the two detectives glanced at each other, too.

"I was just wondering if he approached the top of the stairs in anger."

"No, he did not."

"You never argued with your husband?" Giano asked.

"I didn't say that. Of course we argued. I'm pretty sure all married couples occasionally argue."

"I'm sure you are correct, Mrs. Chandler," Mason said. "On those occasions when you *did* argue, did you two ever get physical?"

"No, only verbal," Mommy said shooting me another look.

"What did you argue about?"

"Mostly about money – there never seemed to be enough. We rent this house and wanted a place of our own, but saving up enough for a down payment was difficult."

"Do you both work?" Mason asked.

"Yes, Jim was a junior draftsman at Canfield Engineering in Manhattan. I work as a school aide in the early morning through the lunch hour at Maywood High School here in Levittown."

There was a knock at the door and Officer Boyland let a man in who introduced himself as Doctor Woodson, a deputy medical examiner. He went down into the basement with Detective

Mason. Just then two more men came in, "Crime scene guys," Boyland said and they also went downstairs.

They were down there a long time and when they all came up Detective Mason said, "We're just about done here, Mrs. Chandler. Let's move to the den while they remove your husband's body."

The ambulance guys took Daddy away and the doctor and the crime scene guys left too. Detective Giano said, "All we need Mrs. Chandler is your written statement. We can do it now if you are up to it, or tomorrow afternoon in our office if you prefer."

"I'd like to do it now," she said. "Can I put Frankie to bed first?"

"Sure," Giano said. He knelt down in front of me and said, "I'm very sorry about your Dad, Frankie. Try to be strong for your Mom. She'll need you by her, especially the next few days."

"I will," I told him. "I love my Mommy."

"While you're putting Frankie to bed," Boyland said, "is there anyone you'd like us to notify? Maybe someone to come over and stay with you awhile?"

"No," Mommy said. "There are no nearby relatives, and we really don't know the neighbors that well. Frankie and I will be fine."

Mommy brought me up to bed and tucked me in. I fell asleep thinking about Daddy and the brand new bicycle he got me last Christmas. I hoped Mommy would be okay. I hoped she hadn't pushed him down the stairs. I hoped she wouldn't have to go to jail and leave me all alone.

CHAPTER TWO

Danny

I got the call to respond to 7721 Linden Street, Levittown for an aided case. The dispatcher said, "Possible serious physical injury. Ambulance is also responding."

I logged the date and time of the call on my clipboard, switched on my roof-rack lights, hit the siren and sped to the house. I was there in a few minutes and the ambulance pulled up right behind me. I was met at the door by a nice-looking, but obviously distraught woman who identified herself as Angela Chandler. The not unpleasant odor of garlic, probably remaining from their dinner, reached my nose. I noticed a young boy seated at the kitchen table as Angela directed me and the AMT ambulance driver to the basement where she said her husband had fallen down the whole flight of stairs.

We examined the body and it didn't take us long to determine that Mr. Chandler was dead, most likely from hitting his head on the hard cement floor. One of his legs was twisted behind him and appeared to be broken. We came upstairs to give Mrs. Chandler the grim news, and as I reached the top of the stairs, I noticed it – a large, highly-polished gray block of marble or granite that was being utilized as a doorstop to keep the basement door open. It was about four inches high, eight inches long and two inches thick – very similar to the dimensions of an ordinary brick – and it looked as if it weighed a few solid pounds. I resisted the urge to pick it up to examine it, but knew it would have to be checked out at a later time.

Angela Chandler seemed genuinely upset over the news of her husband's death and the boy who she told us was her son Frankie, began to cry. But something was not quite right. Angela seemed disturbed when I told her detectives and crime scene personnel would have to show up and Frankie, well Frankie just seemed to parrot what "Mommy told me," with little emotion. I kept thinking about that heavy block of granite.

After I made all the notifications on the radio, I called the detective squad on my cell phone and filled in Wally Mason, who was catching cases this tour, on the situation and my suspicions. When he pressed me for particulars I couldn't give him any. "Okay, Danny," he said. "We'll kick it around afterwards. Me and Joe will be there soon."

When Wally – whose size and gruff demeanor could be intimidating – and Joe Giano arrived, and we were safely in the basement and out of earshot, Wally said, "Well, my young rookie police officer have you thought of any particulars for your suspicions?"

"Yeah, Wally," I said not upset over the rookie label for that was what I was after all. "Angela seems a bit defensive and Frankie is kinda…well, creepy."

"Are those the elements of a crime heretofore unknown to me?" he asked with a serious look on his face.

I had to laugh and said, "No, but the heavy doorstop at the top of the stairs could be a murder weapon."

"Well, Sherlock," Giano said with a grin, "we will most certainly check that out very carefully."

"Before we left the office," Mason said, "we ran this address through the database. There are no reports of domestic disputes or violence here, nor have there ever been any occurrences or complaints that warranted a police response."

"And," Giano said, "neither Angela nor James Chandler have any arrests or priors or complaints against them – not even a traffic ticket."

"That doesn't mean she didn't clock him with that brick though, does it?" I asked.

"No, it does not," Mason said, "but let's not form an opinion until Joe and I speak to the grieving widow, and until the medical examiner has his look-see, and until crime scene processes the area. Is that okay with you Detective, uh, I mean, *Police Officer* Boyland?"

"Sure," I said, feeling pretty well shot down.

"Good, Danny Boy," he said referring to the name conferred upon me practically the minute I entered the Police Academy almost a year ago. He smiled and there was no sarcasm in his voice when he said it. Wallace Mason was a damn good detective, albeit a tough, rough-around-the-edges one, and I'd best be served by just keeping my mouth shut and listening and observing him and Joe work. I vowed to do just that – that is after I couldn't resist silently pointing out the doorstop to him as we reached the top of the stairs. Joe grinned and whispered, "The butler did it, in the study, with a brick."

I listened carefully as Wally and Joe interviewed Angela and Frankie and I caught, on two occasions, Angela shoot a look at her son, a look that said, "Say nothing," or "Back me up on this." I knew that both detectives also noticed those glances. Maybe this rookie was onto something.

When the crime scene guys came, Wally Mason went with them toward the basement. I was certain he would now tell them to inspect a certain block of gray granite *very* carefully.

After Doc Woodson and the body and the crime scene techs left, Wally and Joe let Angela put Frankie to bed and then they took her statement. We all gave her our condolences once again and left her to her grief and loneliness. As we were walking to our cars Wally Mason turned to me and said, "Come back to the stationhouse and meet us in our office. Doc Woodson and the crime scene guys are en-route, too. We're all going to have a little pow-wow on this caper."

"Are you now thinking this was not an accident?" I asked.

"We'll see, Sherlock," Joe Giano said.

● ● ●

When we were all assembled in the detective's squad room Wally Mason said, "Doc, could you give us your opinion on this? And then you can get out of here and back into bed."

"It appeared to me that his death was caused by the fall – specifically the blow his head received when it hit the basement floor."

"Could Chandler have been hit in the head by a heavy object causing him to fall down the stairs?" Mason asked.

Woodson raised his eyebrows in surprise and said, "You think this was not an accident?"

"We don't know," Giano said.

"Got a possible weapon?"

"Maybe. A heavy granite doorstop. And maybe Bob Stans from crime scene here can tell us what he thinks."

Stans put on a pair of glasses and looked at his notes. He said, "I examined the doorstop using binocular magnifying glasses. It has a very smooth polished surface and I was unable to detect any bloodstains, or hair or fibers, or any other material on it."

"How about fingerprints?" Giano asked. "Should be a good surface for them."

"Good surface, indeed, but not even a smudge. Sorry, guys, but if you think she crowned him with that block, I couldn't find any evidence of it."

I was sorely disappointed by Officer Stans's findings, but bit my lip and said nothing. Wally must have read my mind because he asked Stans exactly the question I had wanted to burst out with.

"Bob, could any evidence on that block be easily washed off?"

"Very easily. The only thing I can suggest is to retrieve it and submit it to the Lab, but I doubt if they could find anything either."

The doctor got up to leave and said, "Maybe I can find something at the post-mortem in the morning. Anyone want to join me? Company is always appreciated at the morgue."

"I'll be there," Mason said. "Nine o'clock?"

"Nine-thirty," Woodson said. "See you then. Goodnight all."

"Uh, Doc," I said. "Would it be okay if I observed, too? I've not seen a complete autopsy yet."

"Sure," he said with a smile. "I'll be glad to further your forensic education."

"Danny," Giano said, "I don't know if your boss will approve overtime for that."

"No problem. I'll be there on my own time, in civvies," I said.

"I see, Danny Boy," Mason said, "that you are all juiced up over this caper. I'm starting to get that way, too."

"Really?"

"Yeah, there was something going on between Angela and Frankie all right. Something stinks here."

I was relieved to hear that from Mason and we broke up with a lot of suspicions and questions that might, with any luck, be answered in the morning.

• • •

My first autopsy was not a pleasant experience – neither was my fiftieth one many years later – but, despite the sights, sounds and smells, I got through it with nothing more than wobbly knees. When the gruesome task was over and the morgue attendant was sewing up the corpse of James Chandler, Doc Woodson said, "Well, that does it. One wound to the head and a broken left femur."

"Nothing suspicious at all?" Wally asked.

"Nothing to prove that it didn't happen the way the wife said it happened."

"Only one wound on the head," I said. "Maybe she didn't hit him with that doorstop. Maybe she just pushed him down the stairs. Or he could have hit his head on the same place that she hit him with the block."

"Or maybe she poisoned him," Mason said, and he wasn't smiling at all.

"I'll let you know the results of the toxicology reports as soon as they are complete," Woodson said, "but I didn't see any evidence of poisoning in his organs."

"Okay, I know when I'm beat, Doc. I'll close this out as accidental pending tox results. But I'm still suspicious about this. How about you, Danny?"

"Still suspicious, too."

"Suspicions are not proof gentlemen," Woodson said. "Be happy it's an accident – a lot less paperwork. I'll have my secretary call Mrs. Chandler so that she can have the funeral parlor come get the body."

We left the morgue without a word, Wally heading toward his unmarked squad car and I for my private vehicle. We went our different ways, but I knew our thoughts about Angela Chandler were not different at all.

● ● ●

The tox report came back negative and Wally Mason officially closed the case as "Death-Accidental." He had conferred with the Homicide Squad and they agreed with his conclusion and left the case with the Nine-Eight squad. If it was not a *whodunit*, they were not interested.

Jimmy Chandler's wake and funeral were sparsely attended – Wally had made an appearance at both – and things went back to normal for Angela and Frankie. Normal lasted only a brief few days though, as I found out on the following Tuesday when I was patrolling on a day tour. The radio dispatcher said, "Car 9806, respond to 7721 Linden Street, Levittown – unknown trouble."

The Chandler's house! What could have happened now? I punched the accelerator and was there in four minutes. Everything looked normal, from the neatly-trimmed lawn to the closed front door, as I pulled to the curb and jumped out of the car. I knocked on the door, and as if he had been waiting on the other side, Frankie Chandler opened it and looked up at me with what I could only describe as a look of utter despair. His eyes were wide-open but there was no life in them. I said, "Frankie, what's the matter?"

He sniffed and blinked his eyes, obviously on the verge of tears. He took my hand and silently led me into the kitchen. He pointed to the table. I saw only an empty glass, but as I got closer I saw a piece of paper with writing on it. When Frankie broke his silence he startled me. "It's from my Mommy," he said. "She's gone."

My fingers trembled as I picked up the note. I read,

Dear Frankie,

I'm sorry but I had to leave. Call the police at 9-1-1. They will know what to do. Maybe someday we will see each other again and then you will understand why I did this. Until then, I love you.
Mommy

That heartless bitch! Now I *knew* she murdered her husband. And now to abandon her only child! I hadn't been on the Force for long, but I was certain it would be a long time before I came across another cruel, cold-blooded act such as Angela had just committed. I put down the note and said, "Was this all she left?"

Frankie nodded yes. I looked at the empty glass and said, "Sit down, Frankie. I'll get you some milk. Then I have to call Detective Mason to come over. Okay?"

"Okay," he said.

I paced around the house while waiting for Wally to arrive, my attention focusing on the shiny granite doorstop which now sat adjacent to the wall next to the closed basement door. I was sure I would have no trouble convincing Wally to take it with us this time when we left.

He arrived in ten minutes and I pointed out the note to him. He said, "What time did you get home from school, Frankie?"

"Same as always, around three."

"And mommy wasn't here?"

"No. I called for her…uh, I yelled, 'Mommy, I'm home', but she didn't answer. I went into the kitchen. Mommy always has a glass of milk and cookies for me, but they weren't there. Uh, the glass was, but it was empty. And then I saw the note under it."

"Did you check around the house to look for her?"

"No, I just did what the note said. I called 9-1-1 and waited. Officer Boyland got here right away."

"Can you show us mommy's bedroom?"

"Sure, it's upstairs."

We followed Frankie upstairs and Wally looked at me shaking his head and mouthing the word, "Unbelievable!"

A quick check of the room determined that most all of Angela's clothes and personal effects were gone. Jimmy Chandler's suits and jackets and slacks remained neatly arrayed on one side of the large closet.

"Frankie," Mason said, "what kind of car does mommy have?"

"It's a green Chevy, but it wasn't in the driveway when I got home."

We went back downstairs and Wally picked up the phone and called Central Detectives. "I want a crime scene team at this address. And give me a DMV check on any vehicles owned by a James or Angela Chandler also at this address."

Central came back with a 1986 Chevrolet, dark green, four-door sedan registered to James Chandler. Plate number was FSV-7624.

"Thanks, Wally said. "I want you to put out a multi-state alarm for that vehicle and its driver – Angela Chandler, age 31, five-foot five-inches, a hundred fifteen pounds, dark brown hair and eyes. Wanted for murder and child abandonment."

I knew, and I knew that Wally knew, the murder charge was really pushing it, but that charge would certainly get every cop's attention from Maine to Florida.

"Frankie," Wally said, "do you have any relatives, uh…aunts or uncles that I can call to come over to be with you?"

He shook his head no.

"How about grandparents?"

Again, a shake no.

"Did mommy have an address book with telephone numbers of her friends?" Wally asked.

Frankie walked over to the kitchen counter by the wall telephone and looked it over. "It's a red book. It usually was on the counter, but I don't see it now."

I noticed a name and number on a piece of paper stuck on the side of the refrigerator with a magnet. Frankie, do you know who Mrs. Mary Bennett is?"

"She's the landlady."

"Frankie," Wally said, "would you mind going into the den and watching TV for a while? I have to discuss some things with Officer Boyland."

"Okay," he said and shuffled away.

Wally was livid. "That poor kid. A week ago he was part of a family and now he's an orphan. That rotten murdering bitch. I guess we have no choice but to get Child Protective Services over here right away."

"That's too bad," I said. "That system sucks. If Angela isn't found, Frankie's future will not be a happy one."

"Sounds like you speak from experience, Danny Boy."

"Oh, yeah," I said. "A story for another time."

"I see Crime Scene pulling up," Wally said, "and I'll tell you this – that fucking doorstop will leave with them this time."

CHAPTER THREE

Angela

It was well past two in the morning when the detectives finally left, and I felt I had toughed it out pretty well despite their questions about the arguments that Jim and I had, or didn't have, engaged in during our marriage. I was sure I had convinced them Jim's death was caused by what I had claimed – an accidental fall – and that they left seemingly satisfied with that scenario.

I went upstairs to check on Frankie. He was sound asleep. I went back downstairs and over to the basement stairwell, flicked on the light and went down. I stepped over to the congealing puddle of blood, now giving off a coppery odor, and walked over to the small twelve-bottle wooden wine rack. I selected a bottle of Shiraz and took it upstairs to the kitchen. As I extracted the cork I wondered if this bottle would have been the one Jim was going to choose had he gotten this far, that is if I hadn't crushed his head in with the doorstop and pushed him down the stairs.

The kitchen still smelled faintly of garlic, tomato sauce and the veal that we had for dinner. Veal parmigiana, a rare treat due to the cost of the meat, was Jim's favorite meal, and since it would be his last, why not go for it? I poured a full glass of the dark, red wine and raised it out and up to toast my dear, late husband. "Here's to you, you bastard," I whispered. "May you rot in hell." I took a long swallow of the wine and sat down to think things out. Right now, it appeared I had gotten away with it. I didn't know if any of the cops made a connection between the doorstop and its possible employment as a murder weapon, but even if they did I was certain that I had cleaned it very thoroughly. But to be sure, I would do that once more.

I went over to the basement door and brought the heavy block back to the kitchen and placed it in the sink turning the hot water on to flow over it. I scrubbed all its surfaces for a good five minutes using dish detergent and bleach, then rinsed it thoroughly and dried it. After inspecting it I put it back in its place. I was bone-weary tired, and knew I should clean up Jim's blood before it dried. But then, I realized, it really didn't matter. My plans did not include the condition of this basement anymore.

• • •

I slept until eleven the next morning and when I got up and looked in on Frankie he was still sleeping on his back. As I looked at the poor kid a picture of Jim came to me; they looked so much alike – a spittin' image as the old cliché goes. I hoped that good looks were all he shared with my late husband. I hoped he wouldn't grow up mean and nasty – a wife beater like Jim, and my father. And I hoped that he would earn enough money to *buy* his wife a house instead of renting the cheapest place in the neighborhood.

I wished this all for Frankie because I knew I'd never be around to find out.

Drinking my second cup of coffee I reflected on last night's events. Had I covered all my bases? Had I slipped up somewhere? Would they find anything after the autopsy? I glanced up at the wall clock and realized it was probably over by now. Had all my careful planning before the murder – a preemptive strike I knew I had to make – have a flaw in it? I didn't think so. And I didn't doubt the fact – then or now – that I *had* to kill Jim. The verbal abuse had escalated to physical abuse and I knew where that would lead – to my death. Just as my father had finally killed my mother. Way back then I had vowed to never let what happened to her happen to me. I would not endure what she endured all those long suffering years, and I hadn't. I began to re-hash last night once more when Frankie walked into the kitchen rubbing the sleep out of his eyes. I got up and hugged him and said, "You slept a long time. That was good."

"I'm hungry," he said.

I fixed him some scrambled eggs and toast and a big glass of orange juice and he wolfed it down and went into the den to watch TV. I didn't press him to talk about his father and I was happy he didn't bring it up either. I poured a final half-cup of coffee and got back to recalling last night's chain of events. I needed to go through them one more time just to be sure that I hadn't made a mistake.

I had put Frankie to bed after dinner, came back downstairs and suggested to Jim that he get a bottle of wine to "celebrate."

We had had only a small glass with dinner from a three-day old bottle that had a third left in it. He had come home from work that day and informed me he had gotten a good review, but only a small bump in salary. Big deal, a ten dollar raise! But he was in a good mood and insisted he was next in line for a promotion to journeyman draftsman probably within a year. I had smiled and said, "That's great news, Jim," while thinking that the cheap outfit he worked for would give him another big ten bucks a week for it.

I followed Jim to the basement door. He opened it and placed the granite doorstop in front of it to hold it open and started down the stairs. I picked up the block with both hands not deterred by its bulk or weight – I had practiced with it – and hit him hard on the back of his head. He said, "Oh," and fell to his side on the handrail. I pulled him upright and shoved him down the stairs. I picked up the doorstop once more and went down to make sure he was dead. If not, I would have hit him again to finish the job. Fortunately, I didn't have to do that. He was definitely not breathing.

I came back upstairs, washed and dried the doorstop and placed it back in front of the basement door. I rubbed some table salt into my eyes and began screaming until Frankie awoke and came downstairs. Then I checked Jim out and called the police. I had already gone over that part of the evening many times. Yes, I believe I had it wrapped up neat and clean. The next few days would tell, but I vowed to keep my composure through them all. Then I would be home free – finally.

The phone rang and my bravado evaporated. I picked it up and answered. A female voice said, "Hello, Mrs. Chandler? This is Elle Masters, the medical examiner's assistant. You can call your funeral director now and tell him it's okay to pick up your husband's body."

"Thank you," I said. "I'll make that call now."

I breathed a sigh of relief and hung up the phone.

● ● ●

Hardly anyone showed up for Jimmy's wake and funeral. I was an only child and my father was in jail serving twenty-five years to life for murdering my mother. Had they both been able, however, they probably wouldn't have come anyway. But then they would have been happy to see him dead, so it would have been a toss-up. They had been vehemently opposed to our marriage. Unless Jimmy found a way to miraculously change into an Italian Roman Catholic he would never be accepted into the Capozzi clan. And when our marriage took place in a Lutheran church, I was as good as dead in their eyes.

Jimmy's parents were not much better than mine and they didn't show up either. Wealthy world travelers they had disinherited their only son when he chose to marry a "low-class Wop" from a poor family. We had not heard from them – not even a card – in over four years, and my attempts to reach them about their son's death were in vain. They were probably off to Paris or Vienna, or who knows where again, and the messages I left on their machine at their home in Colorado were not returned.

Only a few friends from Jim's office and my school came to pay their respects at the one-day viewing and funeral service and he was put in the ground on Saturday, October 15. I sent Frankie back to school on Monday and took two bereavement days off from work. They were very understanding and encouraged me to take the whole week off. Little did they know I would never be back.

I drove to the bank and withdrew all the money from our checking and savings accounts – a whopping $2,700 – and filled up the gas tank on the way home. When Frankie came home that afternoon I gave him his usual glass of milk and plate of cookies. He took a swallow of his milk and said, "What will we do now, Mommy?"

"I don't know," I said. "It will take awhile to figure things out."

"I miss Daddy," he said.

I smiled and said, "So do I, Frankie." It was a lie, of course, but the poor kid was only nine years old and had been in a fairly good relationship with his father. At least Jim hadn't gotten around to beating *him* yet. What I didn't tell Frankie was that I had already figured out what we would do – or at least what *I* would do. Frankie would be left on his own. I felt a little guilt over that. He wasn't a bad kid, but after all he wasn't even my own child, which made even that little bit of guilt fade into the background.

• • •

On Tuesday morning, after seeing Frankie off on the school bus, I began to pack my things in suitcases and boxes. I got them all into the trunk of the Chevy, except my dresses and coats which I laid down across the back seat. I then returned inside the house for a last look and for my final task – a brief note for Frankie telling him what to do. I put the note under his milk glass, locked the kitchen door and went out the front door locking that behind me, leaving this crummy house forever.

I backed out of the driveway and headed for Interstate 495 – the Long Island Expressway. I reached it in ten minutes and drove west to freedom and a new life. I was almost thirty-two years old and all I had was $2,700 and an eight-year old car with over 100,000 miles on it. Jim's meager life insurance policy just covered the funeral expenses and there were no IRA's or 401(k)'s between us. But I had a new start and I promised myself I would make a better life for myself – much better.

• • •

Since it was not yet rush hour I went over the Williamsburg Bridge into Manhattan and crossed downtown on Canal Street, through the Holland Tunnel and onto Interstate 78 to Interstate 81. I got off at the Chambersburg, Pennsylvania exit and found a used car lot where I traded in the Chevy plus $500 for a five-year old Honda Civic with a new Pennsylvania tag and only 43,000 miles on it.

I continued south on the interstate always observing the speed limit and reached the bottom of Virginia in full darkness. I ate a burger and fries from the drive through at a fast food place located on the corner of a large shopping mall. After dinner I drove around the mall's parking lot and found what I was looking for after five minutes – a dark area with an open slot between two vehicles. I unscrewed my new tag and replaced it with the Virginia tags from the car parked to my left. After dumping my old New York tags and the new Pennsylvania one into a large, smelly dumpster at the rear of the mall, I drove off. Four hours later I pulled up to a motel just inside Tennessee. I paid the clerk in cash and registered with a phony name. I planned to go right to bed, be up with the sun and back on the road the following morning. I should arrive in California in four days.

• • •

Sleep would not come. I had been focused on my plans and my escape to a new life, but the old life would not leave so easily. The questions and recriminations shot through my mind – Did I really have to kill Jim? Could counseling have helped? Was his abuse really that bad? And Frankie – what would happen to him? No father and now no mother. When would he find out I wasn't his real mother? How would it affect him?

And finally, oh, my God, what have I done? Should I go back and re-claim Frankie? Or was it already too late?

I lay there tossing and turning until the sun came up. I took a shower and checked out grabbing a coffee and a bagel from the breakfast area to take with me on the road. I approached Interstate 81 and hesitated – do I go north back home or south to Interstate 40 and points west. I took a sip of the coffee and drove up the entrance ramp and onto the interstate. The sun was rising brightly on my left. California, here I come.

CHAPTER FOUR

Danny

Wally Mason's eyes focused on the granite doorstop but he said, "We'd better check for other possible weapons while we're here."

Frankie was still watching TV, seemingly engrossed in SpongeBob Squarepants, so I headed upstairs and Wally went down to the basement. I checked the two upstairs bedrooms, small study and bathroom for other possible weapons, but there were no items that fit the bill. There was a Little League baseball bat in Frankie's closet, but I couldn't see Angela taking it, using it, and returning it while Frankie slept. I looked it over anyway and it was clean and shiny with no visible stains on its silvery surface.

Wally was coming up the basement stairs as I returned to the main floor. "Hardly any tools down there. I guess Jimmy wasn't the handy-man type. The only thing that may have been used as a weapon is this hammer."

He showed me a small claw hammer that he held in his hand with a rag wrapped loosely around the handle.

"The place is a rental," I said. "I guess the landlord fixes what needs to be fixed."

"It doesn't look like there's anything on this thing," Wally said, "but I'll have the Lab check it anyway while they check out the doorstop."

Mason went through the kitchen cabinets and drawers and discovered the red address book mentioned by Frankie. He flipped through it and noted only about a dozen entries and slipped it into his jacket pocket. He was about to go out to the garage when the doorbell rang and Wally opened it and let in a woman. He smiled and said, "Thanks for coming so soon, Pam. We have a case for you."

Pamela Saunders was introduced to me as a veteran case worker in the Child Protective Services area of the State's Social Services department. An attractive blond in her mid to late thirties, she gave the appearance of a harried, worn-out, over-worked civil servant who had seen a lot of tragedy over the years. Mason briefed her on the situation then led her into the den where Frankie was engrossed in the TV.

"Hi, Frankie," she said, smiling at the sad-eyed boy. "I'm Miss Saunders. Can we talk a while? Just you and me?"

I asked Wally if he wanted me to check out the garage and he said yes while he would give one more check to the rest of the downstairs area. The garage was small and there were no tools hanging on the walls. Several cartons of old toys were on the clean cement floor along with a new, blue boy's bicycle resting on its kickstand. A basket of small garden tools and a few packets of seeds rested on a shelf. No obvious murder weapons here.

As I returned inside the house Pam was just coming out of the den. She said, "Frankie claims he knows of no relatives who could take him in, so I guess he's got to come with me."

"Are you going to place him in the State Home?" I asked.

"Yes, until we locate his mother or a relative who's willing to take him in."

"Poor kid. What a fucking world."

"You seem to be taking this personal," Pam said.

"Damn right, I am. I was once a ward of the State of New York. I'm intimately familiar with the *Home* and the joys of foster care."

Wally looked at me and said, "I guess that's what you meant before about a story for another time. Maybe we can locate Angela soon and re-unite her with Frankie. Maybe she's not a murderer. Maybe she just snapped over the death of her husband and the thought of having to raise a kid alone with no money. Maybe…"

"Wally," Pam interrupted. "Frankie just told me that his parents argued a lot – loudly. He told me that Daddy hit Mommy many times, too. He told me that on the night of the accident he thought Mommy was screaming because Daddy was hitting her again."

"Murdering bitch," Wally said immediately reversing his previous speculations.

"Let's go tell Frankie what's going to happen," Pam said.

After she finished explaining things Frankie asked, "What about my toys and bike?"

"I'm afraid you can't take them all. Only your clothes and a couple of toys."

"But my bike! I just got it last Christmas," he said as the tears began to roll down his cheeks.

"Don't worry, Frankie," I said. "If it's okay with Miss Saunders I'll take the rest of your toys and your bike and store them in the storage closet in my apartment until we find your mom."

"That would be fine with me," Pam said. "Is that all right with you, Frankie?"

"Yes," he said, smiling at me. "Thanks."

We gathered up Frankie's clothes and put them in Saunders' car and watched them drive away. Back in the house Mason picked up the doorstop with a paper towel and placed it in a big zip-lock plastic bag. "I'm going to have the experts in the Lab go over this with every test in their arsenal. I *know* she popped him with this."

"Yeah, but that won't help Frankie if you ever hang a murder rap on her, will it?"

Wally put his arm on my shoulder and said, "No, it won't. That kid will have the words on this note burned into his brain forever. Let me call the landlady and let her know what's going on. Then we can get out of here."

Mrs. Bennett told Mason she would come over in the morning to check the place out. "The rent's paid up until the end of the month," she said. "Too bad the boy couldn't stay there with someone."

"There doesn't seem to be anyone, Mrs. Bennett," he said. "We'll lock the place up when we leave."

"Thank you, Detective," she said. "Oh, please turn the heat down to fifty-five?"

Mason turned down the thermostat and left with the note, the address book, the hammer and the doorstop. I took Frankie's toys and bike in my patrol car. "I'll see if I can track down a relative," Mason said.

"Keep me in the loop, okay?"

"Sure, I'll call you tomorrow."

• • •

Wally Mason called me in off patrol at eleven the next morning. When I arrived in his office, Pam Saunders was already there. We poured coffee and waited for Wally to begin. He did not look happy. "I went through the phone book and found a number for Angela's mother and father in Brooklyn, but it was crossed out."

"Both dead?" Pam asked.

"No, just the mother – Maria. Dear dad is serving a life sentence upstate for killing her," he said holding up Cono Capozzi's rap sheet.

"I guess Angela didn't want the same fate," I said.

"I guess not," Wally said, "which lends additional weight to the fact that she probably killed him."

"What about Frankie's other grandparents?" Pam asked.

"Unable to contact them. The local police department in Colorado said the Chandler's notified them a month ago that they would be travelling in Europe for three to four months."

"Any other blood relatives?" I asked.

"Not in this book," he said, tapping it on his desk. "Only a few not-too-close friends from their jobs."

"So I guess Frankie becomes a ward of the state until Grandma and Grandpa come home," I said.

"Maybe I can try to locate them through Interpol. If they use their charge cards over there, it may not be that difficult." Wally said.

"Okay," Pam said. "I'll call the shelter and tell them to make the arrangements to transfer Frankie upstate. I hope Interpol finds his grandparents or somebody finds Angela real soon."

"Me, too," I said with a shudder as Frankie's future as a ward of the state for the next eight and a half years flashed through my mind. The picture was grim indeed.

• • •

A week later Wally Mason called me with some good news. They had not located Frankie's traveling grandparents yet, but Detective Paul McKay from the Blood Analysis Section of the Police Lab had gotten a hit. Wally said, "Paul, using a high-powered microscope, found a slight chip on one of the granite block's corners. Within the chipped surface was a tiny fissure with a small amount of dark-red crust embedded in the bottom of it. He extracted it and was able to get a DNA profile."

"Was it Jim Chandler's blood?" I asked.

"Bingo!" he said. "An identical DNA match."

"What now?"

"I go see the Homicide Squad and set up a meeting with the District Attorney. I try to get Angela indicted in absentia for the murder of her husband. That way we can get the warrant into NCIC, the national criminal database. If she ever gets stopped or background checked, it will pop up and she'll be arrested."

"Any chance of me being at that meeting?" I asked.

MOMMY, MOMMY

"It would be a little irregular, but I'd like you there, Danny. I like your interest and enthusiasm. I'll see if I can clear it with my boss and your boss. I'll let you know."

"Thanks, Wally. I appreciate it."

• • •

True to his word, Wally got the necessary permissions for me to attend the meeting set for two days later at ten o'clock in the morning. I was working a four-to-twelve tour and, although allowed to attend, I would do so on my own time. My commanding officer, Inspector Jack Switzer, while appreciating my eagerness and interest in this case, did not appreciate it highly enough to throw me a couple of hours of overtime pay. It mattered not at all to me. I was really enjoying this investigation and was motivated to help do something to make Frankie's life a little easier. But now – if Angela Chandler was indeed a murderer – his hopes of being re-united with her would be dashed.

At the meeting Wally Mason introduced me to Detective Willy Edwards, a smiling gray-haired investigator from the Nassau Homicide Squad, and to Assistant DA Jesse Regan, Chief of the Homicide Bureau. We all listened patiently, without interruption, as Wally went over the details of the case. When he finished he handed over the lab report and the autopsy report to Regan with a satisfied smile on his face.

Regan laid the reports on his desk, looked at Wally grim-faced through his steel-rimmed glasses and said, "This is it? What else do you have?"

"Whaddya mean?" Wally said. "What the hell else do you want?"

"How about a signed confession from Angela?"

"Very funny. You got the murder weapon and Jim Chandler's blood is on it. That should be plenty for you to present this case to the Grand Jury."

"Really? What do you think, Detective Edwards?"

"We have some problems here, Wally."

"Like what, Willy?" he asked, his annoyance obvious in his voice.

"Jim Chandler lives there. He could have cut himself on that chipped corner once or twice when he picked it up on any number of occasions to block the door. Or Angela could have gotten Jim's blood on her fingers when she went down to check on him and transferred it to the block when she moved it."

"Wait a minute," Wally said. "Chandler blocked the door open prior to going down the stairs."

"Says who?" Regan asked. "And if he did, why weren't his fingerprints on it?"

"Because Angela washed the block clean, that's why," Wally said through gritted teeth.

"Did she admit that to you?" Regan asked.

Wally just glared. I sat there just observing and listening and chose, wisely, to remain silent.

Removing his glasses and softening his usual officious tone of voice, Jesse Regan said, "Wally, I agree with you that she probably did it. I'm sure Willy Edwards and Danny Boyland agree that she did it. But we have to find a way to *prove* it."

"She fucking skipped town didn't she?" Wally asked.

"Yes," Willy said, "which confirms our belief, but doesn't provide proof."

"What do you think, Danny?" Regan asked startling me as all eyes turned my way. I thought for a few seconds and then said, "I don't like your conclusions, but I'm not experienced enough to argue against them."

"Then we're done here?" Wally asked. "No grand jury presentation?"

"No," Regan said. "There's just not enough."

"At least we still have the original alarm out on her," I said. "Maybe if she gets picked up, Wally and Willy can get her to confess."

"Unfortunately, we don't even have that," said a very dejected Wally Mason. "When my boss found out what I sent out, he made me cancel the murder part, and the county won't extradite for a misdemeanor child abandonment charge."

There was silence in the room and there was obviously no more to say so Willy Edwards said, "C'mon Wally, I'll buy you a cup of coffee."

"I need more than coffee," he said. "This system sucks. Angela got away with murder."

"She isn't the first," Willy said, "and she won't be the last."

I knew how Wally felt right now, because I felt the same way – beaten.

CHAPTER FIVE

Frankie

I was sitting alone in a room next to Miss Saunders' office wondering what was going to happen to me now. I was getting hungry and just then she came in with a tray of food and a glass of milk and set it down on the desk in front of me. "I figured you'd be hungry around now," she said. "It's almost six o'clock. Is that the time you normally eat at home?"

I nodded my head yes and she told me to go ahead and dig in. Then she said, "I have a son a couple of years older than you and a daughter about the same age. I have to go home and feed them, too. Someone will take you to the children's shelter to sleep tonight and I'll come over there in the morning to see you. Try to sleep well, Frankie. Good night."

"Good night," I said. "Thank you."

I ate my sandwich and potato salad and drank the milk. There was no TV in the room so I just sat and waited and thought about my mother and the note she left me. I knew all the words by heart, especially the last ones where she said maybe we would see each other again someday and that she loved me. I knew she would come back for me when she could. I just knew it. But now she was probably afraid to because of the police. I know they think she killed Daddy, and I think maybe she did, too.

The next morning Miss Saunders came to me at the shelter and told me the detectives couldn't find my grandparents or any other relatives who I could live with.

"I'm going to have to place you in the state boy's school for awhile," she said. "When we find your mother or your grandparents, they'll come get you."

"How long will it take to find Mommy?" I asked.

"I don't know," she said. "Hopefully, only a few days."

• • •

That was what I remembered, *hopefully, a few days.* That was fourteen years ago. Nine years old and my new life – a life without parents, grandparents, relatives or friends – was about to begin. Two months had gone by before Miss Saunders came upstate to visit me and the news was bleak. "No, Frankie," she said, "the police still haven't found your Mommy. How are you doing here?"

"I hate it," I said. "I hate living with all these other boys. I hate the food. I hate everything about this place."

"I just spoke to the headmaster, Mr. Eglund, and he is going to try very hard to get you into foster care as soon as he can."

"What's that?" I asked.

"It's where you live with a real family in a real home. They treat you like one of their own children. Would you like that?"

"Sure. It sounds a lot better than here," I said.

After Miss Saunders left I felt better and began thinking about leaving this place for a real home and maybe a bedroom of my own. I had been getting nervous and afraid because I had been hearing stories of how the older boys would force us younger boys to do bad things – *dirty* things. I hoped I would get out of here before something like that happened to me. Then I hoped they would find Mommy and she would come and take me back to our home in Levittown.

• • •

Three weeks later I was called into the headmaster's office and was introduced to a Mr. and Mrs. Hammond. After we talked awhile and I answered their questions, I was told to wait outside. I sat on a bench with three other boys about my age and one by one they were called in to the office to speak with the Hammonds. Five minutes after we all had been spoken to, Mr. Eglund called me back into the office and told the other boys to return to the dormitory. He said with a big smile, "Mr. and Mrs. Hammond have chosen you to come live with them and their family. Isn't that wonderful?"

"Yes, sir," I said also smiling. Although it was great to be getting out of here, I couldn't help remembering the dejected faces on the other boys when they were told they would not be leaving.

"I'm Jethro Hammond," the man said standing up and reaching out to shake my hand. "And this is my wife, Pauline Hammond. Of course, you will call us Mister and Misses, but as time goes by you may want to call us Mom and Dad."

"Yes, sir," I said thinking no way would I ever call anyone else Mom and Dad. I had my own Mom and Dad, but then the reality of my situation hit me like a sneak punch to my stomach – Dad was dead. Mom had killed him and it looked like she wasn't ever coming back to get me.

"Go get your things, Frankie," Mr. Eglund said.

"Can I bring my bike?" I asked. "Officer Boyland has it at his home in Long Island."

"That wouldn't be possible," Mr. Hammond said. "We run a working farm way upstate. Between school and your chores there'll be no time for bike riding."

He was not smiling and Mrs. Hammond looked down and said nothing.

So the next day I began a life of hard physical work even on school days – before I left and after I came home. The Hammonds had four other foster children, two girls ages eleven and fourteen and two other boys, ages twelve and fifteen. The Hammonds had no children of their own. The girls mostly did housework – cooking, cleaning and tending to the vegetable garden. We boys did the farm work – hauling, plowing, reaping, planting, weeding, shucking, bailing and loading.

Anthony, the twelve year old, and I hit it off right away. He took me under his wing and gave me advice on how to get along with the Hammonds. "We work hard," he said, "but we have good food, a nice bed to sleep in and they rarely hit us."

"How long can we live here?" I asked.

"Until you turn eighteen," he said. "Then the foster care money from the State stops and you are on your own. That's why you're here. John turned eighteen two weeks ago and joined the Army."

What Anthony didn't tell me then, but did later on, was that the Hammonds turned John out without a thank you, good wishes, some new clothes, or even a few dollars, and immediately turned their attention to finding his replacement. I was beginning to feel unhappy with my situation, but it wasn't until a couple weeks later, when Anthony told me something else, that I knew this was a bad place.

● ● ●

We were bussed to school every day with the other kids from the surrounding farms. There were three grades in each classroom and I spent a lot of time daydreaming about Mommy and my former home. Gone were my friends, the neighbors, the ice cream trucks and the movie theaters of the suburbs, replaced by the wide-open boring farmlands of upstate New York. On the bus ride home I said to Anthony, "You said this was a pretty good place, but the way you said it was kind of creepy. Did you tell me everything?"

"You mean you haven't had a night visit yet?"

"A night visit? What do you mean?"

"So, you haven't," Anthony said. "You're overdue for one. It could be tonight."

"What..."?

"Look, this place is the best one I've been in and I've been in four others, so my advice is to just put up with the old man. If you fight him and don't go along, he'll send you right back to the Home."

Despite my repeated questions, Anthony refused to tell me exactly what the night visit was, finally breaking away from me as we got off the school bus. I had a tough time falling asleep that night, but nothing ever happened. But two nights later…

I half awoke to someone fondling my private parts and I sensed a presence - another body – in my bed. Startled, and now fully awake, I tried to get up but the firm hand of Jethro Hammond held me down. "Now, now, Frankie," he said in a whisper, "just be quiet. I'm just going to teach you a few things, okay? And it wouldn't be wise to make any noise or resist me or tomorrow you'll go straight back to the Home. Do you understand?"

Terrified, I nodded my head.

"That's good Frankie. We'll start slow. Now give me your hand…"

"Yeah," Anthony said, when I told him the next morning of my first night visit. "That's the way he started with me – with all of us."

"The girls, too?"

"Yeah, and it gets worse."

"What do you mean?"

"He makes you put his thing in your mouth and then he sticks it in your behind."

I trembled and had trouble imagining such things. I said, "Does he visit every night?"

"Nah," Anthony said. "There are five of us, so your turn comes up maybe once a week or so."

MOMMY, MOMMY

"I won't let him do that to me," I said.

"And what are you going to do about it?"

"Run away. We could all run away."

"Yeah? To where? You got any money? You got people somewhere who'll take you in? We all don't."

I wondered what to do dreading the next night visit which happened eight days later. Hammond did not make me put his thing in my mouth, but he did use a lot of Vaseline to shove his thing in my behind. I started to scream because of the pain, but he clamped his hand over my mouth and said, "S-s-s-h, quiet boy. This will be over quick and next time it won't hurt as much."

Next time? I shut my eyes attempting to stop the flow of my tears as he pumped away. Finally, it was over. He was panting like an old dog as he got up and pulled up his pants. "Not a word boy, understand? Now go clean yourself up."

A few minutes after he left the room, still sobbing and in great pain, I crawled to the bathroom. I was horrified to see the blood – lots of it – on the toilet paper as I wiped myself, trying to wipe away the filth of Jethro Hammond. What would I do now? I vowed that I would not let him touch me ever again, but how could I prevent it? Mommy, where are you? Help me! Mommy what should I do?

I took a drink of water and then Mommy was speaking in my mind, "Frankie," she whispered. "You know what to do, you know what I would do, what I *had* to do, right?"

"Yes, Mommy," I whispered. "I know."

I knew exactly what to do now. I would *kill* Mr. Hammond just like Mommy killed Daddy. I will smash his head with a brick and throw him down the stairs.

The harsh brightness of the morning sun melted my resolve to kill Jethro Hammond like it would have melted an early spring snow – quickly and completely. Not that I still didn't want to do it, but that I was not capable of doing it. I was not yet ten years old, thin and small in stature, and no match for the rugged forty-year old farmer with the lined face and cold blue eyes who stood a solid, muscular six feet tall. But I had to do something to get away from him before his next dreaded night visit.

• • •

After five days and nights the idea hit me. Anthony was right – I couldn't run away for all the obvious reasons, but I could report him to the police. I could call Officer Boyland. Surely, he would help me. He would know what to do. On the bus ride home from school I said to Anthony, "I'm going to call the police on Hammond."

Anthony turned toward me, eyes wide open in disbelief, and said, "Are you crazy? And keep your voice down."

"I don't want him to do that to me again. It hurt bad and it was disgusting."

"I know, but like I told you there are worse places out there. Besides, the cops'll never believe you."

"They will when you and the others tell them what's been going on."

"No, Frankie, we won't tell. Not a word."

"But..."

"No, buts. Why not tough it out a little longer?"

MOMMY, MOMMY

"No way! I'll just run away. So what if I go back to the Home. Then maybe the next family will be better."

"Yeah, maybe, but when the cops catch you they'll bring you right back here first and Hammond may really hurt you bad."

"Then I'll do something before I run away to make Hammond not want to keep me anymore."

"Like what, Frankie, burn the house down?"

"I don't know."

"Yeah, do something real bad and you'll never get out of the Home again. No other family would take you in."

"Nobody wants me anyway, Anthony," I said as the tears began to run down my cheeks.

"No shit, kid. Nobody wants any of us either. Get used to it."

I turned away from Anthony toward the window ashamed of my tears, looking for an answer, a way out. A big barn came into view. A barn! *Not the house, but the barn!*

CHAPTER SIX

Danny

I was still seething over the results of the meeting with the DA when I got a call on the radio to call Detective Mason on a land line.

"How are you doing, Danny?" Wally asked.

"Still pissed off. What's up?"

"More bad news, I'm afraid."

"Jeez, what now?"

"Yesterday Interpol called me. They located the Chandlers in Switzerland and I was able to speak with them at the hotel. Danny, they want no part of Frankie Chandler. They disinherited their son Jimmy when he married Angela. Obviously she was beneath their class. They had no reaction to Jimmy's death other than could I possibly send them a copy of the death certificate."

"Those heartless bastards!" I said. "And their own grandson. How could they not take him in?"

"Because it would interfere with their lifestyle—and those were Betty Chandler's words."

"Jesus!"

"There's more. Angela Chandler is not Frankie's biological mother. And the Chandler's were not happy with their son's first wife, Ellen Weston, either."

"Wally, this is beginning to sound like a soap opera."

"Indeed it is. Ellen booked on Jimmy and their infant son, and a year or so later he met Angela and they got married."

"She accepted him with a year old boy from another woman?" I asked. "So maybe she isn't bad at all."

"Nobody's *all* bad, Danny. You should know that by now."

"But now Frankie has been abandoned twice – by *two* mothers."

"Life's crummy sometimes."

"Wally, if Angela is not Frankie's biological mother, can she be legally charged with abandoning him if she's ever located?"

"Probably not, but it doesn't matter anyway. Remember, we won't extradite for misdemeanor abandonment? There's no alarm out on her anymore."

"Does Pam Saunders know any of this?" I asked.

"Let's call her and fill her in right now, and then pop the big question to her."

"What big question?"

"Do we tell Frankie that Angela's not his real mother, and that she isn't ever coming back for him?"

"Oh, shit," I said for want of a more appropriate word.

Pam, on the other end of the telephone, remained silent for a good fifteen seconds after we gave her the story. She then said, "How about if I call the Chandlers and try to get them to change their mind?"

MOMMY, MOMMY

"I don't think you will be able to do that, Pam," Wally said. "And even if you do, what kind of life would Frankie have with those two loveless, conceited bastards?"

"You're probably right," she said. "So I guess Frankie's in the system until he turns eighteen. What a rotten break."

"How about taking him in, Pam?" I asked.

"Danny, I am a single mom with two young kids of my own. I earn a civil servant's meager salary and my deadbeat husband misses more child support payments than he makes. Besides, it would probably be a conflict of interest."

"I wish I could do it," I said. "I know what's in store for the poor kid, in and out of foster homes, in and out of the State Home, screwed over by the system. But a single young guy like me working around the clock could not provide a proper home for him, even if the court allowed it."

"How about you, Wally?" Pam asked.

"Been there, done that," he said. "Raised two of my own, a boy and a girl, and two foster kids, a boy and a girl. They are all grown and on their own and I'm looking forward to retiring in a couple years. Just me and the wife touring the U.S.A. in a great big camper."

Pam sighed and said, "We all have great excuses, don't we? That's why there are so many kids without families."

Neither Wally nor I said a word until Wally broke the silence and said, "So Pam, do we tell Frankie?"

"I don't think so," she said. "The only thing left for him is the hope that Angela will come and take him home. Why kill that hope?"

"I agree," Wally said.

"Me, too," I said.

We had spared Frankie Chandler the pain of knowing Angela was not his mother and was never coming back for him, but by not taking him in we also condemned him to a life of sadness, neglect, false hope and possible mistreatment. Good-bye, kid – and good luck. You'll certainly need it.

• • •

Two years had gone by in a hurry – I met a girl, Jean, fell in love, got engaged, got married and had a baby on the way. Occasionally, I would think of Frankie, of maybe visiting him, but I never could seem to make the time. A poor excuse, I know, and when I spoke of him to Jean she said, "You haven't come out and said it, or asked me, but when you speak to me about Frankie I get the impression that you want to take him in to live with us."

"Would you consider it?"

"Convince me, if you can, but I don't think it will work."

When I finished making my case, Jean took my hand and smiled. She said, "You know I always call you my young Sean Connery look-a-like, but now you're jumping into his James Bond character a little strong."

"Bond wants to save the world; I just want to save a young boy."

"This may sound selfish, but we are having our very own baby in six months. He or she will be a full-time job and learning experience for both of us. We will not be able to give Frankie the attention he deserves."

I had to acknowledge that she had a good point and I was beginning to have some doubts myself. I said, "I know what that poor kid is facing, I was there, you know."

"I know," she said. "And look how you turned out – a fine police officer, emotionally stable, with a pretty young wife and a baby on the way. Maybe Frankie will do as well. And I am pretty, right?"

"Yeah, maybe, he'll do okay. And you certainly are pretty, my little blonde honey."

"Flattery will get you everywhere," she said with a seductive smile, "but to get back to Frankie, I just don't think I could handle it at this time."

"Okay," I said, throwing in the towel. ""Let's hope for the best for him."

• • •

Jean and I moved from our apartment in Mineola to a small cape cod in Franklin Square, a hamlet in the western part of Nassau County. The following year, true to his word, Wally Mason retired from the Force and began his journey across America. My son Patrick was born on time and Jean experienced a normal, healthy delivery.

At first I often thought of Frankie, especially when I went to the garage and saw his blue bicycle resting along the wall. One day

I covered it up with a tarp to diminish the guilt I felt over abandoning him, even though I had come to the conclusion that we had made the right decision in not taking him in.

One day, when I was writing up a report in the station house, Pam Saunders walked by and I called out to her. She had just finished up on a sad case of child abuse and was obviously agitated by what had occurred. "You okay, Pam?" I asked.

"No, I am not. Sometimes I wish I had a gun with me to blow some of these so-called parents to hell."

"Bad one?"

"Jesus, they burned their baby with cigarettes all over his body."

"Oh my god," I said thinking of my infant son. "What the hell for?"

"They said he was evil. They were burning the devil out of him."

"Let's change the subject. How are things with you and your kids?"

"Things are pretty good. And you?"

"Great. We have a new baby boy."

"Congratulations. What's his name?"

"Patrick."

She smiled and said, "I was wondering if you might have named him Frankie."

"Ah, Frankie Chandler," I said. "Do you know how he's doing?"

"No, I don't. I've been so damn busy…"

"Me too. How about calling the boys' school and finding out. Would you do that, Pam?"

"Sure," she said smiling for the first time since our conversation began. "First thing tomorrow morning."

"Great. I'm still working days. Have the desk officer get me on the phone if you find out anything."

The next day, Pam reached out for me around eleven o'clock and she was in the same gloomy mood as yesterday. "Bad news," she said. "Frankie spent only a couple of months in foster care with a family that owns a farm in upstate New York. He's back at the state school again."

"What happened? It sounds like that would have been a good life for him."

"The headmaster, Fred Eglund, said the Hammond's – that's the family's name – returned him because he burned down part of their barn."

"That's hard to believe. What did Frankie say?"

"He told Eglund it was an accident. He said he just went out there late one night to sneak a cigarette and he fell asleep. The flames next to him woke him up and he ran out of there and ran back to the house to wake everyone up."

"Sounds reasonable to me. Why didn't they buy it and forgive him?"

"Who knows? Eglund says they're a tough, strict pair."

"I hope he soon finds another family to take him in."

"Me, too," Pam said.

We hung up and I know that Pam felt as shitty as I did – and guiltier than ever.

CHAPTER SEVEN

Ellen

"How awful!" exclaimed Sister Eugene Baptist. "I can't believe a mother could do that. That poor young boy."

"Do what?" I asked looking up from my magazine.

Sister Eugene was still staring at the television and held up her hand toward me. "Listen," she said.

The News 12 anchorwoman said, "So now there is an all-state alarm out for Angela Chandler for the murder of her husband and abandonment of her son. She may be driving a 1986 dark green, four-door Chevrolet, plate number FSV-7624. Any information on her whereabouts should be forwarded to Detective Wallace Mason at the Ninety-Eighth Detective Squad in Levittown."

The name Chandler caused a shiver to pass through my body. I asked Sister Eugene what details I had missed.

"Oh, Audrey," she said. "This Chandler woman is suspected of murdering her husband – but that's not the worst part…"

"What could be worse than that?" I interrupted. "Oh, what was his name?"

"Uh, Jim, they said…James Chandler."

A stronger shiver coursed through me. I said, "And what else did his wife do? What was worse than killing her husband?"

"After the funeral she abandoned her son. The boy came home from school to an empty house and an empty glass with a note under it. How heartless can you be?"

"Why didn't the police arrest the wife right away?" I asked.

"Not enough evidence, but I guess when she fled that kind of proves it, right?"

"Yes, I guess so. What was that poor boy's name? Did they mention it?

"Yes, Audrey. It was Frankie. Frankie Chandler."

Oh my God. Frankie. My son!

• • •

I fell in love with Jimmy Chandler on the rebound after my long-term relationship with Charlie Gerraghty had dissolved. Charlie told me if I wouldn't go all the way with him he would find another girl who would, assuming that there were plenty of them around. I didn't doubt him on that, but I had been raised a strict Roman Catholic and we were just out of high school. We had been boyfriend and girlfriend since seventh grade and no way was I was going to have sex with him or any other guy. No way, that was, until I met Jimmy Chandler.

After Charlie left me, I started to hang out in bars to drown my sorrows in beer or wine. I would socialize with my fellow typing-pool workers one or two nights a week after work in Manhattan, then on Friday in the local places in northern Queens – Bayside, Whitestone and Little Neck.

MOMMY, MOMMY

One Saturday night, I was in Desmond's, an Irish pub in Little Neck, with a high school friend when a good-looking guy struck up a conversation with us. He bought us both a drink and we had a good time laughing and drinking. After about twenty minutes, he said he had to get back to his friends and asked for my phone number. He said, "I'd like to call you soon."

I hesitated a bit and figured, why not? He called me the very next day at my home, where I lived with my parents, and I agreed to go with him to a movie on Wednesday night. And so began our whirlwind romance. Jimmy was older than me – I was eighteen and he was twenty-two – and he had a draftsman's job in the city. He was a nice guy, never pressuring me to have sex despite several steamy make-out sessions where I knew he was ready to burst out of his pants.

About three months later, after we had one beer too many, we were going at it hot and heavy in his car at the rear of Desmond's parking lot. This time he reached between my legs and I didn't stop him and you know what happened next. Still charged up, we got a room at a local motel, and to be vulgar, we screwed our brains out in a wild, steamy night of emotional release.

What I had withheld from Charlie Gerraghty for two years, and what I pledged to my parents and my church I would *never* do before marriage, I did that night, willingly and lustfully, with Jimmy Chandler. And, of course, to pay for my terrible sin, I got pregnant.

After I missed my first period I waited another month before I visited the doctor who confirmed the pregnancy. When I told Jimmy, he was surprised. We always used protection after that first memorable night, but now that proved to be an unnecessary after the fact precaution. He said, "I'm happy, Ellen. I love you and we'll get married right away."

The question of abortion never arose. We were morally against it and were so in love we figured we would be one happy little family. Then reality set in – in sharp hard doses – and things got bad, then worse, then unendurable.

Jimmy had been brought up a single child in Colorado. Although very wealthy, his parent's snobbish attitude and treatment of their son – as if he was imposing on the harmony of their existence – caused Jimmy to leave them as soon as he could, right after he graduated from high school. No sooner was their son's cap and gown off, the Chandlers got on a plane for Europe and Jimmy hopped a Greyhound bus for New York City. The invitation to our wedding was returned by them with a one hundred dollar check and their regrets that they would be unable to attend due to previous commitments.

My parents, George and Eleanor Weston, were also less than thrilled with our planned marriage and when I told them of my condition, they went ballistic. I had to listen to my father's pontifical, Roman Catholic ranting, including that I was forever destined to burn in hell, that I was a no-good tramp, that my child would be illegal and condemned to limbo when he or she died. Or was it purgatory? The damnations were coming so fast and furious I couldn't keep track of them. When he had vented out, I was given a week to get out of the house, and out of his life forever.

The wedding ended up to be a small affair – only friends attended – our party being boycotted by my relatives after a call from my dear old dad. And Jimmy had no relatives he was aware of. So we had a civil marriage and a reception where the bride did not get to dance with her father and the groom did not get to dance with his mother. Not a great start to a life of wedded bliss, but we vowed to be happy despite it. Jimmy and I and our baby would not only survive, we would prosper – or so I planned.

I moved in with Jimmy in his small one-bedroom apartment in Whitestone and we eagerly awaited the birth of our child. Frank Chandler arrived on time, a healthy eight pounds, with no complications. There was no doubt who his father was – the likeness was apparent even at that early age. But our initial euphoria with our new baby quickly wore off. Things went downhill in many areas. Experienced couples would say there are only three things that cause trouble in a marriage – sex, money and children. And it seemed we had all three problems at once.

My sexual desires and responses took a steep nosedive after Frankie's birth. I just wasn't interested in making love to Jim anymore. I didn't know if it was physical or mental, but I do know the guilt put upon me by my parents and the guilt by being brought up in the Catholic Church weighed heavily on me all the time. And the more I rejected Jim's attempts at lovemaking, the madder he got, often leaving the apartment and coming home hours later with the smell of alcohol on his breath.

Then there was Frankie himself. He was forever crying and never slept through the night even after six months had passed. He was always sick, nose running, fever spiking, coughing all the time. It seemed I was always at the doctor's office with him writing checks for co-payments. Babies cost a lot of money and we didn't have much to begin with, just Jim's meager salary and me not working. We had no car and had trouble making the rent, and unlike other couples in our position, we had no parents or relatives to turn to for short-term assistance.

I became desperate and sought refuge in the church, not my former parish of St. Gregory's where the place would explode in flames if I walked in, but in St. Barbara's a couple blocks away from the apartment. I would wrap Frankie up and get down on my knees in a rear pew and pray to God for help and guidance, but none came. I was afraid to speak with a priest, afraid to confess my mortal sin, afraid of their scorn, rejection and condemnation.

By the time Frankie was nine months old, I was desperate. I hated Jimmy, I hated my life, I hated myself and God help me, I hated Frankie. Thoughts of suicide became attractive – how else could I end my misery? But my Catholic teachings once again intervened. I had committed a terrible sin in that car. How could I now compound it with an even worse sin in the eyes of the church?

I stopped going into St. Barbara's, but one mild, spring day with a light breeze blowing, as I walked past it pushing Frankie in his stroller, trying to clear my mind of my troubles, a very old nun walked down the church's steps and stopped to admire Frankie. For once he was not fussing or crying and the nun stroked his cheek and said, "God has given us a beautiful baby and God has given us a beautiful day."

"Thank you," I said as the nun stood up.

She looked me directly in the eyes, still smiling as if she were looking into my soul. "God bless you," she said. "I will pray for both of you. Find peace in the Lord."

MOMMY, MOMMY

As she walked away I felt that she had seen into the very core of me and sensed my troubles. And she had somehow given me the answer to them.

• • •

Jimmy used to come home from work promptly at six o'clock until things went sour. Now it was rare for him to make an appearance before nine, smelling of alcohol, not asking about dinner, plopping himself on the couch in front of the TV. On this day, a Wednesday, I was fully prepared by four o'clock. My clothes were all packed and Frankie was sleeping soundly. I had deliberately kept him up past his usual nap time weathering the hysterical crying that resulted, but now I hoped he would sleep for at least four to five hours.

Before putting the note in the envelope marked "Jimmy" I unfolded it and read it slowly one more time:

Dear Jimmy,

I know I have made all our lives miserable. By leaving now, I sincerely believe that you and Frankie will have a much better life and future without me. My sins are unbearable and will continue to drag us down if I stayed. I must seek my redemption elsewhere. Maybe you would be better off if you put Frankie up for adoption. He might be too much of a burden as you try to make a better life for yourself. I am sorry for what I put you through. Ellen

I did not sign it, *Love Ellen* – that would have been hypocritical. I sealed the note in the envelope, picked up my suitcase and went out the door, locking it behind me. I did not kiss Frankie good-bye. I just left.

When I walked out of our Queens apartment that day I knew exactly where I was going. I had done internet research and located several convents that were open to accepting new members to the novitiate – not only accepting, but begging girls to join. It seemed the church's problem in recruiting new members of the priesthood spilled over to the sisterhood. I'm sure I could have given the bishops and the cardinals a few good reasons for their problem, but I was not out to criticize the church – after all, I needed it for its ability to hide me for the rest of my life and for me to eventually, hopefully, prayerfully, earn my redemption and salvation.

I chose one way out east on the south fork of Long Island. It was called St. John of the Cross and was spread out over a hundred acres in an idyllic, pastoral setting. I had already decided to tell them the truth, well not *all* of it. In my interviews I told the Mother Superior I had a baby out of wedlock and gave it up for adoption. I was now grievously sorry for my sin and wished to devote my life to God. After I confessed this sin to the kindly priest who served the convent, Father Francis Mulvey, I was accepted as a novice in the Dominican Sisters of St. Joseph. I cut my long blond hair, removed the liner and mascara from my blue eyes and scrubbed the magenta lipstick from my mouth. I was ready to don the habit of a nun for the rest of my life.

St. John's parish operated an elementary school which served the affluent surrounding communities providing a religious education from kindergarten through the eighth grade. I served as an aide to the teaching nuns while I went to college at night to obtain my teaching degree and credentials. By the time I completed my requirements I was there for six years and received my first assignment to teach the second grade, replacing Sister Amelia who retired at the age of seventy-five.

When I stepped into the classroom that September I could not help remembering that my son would probably be starting second grade himself this term. Not that this was the first time I had thoughts of Frankie – oh, no, I thought of him often, of how he was doing, of how Jim handled his upbringing, if he gave him up for adoption, if Jim ever told him of me, if Jim ever tried to find me – yes, I had a lot of thoughts and second guesses and self-recriminations, and I probably always would.

So, two years later, when Sister Audrey brought my attention to the television news and I learned that Frankie was now an orphan, I didn't know what to do. Should I claim him and leave the convent? I could get a public school teaching job and support him, but what did I know about raising a child? And I was content in my life – but would Frankie be content in his? I agonized and prayed constantly for several days and finally reached my decision. I would do nothing. I had willfully abandoned my son eight years ago and I would now willfully abandon him once more. I was a wonderful God-loving Christian, wasn't I?

CHAPTER EIGHT

Frankie

The next night, after I was certain that it was too late for a visit from Hammond, I slipped out of bed, put my bathrobe and slippers on and glanced at the alarm clock as I left the bedroom. It was 2:17, and I was pretty sure everyone was sound asleep. I went slowly down the stairs to the kitchen. My heart was pounding – I remember that distinctly. There on the kitchen table, where they always sat, were two packs of cigarettes belonging to Mr. and Mrs. Hammond awaiting the first puff of the day for the early risers.

Sitting atop Mrs. Hammond's box of Marlboro lights was a box of wooden matches. A Bic Lighter rested on Mr. Hammond's red box of Marlboros. I took the Marlboro lights and the box of matches and carefully eased out the kitchen door, not making a sound. I was in the barn a few minutes later and struck a match and glanced around. I spotted the half dozen milk cows in their stalls and opened the half doors to shoo them out. They were not in the mood to move, but I'm sure they would when they smelled the smoke. And I sure wouldn't miss their foul smells when I got out of here.

I piled a mound of straw in the far corner of the barn away from the door that I had left open for the cows to run out. I took out a Marlboro and lit up drawing in the smoke, but not inhaling. I was not an experienced smoker and didn't want to have a loud coughing fit. When the cigarette was halfway smoked, I pushed it under the pile of straw and then lit the straw on fire with a match. As the flames grew higher I backed away and placed the boxes of cigarettes and matches on the floor. The cows started to move their feet and snort a bit and only needed a bit of coaxing now to bolt from their stalls and gallop toward the open barn door. I stayed a moment longer to make sure the dry wooden walls in the corner where I'd started the fire were burning. As the flames reached up toward the inner roof, I ran back into the house, put on the kitchen lights and began screaming, "Wake up! Wake up! The barn's on fire!"

I ran upstairs yelling all the way and burst into the Hammond's bedroom. "Get up! The barn's on fire!" I yelled.

When I saw them arise I ran out to the other bedrooms and awakened all the kids. I heard Mr. Hammond tell his wife to call the Fire Department and then get over with him to the barn. "And bring all the kids," he shouted. "Maybe we can put this out."

We couldn't put it out though, and when the fire department arrived and did their job, about one third of the barn was gone. "What happened here?" the fire chief asked.

"Danged if I know," Hammond said. "I was in a sound sleep and one of the kids woke me up yelling that the barn was on fire. Frankie, it was."

"Frankie?" the chief said.

"Uh…yeah, it was me that woke everyone up."

All eyes now turned toward me and the chief asked, "Did you start the fire, son?"

"Uh….yeah…but it was an accident!"

"Why you little…" Hammond started to say, reaching for me.

"Hold on, sir," the fire chief said. "How did it happen?"

"I couldn't sleep, so I went down to the kitchen for a glass of water and I saw the cigarettes on the table," I said with my eyes focused on my feet.

"And then?"

"I took a pack of Marlboros and the box of matches and went in to the barn to try to smoke."

"You little son-of-a-bitch," Hammond said.

The chief put his hand up and said, "Please, let Frankie finish."

"I sat down in the straw and lit the cigarette. I was so tired. I took a few puffs and then the next thing I remember I was coughing on the smoke, but the smoke was not from the cigarette, it was from the straw. Then I saw the flames and I got scared and ran for the door. But I thought about the cows, so I opened their gates and shoved them out."

"Thank the good Lord for that," Mrs. Hammond said touching my shoulder.

"And then I ran into the house and yelled for everyone to wake up."

The chief sent a couple of his men into the barn and in a few moments they came out with a water-soaked box of Marlboros and the matches.

After the fire department rolled up their hoses and drove away, Mr. Hammond smacked me across the face with the back of his hand, drawing blood from my nose. "I don't care if it was an accident," he said, "and I'm not so sure I believe it was – but you're outta here tomorrow. Pack your things, Frankie, you're history."

"But, sir, please, I didn't mean to, I…"

"Shut up," he said, "I ain't finished with you."

He removed his thick jeans' belt and whacked me across the shoulders with it. "Jethro," the kindly Mrs. Hammond said, "maybe…"

"Be quiet, woman. He needs a good beating. Like I said, I ain't finished with this little bugger yet."

• • •

By nine o'clock the following morning, despite their lack of sleep, the kids were awake to say good-bye to me – their newest and shortest stay member. Although there was sadness in their faces, there also seemed to be a bit of wistfulness, as if they too might be wishing they were leaving the Hammond farm. "Let's go," Mr. Hammond said. "Anthony, take that other bag."

Anthony and I walked behind Hammond as he headed out to the pickup. "Well, you did it," Anthony whispered. "You're outta here, you son-of-a-gun."

"It was an accident," I said with a big grin on my face.

"You're pretty smart for a nine-year old. I'll give you that."

"I'll be ten in a couple of weeks," I said.

"Well, Frankie, wherever you end up I hope you make it to eleven. I sure hope you did the right thing."

Hammond grabbed my arm and said, "Get it the truck."

"Bye, Anthony," I said.

The ride back to the Home took well over an hour and Hammond never uttered a word to me. I didn't care. I was getting away from him and his night visits. He pulled up in front of the front entrance. He opened the door and grabbed me by the arm saying, "Get out you little bastard."

I wanted to curse back at him but kept quiet. He sat me in a chair outside the Headmaster's office and walked inside. He came out a few short minutes later leaving the door to Mr. Eglund's office open. He walked past me without looking at me and without saying a word. Fine by me, I thought. Walk out of my life forever you dirty, old bastard.

Eglund said, "Come in Frankie," and when I did he kept me standing in front of him and asked if what Hammond had told him was true.

"What did he tell you?" I asked.

"That you set fire to his barn."

"Yes, sir, I did. But it was an accident. I snuck out there to smoke a cigarette and I guess I fell asleep."

"Where did you get the cigarette?"

"I took the pack and the matches from the kitchen table."

"So you stole them?"

"Yes, sir."

"Did anything happen in the time you spent with Mr. and Mrs. Hammond that made you set that fire?"

"Oh, no sir. They treated me fine. Like I said, the fire was an accident. I would have no reason to set it."

"I'm going to send someone out there to talk to the other children about this."

"That's okay. We all got along."

"You know that this is a serious mark against you. Prospective foster parents and those interested in adoption may not want a boy who steals and set fires."

"I did steal the cigarettes, but I didn't set the fire on purpose," I said with determination. I didn't like lying to Mr. Eglund. He was a pretty nice man, tall, thin always well-dressed in a three-piece suit. But when he smiled he sometimes reminded me of a long skinny snake ready to sink his fangs into me.

"All right," he said, "let's get you a place to sleep. Bring your things."

On March 22, I celebrated my tenth birthday. The 137 boys with me at the Home sang an out of tune Happy Birthday song to me and I received one extra chocolate chip cookie for dessert. There were no gifts. Mommy didn't come. She did not send a card. She did not call me on the telephone.

The school had taken in some older, mean, tough kids during my stay on the farm and they had taken to bullying the younger ones, me included. Four of them, all around sixteen years old, grabbed me one day and terrorized me. They were about to sodomize me when one of them thought he heard someone coming not too far away. He said, "You got a reprieve for now kid, but we'll get you someday."

And get me they did—repeatedly. Gang raped me and forced me to suck their penises. I was too small to fight them off and too afraid to inform Mr. Eglund. I wasn't the only young boy to get sodomized – there were several others, some as young as six years old, who fell victim to the predators. Finally, some boy got up enough courage to tell Mr. Eglund what was going on, but Eglund ignored the complaint and reprimanded the boy for concocting a lie. "Son," he said, "if anything like that were going on here my staff would have notified me at once."

The night staff, when all the acts took place, consisted of one dorm supervisor who was fast asleep thirty seconds after he turned off the lights. The sodomy continued unabated for almost a year when a rare occurrence took place. A mother came to the school to re-claim her eight-year old son after placing him there over two years ago. Her economic situation in life had dramatically improved and for once there was much joy as they prepared to leave. When the boy, Kevin Morton, was safely at home only then did he tell his mother about the repeated acts of sodomy he was subjected to. She believed him and took him to a pediatrician who confirmed it.

Enraged, Mrs. Morton made an appointment to see Mr. Eglund and threatened to sue the school, the state, and him personally for several million dollars. Eglund calmed her down, and after a long discussion, she agreed to accept a deal that included medical care and psychological counseling for her son up to age eighteen and a cash settlement of $50,000. Her part of the deal was silence.

Realizing he had dodged a big bullet in the form of scandal, lawsuits and his career, Eglund fired the night dormitory attendant and replaced him with four new ones who assured him they would not sleep while on duty. The predation finally stopped and my eleventh birthday passed uneventfully and in similar manner as my tenth, although this time the one extra cookie was an Oreo.

• • •

That summer a middle-aged couple came in and spoke to me and a few other boys. My hopes were not high as this would be my seventh interview since my return. I guessed the barn fire had a lot to do with no one selecting me. Mr. and Mrs. Ryan asked the usual questions and then Mrs. Ryan asked me about the fire. I related the story, just as I had told it to Mr. Eglund. Mr. Ryan whispered something to his wife then said, "I like a boy who admits what he did, like taking those cigarettes. Most kids would lie about that."

"And the fire was definitely an accident?" Mrs. Ryan asked.

"Yes, ma'am," I said.

The Ryan's chose me to come live with them and, to my most pleasant surprise, they lived in the suburban hamlet of Bethpage, about two miles from where I had grown up. The Ryan's were decent people who had lost their son the year before. While riding his bicycle after school he was struck by a delivery truck and killed. His name had been Peter and he had been about the same age as me. The Ryan's had one other child, a daughter named Margaret, who was approaching thirteen years old.

MOMMY, MOMMY

The first day in the Ryan home, a pleasant three-bedroom ranch with a spacious backyard, Mr. Mike Ryan, a genial, twinkly-eyed man, explained to me that they were not looking for a replacement for their lost son – not exactly, that was.

"What the mister is saying," Mrs. Nora Ryan said, "is that we were all geared up for two children – a boy and a girl. We figured that another boy could use the things our son had – the bedroom, the baseball equipment the video games – all that. We don't expect you to be our Petey. We expect you to be your own self."

"Thank you, ma'am," I said to the woman, who seemed even nicer than her husband, beginning to feel some happiness for the first time in over two years.

"Of course, there's no bicycle now," Mr. Ryan said, "but if things work out here, maybe we can get you one."

"I have a bicycle already," I said. "Officer Boyland is keeping it for me. He also has a box of my toys."

"And who is Officer Boyland?" Mrs. Ryan asked.

"He's the one who came to the house when my Mommy left me. He works in the precinct around here."

"Well, we'll call this Officer Boyland tomorrow and see what we can do about getting your things over here," she said.

• • •

The next night after supper there was a knock on the door and Mr. Ryan let Officer Boyland in. He was wearing regular clothes and smiled when he saw me. We shook hands and he said, "You certainly got taller since I last saw you, Frankie. How are you doing?"

"I'm doing okay," I said.

"Well, come on out and help me get your things out of my truck."

"I'll give you two a hand," Mike said. "And when we're done, we'll have some cake and coffee."

I wheeled my bicycle into the garage and stared at it. "It still looks the same," I said. "Like brand new."

"I cleaned it up a bit," Boyland said. "Tightened all the bolts and oiled up the chain."

"Thank you," I said as I ran my hands over the gleaming chrome and blue enamel frame.

"Come on inside," Mr. Ryan said. "Don't worry Frankie, it'll be here in the morning."

My bike was back! And my toys! It was as if my former life was slowly returning. And now all that was missing was Mommy. Maybe now she would return too.

CHAPTER NINE

Angela

During my first few weeks in Los Angeles my main concern was getting stopped by the police who would discover that I was wanted by the New York police for murdering my husband. On November 17, I turned thirty-two years old. Now a month out of Long Island, I began to relax and sought out the L.A. street people who, for a few dollars, directed me to the underground document forgers. For the right price – a hefty one – I was now Maria Theresa Ferraro, in possession of a New York State Department of Health official certificate of birth with a raised seal, to prove it.

With this single document and proof of residency – my six-month lease on my seedy apartment – I was able to get a driver's license, new California plates for my car and a new social security number. I took my original birth certificate, New York driver's license and original social security card and carefully burned them over the gas stove and flushed the ashes down the sink drain. My old life was now behind me and a new one ready to begin – with a new name, and soon a new job and a new look. And maybe, just maybe, in the far future, a new husband.

Good-bye and good riddance to Angela Dolores Capozzi Chandler and welcome to the brand-new Maria Theresa Ferraro!

• • •

With my money just about gone, I had to find a job – soon. I applied to the local school district, but backed off when I learned I would have to be fingerprinted and background checked. There was no way I could do that. And, unfortunately, private schools had the same requirement. I knew very little else other than being a teacher's aide, except waitressing which I had done while attending community college. I had no choice, so I checked the newspapers want ads and selected three restaurants that were near a bus line and within a reasonable distance from my apartment.

The first restaurant I applied to hired me on the spot after a ten minute interview. The manager had been desperate for help – two waitresses quit recently, one for marriage and one who wanted to see the world. I was attractive and intelligent and had some experience. "Maria," Mr. Damiano said, "you will do very well here. Business is booming. We do a lot of expense account lunches and dinners here at Maxwell's and, as you know, the bigger the bill, the bigger the tip."

Maxwell's was essentially a steak house, but they now offered a variety of veal, pork and excellent fresh seafood. Dinner for two, which usually included a cocktail or two, or a bottle of wine, or both, ran to $150, sometimes more. And the patrons of Maxwell's were generous tippers most in the 20% plus range. I did very well and when my lease expired I got a better apartment, closer to the restaurant and forsook the bus and used my car. Tony Damiano was pleased with my work saying, "You're doing great, Maria, the customers love you. Don't you leave me. Don't do something foolish like getting married and running off like Caroline did."

"I'm not interested in marriage, Mr. Damiano," I assured him. But I certainly had offers – not for marriage, but for dates, all of which I declined. Tony Damiano frowned on it as bad for business and I agreed. If I were going to go out on a date it would not be with a customer, but where else would I get one? I worked six days a week from 11:30 in the morning until the dinner crowd left, most nights after 11:00 p.m. My one day off, Monday, when Maxwell's was closed, I spent cleaning my apartment and grocery shopping. I resigned myself to working, socking away the money and putting my social life on hold for awhile. Besides, it was too soon after Jimmy and maybe I wasn't ready for a serious relationship now anyway.

• • •

One evening about a year after I started there and after the restaurant closed up, I was walking to my car in the parking lot when a voice called my name. I turned around to face one of the restaurant's most frequent, and best, customers – Thomas O'Shea.

"Oh, hello, Mr. O'Shea," I said. "You startled me."

"I'm sorry, Maria, but I wanted to speak with you – ask you something. I didn't want to do it inside the restaurant because I know Tony frowns on his staff fraternizing with the customers, a wise policy I must agree."

"What can I do for you?" I asked, sizing up the affable O'Shea.

"Would you join me for a drink? Just one before we both head home?"

I looked at him and, to my own surprise said, "Sure, why not?"

We walked a block and half to a decent cocktail lounge and went in and got a small table in the bar area. O'Shea ordered a Chivas on the rocks and I a glass of Pinot Grigio wine. I knew O'Shea well and he always asked for a table in my area. He was a generous tipper and always a gentleman. He smiled at me often, but never openly flirted or made suggestive remarks as some of my other customers did. I could not say I was overly attracted to him, but because he was an apparently decent guy, maybe that's why I accepted this invitation.

We spent almost two hours together and had several drinks and truly enjoyed each other's company. O'Shea insisted on putting me into a cab for my trip home and offered to give me return fare for the morning ride back to the restaurant. I had protested that I was okay to drive but he said, "Not with the DWI crackdown, Maria. I'm taking the next taxi home myself."

As the cab headed home, I felt happy with Tom O'Shea. He had not come on strong – he had not even asked for my telephone number. I hoped he would soon do so. Maybe I had finally found a decent man.

• • •

On his next meal at the restaurant Tom O'Shea took advantage of a chance meeting with me at the waiter's area to ask me out on a formal date – dinner and a show. I accepted and wrote my phone number down on a cocktail napkin which he placed in his jacket pocket. Our courtship continued on a regular, but discreet basis and it was only after a dozen dates that we finally made love.

After six months going out together, Tom asked me to marry him, offering me his undying love and a one and a half carat diamond engagement ring. My woman's intuition was that this moment had been imminent and I had thought it over very carefully concluding that being married to Tom O'Shea would be a good situation with no apparent drawbacks. Tom was a happy, genial companion, nice looking with wavy light-brown hair and blue twinkly eyes and we were both friends and lovers. And the fact that he owned a successful business – a trucking company – put to rest any financial fears I might have harbored. So what I – the newly-minted Maria Theresa Ferraro – said to Tom O'Shea was, "Oh, Tom, I love you. Of course I will marry you."

I gave up my apartment and moved into Tom's spacious ten-room house in one of the nicer neighborhoods of Los Angeles. It was not Beverly Hills, but not far from it. He was thirty-seven years old and divorced with no children. We had not discussed having children together and I wondered what we would decide when the topic inevitably arose. I thought of Frankie Chandler then and what I had done to him. How had he fared? He would be almost eleven now and hopefully having a happy childhood with a loving family. If only he had not looked so much like Jimmy…

Tony Damiano shook his head in despair when I – his best waitress – informed him of my decision to get married and leave his employment. "I really enjoyed working here, Tony, but Tom insists that he wants me to be a stay at home wife and help him socially with his business connections."

"I don't blame him," he said, "but the door is always open for you if you get bored or need extra money."

"Thank you, Tony – oh, you will come to the wedding won't you?"

"Wouldn't miss it," he said taking my hand and kissing me on the cheek.

• • •

My life had been a good one with Tom for over three years. We tried to have children beginning about a year after we were married, but nothing happened for reasons that the doctors could not explain. I could not help but think it was God's punishment for having abandoned Frankie. Why should he bless me with another child when I discarded my first one? And if I could remind God that Frankie was really not my child, he would have shaken his head and told me that to him there was no difference at all.

Tom suggested looking into adopting a baby or getting a young child from the State Boy's Home, but I rejected that idea with a weak explanation. "If God wants us to have children he will bless is with one of our own." I could not, of course, tell him, "I know a boy we can probably adopt. He's about thirteen now. You'd love him. There's a slight problem though. I walked out on him four years ago when he was nine. Left him a nice note and an empty glass. Let's see if he wants to come live with us." No, I couldn't say that to Tom, could I?

A few months later I noticed a change in my husband. He began coming home from the office later in the day and I smelled alcohol on his breath on more than one occasion. He also became short with me and was quick to anger over inconsequential things. We were both social drinkers, usually a cocktail before dinner a few nights a week, or a glass or two of wine with dinner. Even when we went out to a social or business function we never over-indulged. What was going on? Was it my refusal to pursue adopting a child? Or was it another woman? Or something else entirely?

Tom's time in the office continued to increase. He came home later and later – and drunker and drunker. I finally decided to confront him. I had to find out what was wrong in our marriage, and hopefully try to fix it. I waited until the weekend and when we were at the breakfast table Sunday morning I said, "Tom, I love you."

He smiled at me and said, "And I love you too, Maria."

"Then you have to tell me what's going on. I'm afraid for you, for us, for our marriage."

"I don't want to trouble you with my problems."

"Is it another woman?"

"Another woman? Of course not!"

"Then what is it? Maybe I can help. Please let me help."

"You can't, Maria. It's the business. Things have been going sour."

"How bad?"

He looked at me directly in the eyes and said, "My accountant says I'm on the verge of bankruptcy."

"I'll go back to work," I said. "Tony Damiano would be happy to have me back."

"No, that's not necessary, yet. I should know in a few days how things will work out. Don't worry, you'll be provided for."

I didn't like the sound of that last comment and pressed him on it. He said, "Bankruptcy doesn't mean we lose all our personal assets. Just the company's assets are at risk and to be reconstructed. We'll be okay. I promise."

I relaxed a bit and said, "You know I'll be with you all the way, Tom. I've never been this rich before and I certainly remember how to make do with a lot less."

"Thanks, Maria," he said. "Thanks for sticking with me. That's why I didn't tell you sooner. I was afraid of what you might do."

"I would never desert you Tom. I love you."

He squeezed my hand and nodded. "I love you, too," he said. "Remember that. No matter what happens, remember that."

Five days later, the company declared bankruptcy and two days after that my dear husband, Tom O'Shea, hung himself from a rafter in the garage. He left no note – I guess he felt he didn't have to. And he had taken care of me with a sizable insurance policy, which paid off regardless of the manner of death, as well as the house and cars.

After the funeral, I put the house on the market. It sold quickly as I had priced it a bit below market value. I also sold our three cars. I bought a small house in a nice neighborhood only a few miles from Maxwell's restaurant where I resumed working. I was financially secure, but now had two dead husbands in my past.

MOMMY, MOMMY

I couldn't help but think that God was exacting his revenge on me – taking Tom's life in return for my killing of Jim and abandonment of Frankie. I hoped and prayed He was finished with me.

CHAPTER TEN

Frankie

The months flew by and I settled into my new home with the Ryan's. Things seemed to be finally going well for me. My school grades were not *excellent* as were Margaret's, but *very good*, the category just below hers.

I rode my bike all over the neighborhood and even back to Levittown where I used to live. While there, I played with some of my old friends and stared wistfully at my old house. I missed my mother and father terribly, but Daddy was buried in the ground, never to return, and Mommy – where was Mommy? I was beginning to believe that she would never return either.

I had been thinking these thoughts while sitting on the sidewalk, my back resting against a sycamore tree, with my bike on its kickstand parked next to me. I was startled by a hand gently touching my shoulder. An elderly gray-haired woman with a kindly smile said, "Son, may I help you with something?"

I scrambled to my feet and said, "Oh, no, sorry, ma'am. I'm just leaving."

"I've seen you ride your bike around here and look at my house. Now you've been staring at it for almost ten minutes. Care to tell me why?"

"I used to live here."

"Ah, I see. Were you happy here?"

"Yes, ma'am, for a while. Until my Dad died and my Mommy ran away."

"Oh, yes, Mrs. Bennett told me the story when we moved in. How dreadful. So, you must be Frankie Chandler."

"Yes, ma'am."

"Where do you live now?"

"A couple miles away with Mr. and Mrs. Ryan and their daughter."

"And are you happy there?"

"Yes, ma'am, they are all very nice to me."

"Would you like to come inside? Perhaps see your old room?"

"I…I…don't think so," I said.

"You're probably right. I shouldn't have asked. If you're happy now, let the past stay in the past, if you know what I mean."

"I think so. I'd better be going home."

"Good-bye, Frankie. I'm glad you're happy now."

My twelfth and thirteenth birthdays were spent with the Ryan's and they were much better and memorable than the previous two at the State Home. They over-indulged me with gifts and hugs and good wishes, and I had overheard Mr. Ryan speaking of adopting me.

"Well, he is a good boy and, yes, let's look into that," Mrs. Ryan had said. "That would be fine with me."

Shortly after the Ryan's informed me that they had filed the papers to officially adopt me, tragedy struck the household. Mike Ryan, age 47, had a severe heart attack at his job as a construction supervisor in Brooklyn. Despite the heroic efforts of the responding EMT crew and the ER doctors, he died a few hours later. The family was devastated, especially me. I had now lost a man who had become like a second father.

In the weeks after the funeral, a lot of businessmen and lawyers visited the Ryan home and I picked up snatches of conversations – "the life insurance just about covered the funeral expenses," "the stock market has been in a severe downturn," "What job skills do you have?"

Two months after Mr. Ryan's death, Mrs. Ryan called me into the den with Margaret and she motioned for us to sit down. I could see the tears in Margaret's eyes and I knew that she already knew what her mother was going to say – and it wasn't going to be good. "Frankie," she said, trying to keep her voice steady. "We are in a bad situation now that Mike is gone. It's money. There really isn't any. I've talked to a lot of people and here's what I have to do – I have to sell this house and I have to get a job. Me and Margaret have to get an inexpensive apartment, and she's going to have to work part-time till she finishes high school."

When I heard "me and Margaret" I knew what was coming next. "Frankie, I just can't keep you anymore. You have to go back to the Home."

"But Mom," I cried out, "you can forget about adopting me and just keep the foster care money. And I'll work part-time too. I'll be a help."

"It just won't work, Frankie. They worked out all the numbers for me. I can't make my bills with supporting you. I just can't"

I looked at Margaret, who was sobbing hard now, and I began to cry too. She ran over to me and said, "Oh, Frankie, it's like losing my brother Petey all over again."

That got Mrs. Ryan crying too and when we finally all calmed down, I quit the fight and accepted the situation. "When are you taking me back?"

"Tomorrow morning."

"Could you let Officer Boyland know?"

"Sure Frankie…oh! Your bicycle. Maybe the officer will take it again for you."

I was bitter and told her to sell it when she moved. "Sell all my things," I said. "I just need some clothes."

"Oh, Frankie," she said, and started crying again.

• • •

When Police Officer – now Detective – Boyland got the call from Mrs. Ryan later that afternoon he volunteered to pick me up himself and transport me back to the state school for boys. It was obvious that Mrs. Ryan was extremely thankful to be relieved of the long drive and the need to repeat our sorrowful good-byes of the previous day. Between Petey and now me, she probably feared that further emotional pain could put her right in the ground next to her beloved Mike.

We hugged and said good-bye at the front door, all of us resolving not to cry again and we all held up well. With a simple suitcase in my hand, I joined Detective Boyland on the sidewalk.

"Ready?" he asked.

"No," I said. "I'm never ready to go back to that place."
"I understand."
"Sure you do," I said sarcastically.
"I spent a few years there myself."
"No kidding?"
"Yeah, no kidding. Listen, I'm not going to bore you with the details of my life and troubles, but I want to say this to you. Life is not fair and I've found out that life was not meant to be fair."
"What do you mean?"
"Frankie, we just gotta deal with what comes our way whether we like it or not. That's what I mean."
"You mean like your father falling down a flight of stairs and getting killed and your mother running away?"
"Yes."
"And some guy always wanting to stick his dick up your ass?"
"What?"
"Never mind. And how about being happy in a foster home and the man ups and has a goddamned heart attack and dies and now you're back to square one? So I'm supposed to roll with all those punches according to you, right?"
"Frankie, I..."
"Hey, *Detective* Boyland, leave me alone, okay? Just take me back to where it seems like I belong."

● ● ●

On my fourteenth birthday I was still in the State Home. My age was now working against me both for another foster home and on any adoption candidates. I began a growth spurt and began to fill out my thin frame. There were few leftovers at the communal dining table and Mr. Eglund, who had grown to really like me over the years, shook his head one night and said, "My God, Frankie, where do you put it all?"

"I don't know, sir," I replied. "I'm just hungry all the time."

"Well, come over to the staff table if you're not getting filled up here. I'll give you some of our food."

Just after my fifteenth birthday, a couple came in and interviewed me and a few other boys my age. The man, Mr. Harold Jonas, had actually felt my shoulders and biceps as he looked me up and down. When Jonas and his wife went into the office with Mr. Eglund, the four other boys who were interviewed and I compared notes.

"Jesus," Jason said, "the fuck was feeling me all over."

"Me, too," Stanley said. "He must think he's buying a slave."

"Whatever he wants us for," I said, "I guarantee there'll be hard work involved."

"I hope it's not a farm," Willy said. "I hate fuckin' farms."

"You'll take it though, won't you?" Jason asked.

"Yeah, anyplace is better than this place. The food sucks, the beds are hard and we gotta work our ass off here too."

"I can't wait till I'm eighteen and outta the system," Stanley said.

"Then what?" I asked.

"I'm joining the Navy."

"To see the world?" Jason asked.

"Why not?"

"Yeah, why not?" Willy said. "We won't have too many other options, will we?"

Mr. Eglund stuck his head out of his office and said, "Jason, please come in."

The rest of us started to leave the outer office area, but Eglund said, "Stay awhile. The Jonas's may again wish to speak to one or more of you."

I was called in next and the Jonas's asked me more questions. Mrs. Jonas, a very pretty brunette, smiled a lot at me and occasionally licked her lips which made me feel uncomfortable. I went back outside to await the decision and five minutes later Mr. Eglund called me back in and told the other boys they could return to the dormitory.

"Frankie," Eglund said. "Mr. and Mrs. Jonas would like to take you to their home – their farm – in the Mohawk Valley. How does that sound to you?"

Shit! Another farm! I said, "That would be fine. I'd like to go."

"Wonderful," Mrs. Jonas said. "A fine looking boy, and strong, too."

Vicky Jonas was right about me – on both counts. I was now five eight and a solid 155 pounds and I hoped a girl would find me attractive. I had dark-brown curly hair, clear light-brown eyes, a square chin with a small dimple in its middle, bright, white teeth and a nice smile – when I smiled, of course, which wasn't often.

"Can he come with us now?" Harold Jonas asked.

"I don't see why not," Eglund said. "I'll help Frankie get his things together and he can say good-bye to the boys. We should be no more than fifteen minutes."

"Fine, we'll wait here." Jonas said.

"So, you're outta here again?" Willy said.

"Yeah," I said, taking my shirts out of the dented metal clothes cabinet next to my bed, "to another fuckin' farm."

When we finished packing up my things, I waved a general good-bye to all the boys and said with a smile, "I hope I never see your ugly mugs again."

"With your track record you'll be back here before Christmas," Jason said with a laugh.

Then they all laughed and wished me luck. No one at the time realized just how accurate Jason's predication would be.

CHAPTER ELEVEN

Frankie

The Jonas's place was a small dairy farm – a dozen milk cows, scads of chickens, some pigs and a few sheep. What they grew on their few acres was primarily for animal feed. Mrs. Jonas also tended a vegetable garden for the family's use which consisted of the two of them and now a third – me. My chores were many and varied – weeding the vegetable patch, slopping the hogs, milking the cows, crating the eggs and loading the truck for Mr. Jonas's trips to the wholesaler.

The work was not back-breaking, but it seemed to be never-ending. After a few weeks it became repetitive and boring – the same chores over and over again. On a warm day in early June I helped load up the big truck with full milk cans and crates of eggs and Harold Jonas left for the long ride to sell his goods. "Frankie," Vicky Jonas said to me, "let's have a cold drink and then you can help me weed the vegetables."

I drank two tall glasses of sweet lemonade and headed out to the vegetable patch with Mrs. Jonas. Vicky, as I noticed when I first met her, was a fine-looking woman in her mid-thirties and today she was showing off her attributes. She wore denim cut-off shorts – and short they were – with the bottom of her left cheek occasionally showing, and a thin, low-cut tee shirt tied at her midriff, which just about contained her firm, ample breasts. I walked behind her out to the garden and felt a little dizzy as the sun hit me.

We worked a few yards apart for a while then Vicky came over and knelt beside me. She turned to me and smiled. I noticed the full red lips, the white teeth, the cheery blue eyes and the droplets of sweat on her forehead just under her dark brown hair. I also noticed her breast as she bent over to pull a weed. I could see all the way down, almost to her nipple and I felt myself getting an erection. Suddenly, I wavered and had to put a hand down to the ground to keep from toppling over.

"What's wrong, Frankie?" she asked.

"I don't know. I just felt a little weak – dizzy."

"Poor boy, probably still not used to the summer sun. It *is* hot and close. Come on inside and have another glass of lemonade."

I made it back to the kitchen with Vicky holding my arm and I gulped down another glass of lemonade. But the dizziness did not go away and Vicky said, "I think you'd better lie down awhile."

She helped me to the bedroom and took off my work boots and socks. "Here let me help you out of your work clothes. You'll feel better just in your underwear – cooler."

But she didn't stop there and had my tee shirt and jockey shorts off in a flash. Then her tee shirt and cut-off jeans came off even faster and she was on me in an instant kissing me full on the mouth, moving her naked body over mine.

"Mrs. Jonas, what…?

MOMMY, MOMMY

"Hush, now," she said. "Relax and enjoy this. It will make you feel better, I promise."

I had a full erection now – I just couldn't help it – and when she wriggled down my body and took me in her mouth I almost couldn't stand it. After a few moments she slid me inside her and said, "Just lay back, Frankie, I'll do all the work."

It was over quickly – much too quickly for Vicky Jonas. She told me that this was okay for starters, but she had a lot to teach me and assured me that I would love every minute. Still dizzy, I slipped into a deep sleep. When I awoke, Mr. Jonas was already home and dinner was getting ready to be served. I dressed and went cautiously downstairs sure the guilt of what had happened would be all over my face.

"How're you feeling, Frank?" he asked. "The missus told me how you almost fainted out there."

"Oh, much better," I said. "I guess the heat got to me."

Now I was wondering if it was *just* the heat or something Mrs. Jonas might have slipped into my glasses of lemonade.

"Yeah, you city boys need some time to adapt to the outdoor world. You'll get used to it."

A few days later when Mr. Jonas headed into town to get the truck serviced, Vicky approached me and asked, "Would you like another lesson in love?"

"Uh...Mrs. Jonas...er...I don't think this is right."

"What, Frankie? What's not right?"

"You know, doing what you're doing. I mean, you're married."

"That's beside the point," she said. "My needs are not being met, but you, Frankie, can be taught to meet them."

"But, Mrs. Jonas…"

"No buts about it, and call me Vicky when we're alone."

"This isn't right."

"You liked it though, didn't you?" "Well, yeah, but…"

"Listen, Frankie and listen close. You and I are going to make love whenever we get the chance, so you'd better get used to it."

"And if I won't?"

"Then I'll tell my husband you raped me. He's a powerful man – and a jealous one. If he doesn't kill you, then the police will arrest you. Do you understand?"

Although I said yes, I did not understand at all. I did not understand that because of my young age, I was the victim regardless of what Vicky Jonas asserted. She was the predator and she was guilty of rape and endangering my welfare. But I did not know that at the time. I was frightened so I went along with Vicky's demands and desires. I certainly did not want to go back to the Home once again.

• • •

June turned into July and Vicky took every opportunity to have sex with me. "You know," I said, "you better be careful. You might get caught someday."

"You mean *we* might get caught someday, don't you, Frankie? And if we do, you're the one that's in for it for raping me. Harold would never believe I did it willingly with a boy like you."

"You're an awful person," I said.

"Could be," she laughed. "Now get those clothes off."

MOMMY, MOMMY

On August 14, it finally happened – Harold Jonas came back home from town sooner than expected and found his naked wife beneath me. Jonas grabbed the heavy table lamp and shouted, "Son-of-a-bitch!" and whacked me across the back of my head with its marble base. As I collapsed on top of Vicky I heard her say, "Jesus, Harold, your timing couldn't have been worse. I was just ready to come."

Then just before I blacked out completely, I heard Mr. Jonas say, "Well, ain't that just too bad. Come on and help me tie him up."

When I came back to consciousness ten minutes later I found myself still naked on the bed and bound tightly with rope and duct tape. My eyes widened as they focused on Harold Jonas standing over me with a shotgun in his hands. "Rape my wife, you little bastard? I'll fix you."

I struggled to break free but couldn't move. I wanted to speak, to tell Jonas that this wasn't my fault.

"You know, kid, I just had a better idea than just shooting your balls off. Fuck my wife? Well, now I'm gonna fuck *you*. See how you like it, boy."

My god, it was happening again! He turned me over onto my stomach and I heard him unzip his trousers. I felt a greasy substance being spread between my cheeks and then the pain of penetration.

"There, you little bastard. Do you like it? Well, maybe you'd better get used to it. You'd better learn to take it or I'll kill you."

When it was over and Jonas left the room, I sobbed and my body shook uncontrollably. I hadn't yet calmed down fifteen minutes later when someone sat on the bed and I felt a warm hand caress my back. "Oh, Frankie," Vicky said, "I hope you're all right. I just had a long talk with Harold. Things may not be so bad after all. Here, let me get these ropes and tape off you."

When she removed all my bindings she handed me my clothes and said, "He knows you didn't rape me now. I just told him."

"Why didn't he beat you up or something?" I asked.

"Because deep down he knows that he can't satisfy me – or any other woman. His passion is for boys – like you. He agreed to let us continue our affair, but you have to let him have his way with you when he wants."

"This is sick, Vicky."

"No, this is the real world, Frankie. I'd go along if I were you."

"And if I don't? If I run away?"

"Where are you going to run to? He'll come after you and if he can't find you he'll go to the cops and press a rape charge against you. The cops will pick you up right away, and you'll go to jail for a long time."

"Not if you don't testify against me. Not if you tell the truth," I said.

"Oh, but I will testify against you – how you forced me to do your bidding, how you threatened to kill me if I said a word. I'll tell them that, Frankie, because if I don't, Harold will surely kill me."

"I'm confused," I said. "I need sleep."

"Of course, Frankie, you rest now. I'll leave you a plate of dinner on the countertop if you wake up hungry later. It won't be so bad, you'll see."

MOMMY, MOMMY

She kissed me goodnight and closed my bedroom door. I had told her I was confused so I could buy some time, but I was not confused at all. I knew exactly what I was going to do – I was going to kill Harold Jonas and, if necessary, I would kill the treacherous Vicky Jonas, too.

● ● ●

I slept solidly for a few hours and awoke around ten p.m. The house was quiet. I walked softly into the bathroom and washed up. I realized I was starving, so I crept quietly down the stairs into the kitchen and, just as Vicky had promised, there was a plate of food, covered in aluminum foil, on the countertop.

I uncovered the plate and placed it in the microwave. I pressed the "reheat" button and went over to the fridge to get a Coke. I ate and drank slowly, planning my next move. There really was nothing to plan – I had to wait for the opportunity to present itself. But I know one thing for certain – it would have to be soon. I would not allow myself to be sodomized again. Jethro Hammond did it and I took care of that situation. I would take care of this one, too, but probably couldn't set another fire this time.

Two days later while cleaning out the stalls of the dairy cows in the barn, I spotted what could be the way to dispose of Harold Jonas – and make it look like an accident – much as Mommy had done years ago to my father. A truck engine was suspended by chains from a beam in the ceiling of the barn. The chains were around the engine and the four ends were hooked onto a large hook screwed into the bottom of the beam. Jonas planned to eventually replace the one in his truck with this one.

The bottom of the engine was about eight feet off the floor of the barn. Harold was building a sturdy, wooden bench which he would slide under the engine and use it to overhaul the big eight cylinder unit. It was not a priority for Harold as his truck was running fine for now, but he knew its engine wouldn't last forever. This spare engine had been hanging there for a couple of months. It was not in the way of any chores, and would probably remain there until the truck was on its last legs.

Harold was away delivering milk and produce to the market and I studied the engine and the chains. My concentration was interrupted by the entrance of Vicky who said, "Come inside, lover boy, mamma needs to get laid."

I followed her inside and we headed upstairs to the bedroom. After a heated session of love making, Vicky said, "That was great, Frankie, but remember, my husband needs his lovin' too. Be prepared when he gets back form the market."

"I'll be in the barn," I said, "finishing the stalls and moving bales of hay."

Two hours later I heard the truck return and watched Harold go into the house. He came out ten minutes later and walked toward the barn. I was ready. When Jonas passed through the door, I came out of the shadows behind him and hit him hard on the back of his head with a Belgian block. Jonas went down and seemed to be out cold. I dragged him over and placed him directly under the truck engine. I then got a ladder and pinch bar. I climbed up and inserted the bar into the open eye of the hook. It was a good thing I had checked the hook out earlier in the day. It was screwed in securely and it had then taken all my strength on the end of the bar to free it just slightly from the beam.

I looked down and saw Jonas begin to stir. I came down the ladder, took the Belgian block and hit Harold again. I repositioned him, face down, with his head directly under the engine and climbed the ladder once more. I inserted the bar into the hook, and still with some difficulty, started to turn it. It began to move easier after two turns, and then as I turned some more, it gave way ripping loudly out of the beam and dropping the engine squarely on the head and shoulders of Jonas.

I put the ladder back in its place on the wall and picked up the Belgian block. There appeared to be no blood or hair on it, but I wiped it with an oily rag and placed it back in the obscure corner where I found it. I glanced at Jonas and noticed a puddle of blood growing larger under his head. I moved the straw around the floor where the ladder's four legs had stood. Satisfied, I turned and ran out of the barn shouting, "Mrs. Jonas! Mrs. Jonas!" while thinking, *Thank you, Mommy, for showing me the way.*

• • •

Harold Jonas's death was ruled an accident by the county coroner and the county sheriff's department. Before the sheriff arrived Vicky Jonas looked at me and said, "You did this to him, didn't you?"

"No, ma'am," I said. "I was on the other side of the barn when I heard that thing fall out of the beam and hit Mr. Jonas. I tried to help, but I couldn't move that engine."

Vicky Jonas decided to keep her suspicions to herself. No use bringing up anything that would cause the authorities to interview me at length. She knew the law with regard to sexual predation of minors. Better to just keep quiet and get on with her life. I would have to go, of course. She reasoned that, delightful as it was to make love to me, too many suspicions would arise if I remained. Besides, I wasn't old enough to help her run the farm. She needed a man, an older, stronger virile man who could satisfy her needs and take care of the business. After the funeral, she said, "Frankie, I can't keep you here any longer. I'll take you back to the Home tomorrow."

And then what? I wondered. Where would my lousy life go now? Where are you Mommy? Mommy, I need you now more than ever.

CHAPTER TWELVE

Frankie

The next few years at the Home passed by rapidly. Of course, due to my past troubles and my age, no other family had expressed interest in taking me in. When I turned sixteen I had finally reconciled myself to the fact that my mother was never coming back to claim me. But the nagging question of why she deserted me would not leave my mind. She had obviously gotten away with my father's murder – I was now convinced she had done it – so why not take me with her? I just couldn't banish this past incident from my mind despite plunging into my schoolwork and trying to look forward to the future.

During my last two years of high school I concentrated on vocational skills, especially electrical work and computer repair. Although I turned eighteen years old on March 22 of my senior year, the Home allowed me to reside there until my graduation in June. Mr. Eglund, who turned out to be a pretty good guy after all, arranged an inexpensive furnished room rental in a home in the town of Baldwin, Long island, about five miles from where I grew up. He also got me a job in a local branch of a popular quick oil change franchise.

The day after graduation I packed up my things and thanked Mr. Eglund for what he had done for me. He shook my hand, slipping me a couple of twenties, and wished me good luck. He had a staff member drive me to the nearest bus terminal. I repressed the desire to look back and wave goodbye. I never wanted to see that place again.

After I was settled into my room I called Detective Boyland and he invited me to come up to see him at the Levittown stationhouse the following morning. When I got there he greeted me with a smile and seemed happy to see me. He said, "Look at you, Frankie, all grown up and what a handsome lad you have become!"

And maybe he was right. I had filled out to 175 pounds and was 5' 10" tall. I said, "Thanks, I'm finally out of the Home and I got a room in Baldwin."

"Are you working?"

"At the Rapid Express Oil and Lube on Sunrise Highway," I said. "Doesn't pay much, but with the economy the way it is, it's the best around so far."

"Did you ever get another foster home after the Ryan's?"

"Yeah another farm upstate, but that did not last too long and I was back in the Home for my last few years."

I did not elaborate on my experiences with the Jonas's nor did Boyland ask. He obviously had not heard about Harold Jonas's untimely accidental death. Small talk out of the way I asked the question that had been at the forefront of my mind. "Any word on my mother?"

"No, Frankie, she never turned up. I'm sorry."

"Do you think she killed my father?"

"I'm convinced of it," he said, "and Wally Mason sure thought so."

"Is he still around?"

"No, he retired a few years ago and went out to travel the country with his wife. Knowing you were coming over I went over his entire case file on your dad's death, and I found out a few things I hadn't known."

I perked up a bit and said, "Oh, what things?"

"When your mother took off her car turned up the same day in Chambersburg, Pennsylvania. She traded it in at a used-car lot for a newer Honda and drove off. Wally changed the alarm out for her to now include the new plate number and vehicle ID number of the Honda."

"Did it ever turn up?" I asked.

"No. A week later Wally had to cancel the alarm because your dad's death was ruled an accident."

"But wasn't it a crime to abandon me?"

"Yes, but only a misdemeanor. The county won't extradite anyone for less than a felony level offense."

"Yeah," I said. "Who gives a damn about a nine-year old orphan anyway?"

"Frankie, I feel bad about what happened to you. You know that."

I nodded and said, "Where do you think she was headed?"

"Not Florida," Danny said. "Chambersburg is on I-81 which heads southwest down to I-40 which runs way out west. She could have ended up anywhere from Tennessee to California.

"Danny, could you run that Honda's VIN now and see what turns up?"

He hesitated a few seconds then turned to his computer and said "Sure, Frankie, I can do that," as he accessed the screen and typed in the numbers and letters.

It took about two minutes for the screen to fill with the information and after studying it for a bit, Danny said, "It doesn't list all previous owners, only the last one, a guy named William Lattimore. The car was impounded by the authorities after Lattimore died and left it on a city street. It was crushed for scrap. Happened last year."

"What city?" I asked.

"Los Angeles."

I repressed my internal excitement at this information and changed the subject by asking, "Is the social worker still around… uh…Miss Saunders?"

"No, Pam was fortunate to find the love of her life and get married and quit. Her job was *really* depressing – she saw worse things than I did."

We went to lunch together and Danny asked me how I was getting around town. I told him by bus and on foot as I had no money for a car at this time. He told me he still had my bicycle covered up in his garage and offered to bring it over to my place. He said, "It may be a poor substitute for a car, but you can use it to get from home to your job and to the stores until you get real wheels."

"I'll gladly take it," I said. "Other than you, it's the only tangible item left of my past life."

Danny nodded and said, "When you save a few bucks, I'll throw some money in and help you get a car, but there might be a better path for your life to travel on first."

"What do you mean?" I asked.

"Have you ever thought about going into the service?"

"Yeah, that's what a lot of the guys from the Home do when they reach eighteen. But I really don't want to go to the deserts of the Middle East and come home in a body bag or maimed."

"Join the Navy or the Air Force."

"Were you in?"

"No, but a close friend of mine was in the Navy. He learned a lot in those four years and he was able to save enough money to complete his entire college education when he got out."

"Really?"

"Really, and you don't have to crawl through the sand dunes on your belly."

"You know, maybe I will look into that," I said.

Danny walked with me to the bus stop and told me to call him when I wanted him to bring my bike over. The idea of going into the Navy intrigued me and I made a note to talk to the recruiter soon. It was time to move on as Danny suggested.

I had long ago come to terms with Jethro Hammond and the gang from the Home – what purpose would it do to exact revenge? They couldn't hurt me again. And I *had* to do what I did to Harold Jonas to stop him from sodomizing me again. Yes, it was time to move on. Two months later I was in the United States Navy for a four-year hitch, but thoughts of my mother still refused to be buried with the others no matter how hard I tried. And my bike was once again back in Danny Boyland's garage.

After a year of sea duty, I found my vocation – the world of computers. I knew the basis of their operations from high school, but the Navy opened a whole new world of information. They taught me how to take them apart, re-build them from scratch, and recover data thought lost. They also introduced me to the basics of programming and software development. I now knew what I would spend my education allowance on when I got out – a degree in computer science – the key to a respectful well-paying job.

My last three years in service were spent at the San Diego Naval Base, and as my enlistment neared an end, my thoughts returned to Mommy once more. For the past year or so I had searched several available data bases for her with no luck. I decided to seek advice from an investigator in the Naval Investigative Service whose offices were close by. I recognized one of the guys I had often seen in the cafeteria and approached him. I didn't know his rank because he was in civilian clothes, so to be on the safe side I said, "Sir, would you have time to answer a few questions for me? I'm Petty Officer Frank Chandler from purchasing and provisioning."

"Chief Warrant Officer Alan McDonough," he said sticking out his hand. "How can I help you?"

"I do ordering, pricing and requisitions for the fleet and I'm pretty good at computer research, but I'm not having any luck in locating a person I'm interested in finding."

"Who is the person?"

I figured I'd tell it like it was, well part of it. "My mother. She abandoned me when I was nine years old."

"Sorry to hear that. What's her name?"

"Angela Chandler, and there seems to be hundreds of women out there with that name. But I'm pretty sure that's not her name anymore. She didn't get along with my dad, so I'm assuming she changed it after he…uh…died."

"What was her maiden name?"

"I don't know."

"How about her date of birth and social security number?"

"I don't know."

"Place of birth?"

"Uh, uh," I said shaking my head.

"You have a tough one here, Frank. Almost impossible. But I can give you some direction that may help. Most places of employment would keep records that usually include all the information you are looking for – a date of birth and social security number being the most important. They may not contain her maiden name, though. But her marriage license application certainly would. And the motor vehicle department would also have her date of birth on her license file."

"Suppose she got a new identity all together?"

"Well, if she were willing to give up her original social security number she would have forfeited all her earning credits. She could then have applied for a new number under a new name. I don't see a reason for her to change her date of birth though, unless she wanted to appear younger – or older."

"Anything else, sir?"

"No, like I say you have a tough one there. It's been my experience that if a person wishes to disappear and establish a new identity they can do it without great difficulty."

"Well, thank you very much Mr. McDonough. If you think of anything else please let me know. I'm right around the corner – at least for eight more months."

"Your hitch is up then?"

"Yes, sir and I'm not re-upping. I'm going to college."

"Good for you, son, and good luck locating your mom."

I pondered the advice given me by Chief Warrant Officer McDonough and a few days later an almost forgotten fact jumped into my mind – Mommy had worked! She had a job with the school. She worked at the Maywood High School right in Levittown. And, I decided, when my next leave came up, that's where I would visit.

• • •

A month later, travelling in my naval uniform, I flew from San Diego to New York and took a bus out to Long Island. I registered for one night at a local motel on Hempstead Turnpike at a nice discount because of the uniform. At nine-thirty the next morning I walked into Maywood High School and found the administrative offices with no difficulties. A young lady approached and smiled at me. I hoped the uniform would open the door to any files on Angela Chandler.

"May I help you, sailor," she said.

I turned on a big smile and said, "I hope so. I'm looking to find someone who used to work here."

"Oh, we can't share any employee information with anyone, except with a court ordered subpoena."

"Maybe, you might make an exception, Miss...?"

"Evans. Judy Evans, but..."

"Miss Evans," I said taking out my wallet. "Here is my official identification. Please note my name."

"Frank Chandler," she said carefully examining the document.

"The person I'm looking for is Angela Chandler – my mother."

"Oh, but..."

"I ran away from home when I was fifteen and eventually joined the Navy. I did an awful thing in leaving her. I haven't seen her in seven years and I want to find her and make amends. Will you help me?"

"Let me look her up in the records and I'll see what I can do," she whispered. "Please, have a seat."

A long five minutes later Miss Evans came out with a slim manila folder in her hand and sat next to me. "There's not much in here, I'm afraid," she said opening the folder and handing it to me.

But as I leafed through the pages I had to differ with Miss Evans. On one document alone, my mother's initial employment application, were listed her date of birth, place of birth, social security number and maiden name – Capozzi. Then I noticed the fingerprint card.

"My mother was fingerprinted?"

"Yes," Miss Evans said. "All employees of school districts who come into contact with children – and that's just about all of us – have to be background checked through the state and national criminal record system."

"I see," I said as I continued to leaf through the file coming upon a small black and white photo of Angela. I stared at it and pretended to wipe a tear from my eyes. Miss Evans patted my arm.

"Can I make a copy of a couple of these documents?" I whispered.

"We just got a brand new copier. It's right around the corner. Be quick, okay?"

"Sure," I said. "Thanks a lot."

I copied the employment application, the fingerprint card and the photo and slipped the copies into my pocket. I returned the folder to Miss Evans and said, "You've been a big help, Miss Evans."

Judy Evans, who seemed to have practically fallen in love with me, blushed and smiled and said, "Oh, I'm so happy to help. I hope you find her soon."

"So do I," I said. "I can't wait to see her again."

Judy Evans was a very attractive young woman and I would have loved to ask her out, but Judy, or any other girl, did not fit into my plans at this time. I had a mission now and I had to get focused on it. The submerged desire to find my mother had once more resurfaced – forcefully. I had to find Mommy and have my question finally answered.

• • •

Immediately upon returning to my quarters that afternoon, I changed from my uniform into tee shirt, shorts and sandals, and booted up my laptop. The first database I checked was the Social Security Death Index. I plugged in Angela's number and got no hit. But, what if she had gotten a different number? I concluded that, regardless of what her social security number was, she was most probably alive. Her date of birth, November 17, 1967, made her forty-five years old. She would turn forty-six in four months.

I next checked all available name index databases for both Angela Chandler and Angela Capozzi, and did the same for all fifty state DMV listings. I got almost a hundred hits, but not one with Mommy's date of birth. And, of course, no database that I could access listed social security numbers.

Think, Frank, what do you have? A place of birth – Brooklyn. A maiden name – Capozzi. A date of birth – November 17, 1967. A complete set of fingerprints. If she had been fingerprinted using her new identity and if…no, no she couldn't allow herself to do that – her previous identity would pop up. Their only value would be to positively confirm her identity once I found her – *if* I ever found her. Had she gone to Los Angeles and eventually sold the Honda to William Lattimore? And if so, was she still there?

I took a pad and pencil and wrote: approximately 310 million people in the U.S., so 155 million women. 365 (366) possible dates of birth. About 425,000 women per birth date assuming an equal distribution. But how many just in 1967? Over a span of a hundred years about 4,250. Over 4,000 women born on November 17, 1967! How would I ever find just one? But if I narrowed the search to just one state – California –maybe the task would be a lot less difficult.

CHAPTER THIRTEEN

Danny

Seeing a couple of sailors on leave this fine spring day in Manhattan reminded me of Frankie Chandler who I had not thought of in a long while. I was with my second wife, Detective Tara Brown, on a rare day off together. We spent the day in the city walking around, caught a matinee in the theatre and then had dinner in an expensive Asian fusion restaurant. "Those sailors remind me of Frankie Chandler," I said.

"Who?" she asked.

"Frankie. The young boy whose mother abandoned him."

"Oh, yes, a long time ago, wasn't it?"

"About thirteen years," I said. "When I was a rookie cop."

"Whatever happened to him?"

"He joined the Navy. He had just turned eighteen and gotten out of the State Home. I advised him to do that when he came to see me at work."

"How long ago was that?"

"At least three years," I said. "His hitch should be up soon."

"I hope he has a decent life now, and I hope he settles down and gets a good wife when he gets out."

"Like I got with you?" I asked.

"Best thing that ever happened to you, Mister," she said smiling and poking me in the ribs. Am I right?"

"You bet you are," I said.

Full after the delicious meal we walked to Penn Station to catch the Long Island Railroad back to our apartment in Mineola. By the time the train escaped the tunnel under the East River, Tara's head was on my shoulder and she was fast asleep. And I thought about the life of Frankie Chandler.

● ● ●

My curiosity had been aroused by Frankie's crude remark about being sodomized. I remembered he had said it as we were leaving the Ryan's house for the trip back to the Home upstate. During the ride, I pressed him for details, but he clammed up only saying, "Forget I said it."

When I dropped him off at the front door of the State Home I got out and wished him luck – we shook hands and he smiled a little and said, "Thanks for the ride Detective Boyland."

"Hey," I said, "call me Danny from now on, okay? Remember that the next time we meet. And I'll keep your bike in tip-top shape for you."

"And when will that be?" he asked. "Just when will we meet again?" He turned his back to me and walked in the door.

When I got back to my office in the Nine-Eight Squad, I called Pam Saunders over at Child Protective Services and informed her of the latest sad chapter in the life of young Frankie Chandler.

Then I said, "Pam, have you ever been aware of an attempt at, or an act of, sodomy perpetrated on Frankie?"

"No, why?"

"He referred to it in passing, but declined to elaborate. Can you do some checking for me on that foster home?"

"Sure thing. Give me a few days."

When Pam got back to me she said there was nothing in Frankie's history to indicate that he had been a victim of sodomy. "Maybe at the Home?" I asked. "An unreported incident perpetrated on him by an older kid or a staff member?"

"I guess it could have happened, but I can't recall any incidents like that in my years of dealing with them."

"And the foster home checked out okay?"

"Yes, the Hammonds were long time foster parents of many children and not one complaint over the years."

"But Frankie was there only a short time, right?"

"Right, only a few months, but then they brought him back to the Home after he accidentally set the barn on fire, remember?"

"Yeah, but let me ask you this, if you know. Would foster children put up with being sexually molested if the foster home was otherwise okay? You know, to keep them from going back to the Home?"

"Off the record?"

"Sure."

"Danny, I think that it's very prevalent, but nothing is done about it. You know, no complaint, no crime."

"H-m-m."

"What?"

"Maybe that fire was not an accident after all."

Nothing ever came of my thoughts about this possible scenario until Frankie visited me in the stationhouse after he had gotten out of the Home once and for all. When I returned to my office after having lunch with him and seeing him on his way that day, I called Pam Saunders at her retirement home in Virginia.

After exchanging hellos and bringing ourselves up to date with our lives, I turned the conversation to Frankie Chandler and the fact that he was now out of the Home for good. I told her he mentioned being sent to another farm.

"That's right, and he didn't last long at that place either. The man of the house, Mr. Jonas, died in an accident and the woman couldn't afford to keep him, so back to the Home he went again."

"Jesus, that poor kid! First Mr. Ryan, who was almost like a real father to Frankie, has a heart attack and dies on him, and then another potential father figure dies, too. Oh, what kind of accident?"

"Huh?"

"You said the farmer died in an accident. Was it another fire?"

"No, a truck engine fell on him. Are you suspicious of Frankie?"

"Uh, no. Just my cop instincts talking, I guess."

"It wouldn't make much sense to create accidents that would only get you back into the Home, now would it?"

"No, Pam, it wouldn't, unless…"

"Unless, what?"

"Unless the conditions were worse there than at the Home."

"Are you thinking maybe sodomy again?"

"Who knows? Was there a police investigation?"

"Sure – and they ruled the death an accident. The motor was suspended from a beam in the barn and the hook gave way. No way Frankie, or anyone else, could have caused that."

"I guess not," I said thinking those two events associated with Frankie Chandler's young life were just as Pam had said – unfortunate accidents and nothing else.

I was pleased when Frankie came to visit me in the precinct. He seemed happy and ready to move on with his life. I thought it would do no good to resurrect bad memories of his experiences in foster homes and the State Home, so I didn't press him on the issue. And although he had still seemed interested in locating his mother – I guess I can understand why – he didn't seem obsessed with it, even when I had checked out Angela's car and found out it had ended up in Los Angeles. So I never did tell him the sad fact that Angela Chandler was not his biological mother. I figured it might do him more harm than good, but after he left I looked over Wally Mason's file jacket on the death of James Chandler one more time. Coming across a picture of Jim that I had not really looked hard at before, what now struck me was Frankie's strong physical resemblance to his dead father. Yeah, it would have done no good to have told him – let *her* tell him if he ever does find her one day. And she'll certainly recognize him. In fact, she'll think her husband came back from the grave to exact his revenge on her.

The train screeched to a jolting stop at our station in Mineola bringing me back to reality and causing Tara to wake up with a start. She blinked her eyes and looked around. "Let's go," I said. "We're home."

"Oh, my gosh, I slept all the way?"

"Yeah, bright eyes, you were great company."

"You didn't sleep?"

"No, I was thinking about the sad life of Frankie Chandler, which made me think of the sad life of me and my children."

"Oh," she said. "I know you really miss them. What were you thinking?"

"What happened the last time I saw them, and if I will ever see them again."

"Sure you will," Tara said. "Things change, people change. Stay strong."

I smiled and said, "I'm glad I have you around. I only wish I could share your strength and optimism."

"Forget about it for a while," she said as we parked the car and went into the house. "Let's have a nightcap."

After a good-sized Sambuca, straight up, we went to bed, but sleep would not come to me, and my mind traveled back to the last time I saw my children and, of course, the major screw up in my life that now causes me all this pain.

• • •

While young Frankie Chandler had been making his rounds of foster homes to and from the State Home, I was making my own trips throughout the boros of the NYMPD. After four years on patrol in the Levittown precinct, a year in plainclothes in Brooklyn's Anti-Crime unit and two years in Nassau's Street Narcotics Unit, I was promoted to Detective Third Grade and assigned to the Six-Two Detective Squad in Brooklyn. After a year there, I received a transfer to Nine-Eight Squad, coming full circle back to Levittown where Frankie had found me prior to his stint in the Navy.

One day, about a year after Frankie called me from California, my boss Lieutenant Frank D'Elia asked me if I would be interested in an assignment to a Homicide Squad. I was flattered and said, "Sure, Boss, I'd love to, but that's a fantasy assignment and I'm not sure if I'm qualified."

He smiled, clasped my shoulder and said, "Danny, you're probably my best detective. The boss in Nassau Homicide is Ray Roberts. We came on the job together and I think he may have an opening. Should I drop your name to him?"

"That would be great. I really appreciate this, Boss."

"My pleasure," he said.

A few months after that chat my transfer to Nassau Homicide came through and, after a period of on-the-job training, I was ready to catch cases on my own. I couldn't wait to catch my first *Big One* – a true whodunit – and when I did it almost destroyed me.

To make a long story short, I fell in love with the female murder suspect on my first big homicide case – a mistake of enormous stupidity and fateful consequences. Her name was Niki Wells, and she was as evil as she was beautiful. She actually framed *me* for the murder of her lover's wife, and I spent twenty months in prison before the truth came out. Needless to say this tragic affair cost me my marriage and my family. Jean hasn't spoken to me since the day of the arrest, and my two kids, Patrick and Kelly, still refuse to see me despite my repeated overtures to them.

Fortunately, after I was cleared of the murder charge, I was reinstated to the Force and eventually got my detective shield back. Niki Wells, who stalked me after she beat all her murder charges in court, and managed to put a couple of bullets into me, was shot to death by Tara Brown, my former detective partner, who I am now happily married to. After being re-assigned to Nassau Homicide for awhile, I was transferred to the NYMPD/FBI Joint Terrorist Task Force for a year chasing down a nutty bunch of homegrown eco-terrorists known as the Romens.

When I got back to Nassau Homicide, I caught another big case – two murdered and mutilated men found on a golf course. It was a real whodunit, and with the help of my partner Detective Virgil Webb, nicknamed *Spider* by Manny Perez because "we don't need no Virgil's around here," we solved it to the praise of all. Oh, this time I did not enter into a love affair to screw things up. However, Spider, my tall, handsome, medium-brown skinned partner, almost did despite my warnings and despite his complete knowledge of my disastrous affair with Niki Wells. He fell, like the clichéd ton of bricks, for the gorgeous newspaper reporter, Beyoncé look-a-like, Tiffany Adams-Kim, who fortunately, or unfortunately, depending on your point of view, turned up dead on the very same golf course as had my two victims. We solved that one, too, and no one ever discovered Spider's brief romance with Tiffany, thereby preserving his marriage and family, while my first one still remains in ruins.

CHAPTER FOURTEEN

Danny

A month after Commissioner Cassidy re-instated me, I was settled into the daily routine of the homicide squad and Tara and I decided the time was right to get married. The wedding was a low-key affair with less than fifty attendees, most of whom were fellow NYMPD cops and detectives. Willy Edwards and his wife, Edna, had flown up from Atlanta and Willy stood up for me as my best man. Tara had Queenie Pearson, a fellow homicide detective, as her matron of honor.

With an imminent decision pending on my visitation petition, Tara and I chose a one-week hiking honeymoon in the Virginia mountains to be near Roanoke when the decision came down. We were in a small motel near the Skyline Drive, and after a short hike and a terrific meal at the adjoining restaurant, we made love slowly and tenderly.

The next day we were hiking on the trail toward a waterfall when my cell phone rang. I checked the digital readout before answering. It was Miles Hoffman, my attorney.

"Danny, I have some news."

"What's up?"

"Where are you now?"

"I just happen to be in the Commonwealth of Virginia on the way to Dark Hollow Falls in my hiking boots."

"Can you hike your way to Roanoke tomorrow? Judge Conyers has scheduled our visitation hearing for ten o'clock."

"I'll be there," I said.

The trip down to the falls was easy. Coming back up the steep trail had us both panting and sweating when we reached the top at the parking area.

"Whew," I said, "I'm more out of shape than I thought."

"Anything hurt?"

"If you mean my bullet wounds from the Dragon Lady – no. If you mean my thighs and calves – oh yeah."

"Let's eat our sandwiches and relax a bit," she said. "Then I want to climb Hawksbill Mountain."

"I'm glad I'll be sitting in a courtroom tomorrow," I said.

"But we'll be back here the day after that, and we got a few more days after that."

"You're punishing me, but I'm very happy to be here with beautiful you on this beautiful spring day, and it's comforting you'll be there with me tomorrow, too."

"Worried?"

"Yeah, Jean's lawyer is a real bitch on wheels."

"Well, don't be. We took care of one Dragon Lady, and we'll take care of the nasty Lila Milgram-Haines, too."

● ● ●

Tara and I got to Miles Hoffman's office a half hour before the hearing the following morning after a solid night's sleep. "What's going to happen?" I asked him.

"Judge Conyers has all the background information on the case already. I even called him personally to fill him in on the recent demise of Nicole Wells and faxed him the newspaper articles. All I have to do is plead our case for reasonable visitation and wait for his decision."

"What's reasonable visitation?"

"You tell me. You live several hundred miles away. How often can you get here?"

I'd like to try for a weekend each month and an occasional holiday when they're off from school, and a week during summer vacation."

"Sounds very reasonable to me. Let's mosey on over to the courthouse."

We arrived a few minutes before ten and Judge Conyers promptly took the bench at ten on the button. He looked over his half-glasses and asked, "Where's the respondent and respondent's counsel?"

Since the bailiff and the stenographer were the only ones in the courtroom, Miles rose to his feet and said, "I don't know, your honor. Ms. Haines is aware of the hearing. I spoke with her late yesterday afternoon."

"Bailiff," he said, "get me Ms. Haines office number."

As the bailiff arose, Lila Milgram-Haines hurriedly entered the courtroom. "Pardon me for my lateness, your honor," she said, gulping for air.

"Where is your client?"

"She just informed me she does not wish to attend this proceeding."

"Why is that?" he asked, the color rising in his face.

"She does not wish to see her ex-husband. She…uh, *never* wants to see her ex-husband."

"Before I order her arrest and have her dragged in here, please tell me that you are empowered to act fully on her behalf."

"I am, your honor."

"Wonderful. Let's proceed. Mr. Hoffman?"

Miles briefly and professionally made the case for reasonable visitation, emphasizing that I had been cleared of all criminal charges and departmental charges and had been retroactively re-instated to the New York Metropolitan Police Department. Lila's position was that I had willfully abandoned my family for an extra-marital affair causing them irreparable harm, and to now allow me to interact with my children would re-kindle the sordid affair and damage them further. She said in her most venomous voice, "The children, as their mother, have expressed their desire to never see their father again."

That gave me a sinking feeling in the pit of my stomach and a feeling of light-headedness. I grabbed Tara's arm for balance and she whispered, "Easy, now."

"Where are the children now?" the judge asked.

"At home with their mother."

"I want them produced. I want them here in this courtroom for an interview in my chambers with both attorneys present."

"Yes, sir," Lila said. "I'll try…"

"No, Ms. Haines, you *will* have them here within the hour. Is that clear?"

"Yes, Your honor. I'll call right now."

"Good. Mr. Hoffman, you may remain. Mr. Boyland, why don't you come back at two o'clock? By that time I will have interviewed your children and should be in a position to render my decision. Court's adjourned until then."

• • •

Tara and I returned to the courtroom at 1:45 and waited. We had eaten a light lunch and even that small amount of food – a cup of soup and a half a sandwich – did not go down easily into my stomach. Ten minutes later the judge entered from his chambers with Miles and Lila following. When everyone was seated in their proper place the bailiff called the court to order and Judge Conyers said, "Does either attorney have anything further to add before I render my decision?"

They both said, "No, your honor."

"Fine. I rule in favor of the plaintiff. Daniel Boyland will have the visitation requested commencing immediately. Can you two attorneys work together to draft this agreement in an expeditious manner?"

They both answered in the affirmative.

"Then this case is closed except for my following remarks, which I want on the record. You have won your quest to see your children, Mr. Boyland, but the road going forward may be more difficult than the one you've already traveled. Your children

– Kelly and Patrick – do not wish to see you. Their mother has poisoned their minds beyond my ability to reason with them. They believe you are a monster, a murderer, a betrayer, and evil on a par with the devil himself. I believe only intensive therapy with a competent child psychologist could get them to believe otherwise. I truly hope, Ms. Haines, that you had no part in this process of twisting their minds."

"No, your honor, of course not."

"Good, because I am giving you the task of convincing your client of the error of her ways. But first I will speak to her privately in my chambers tomorrow morning. If she fails to appear, I will issue a warrant for her arrest. Is that clear, Ms. Haines?"

"Yes, your honor."

"Mr. Boyland, I have made a room available for you to see your children. I would like both attorneys to be present at this first meeting. I might also suggest that it might not be a good idea to have your new wife present this first time."

"He's right," Tara whispered.

"Yes, your honor," I said. "I agree with all your suggestions."

"Good. Proceed to room 317, and I'll also see you tomorrow morning, Ms. Haines – with your client."

I arose on shaky legs as Tara grabbed my hand and said, "Good luck. I'll be waiting here for you or outside in the hall."

I nodded and followed Miles and Lila to room 317. We entered to find Patrick and Kelly seated glumly in spoke-backed wooden chairs. The last time I had seen them had been the day before my arrest almost three years ago. Patrick had just turned eleven in

April and Kelly was now eight. And, of course, they had changed dramatically in those three years, both in size and appearance. The lump in my throat almost prevented me from speaking. I choked out, "Hi, Pat. Hi, Kelly."

They glanced at me then looked down without saying a word. I pulled up a chair close to them and said, "I know you are not happy to have to see me, but I am very happy to see you. I plan to visit with you as often as I can get down from New York."

Patrick looked up with defiance in his eyes and said, "I don't ever want to see you again. Why do you want to see us?"

"I am your father and I love the both of you very much, and I miss you both – that's why."

"You're not our father anymore. You left us and mom. And you're a murderer – an evil man."

"Yes, I did leave you and that was the greatest mistake I ever made in my life. But I am not a murderer, and I am not evil. I'm just a regular guy who screwed up big time. Now I want to set things straight and be a small part of your lives."

Patrick looked over at Lila and said, "Can we go home now, Ms. Haines?"

Lila looked at me and I nodded. "Sure, children," she said, "we can go now."

They went out the door, Lila first followed by Patrick then by my golden-haired little girl. She turned and there was a tear in her eye. She said softly, "Bye, Daddy."

That broke my heart. I sank back into my chair and wept for several minutes before I began to calm down. Miles patted me on the shoulder and said, "The worst is over. Things will get better from here on."

• • •

When I had returned to the courtroom from the meeting with my children I must have looked awful. Seeing my red-rimmed eyes and red nose Tara knew I had been crying – a lot. "Let's get out of here," I said. "I'll tell you about it on the drive back north." But, so far, as Tara drove north on I-81, I had told her nothing.

Tara finally broke the silence saying, "It's getting near six o'clock. You want to stop and get something to eat and look for a motel?"

"Whatever. I'm not hungry."

I knew Tara wanted to snap me out of my mood, but she wisely kept quiet and continued driving. She exited at Staunton and pulled up to a Best Western that had an attached restaurant. "I'll be right back," she said leaving the car parked near the lobby. She was back in five minutes with a key and drove the car around to the side of the building. "Let's go," she said. "We're in room 142."

We carried our bags in and washed up. "I'm hungry," she said. "Let's walk over to the restaurant."

"Let's stop in the bar first," I said.

"Sure, I could use a drink myself."

We sat at a small table in the lounge area of the bar and I took a large swallow of my Jamison's on the rocks. "They hate me. My kids hate me."

"Tell me about it."

I did and when I finished I said, "Oh, on the way out Kelly said 'Bye, Daddy.' It damn near broke my heart."

"Then why are you so down? Those two words show that Jeanie didn't completely twist that little girl's brains. She called you *Daddy*, after all."

I straightened up a bit and looked Tara in the eyes. "Yes, I guess she did."

"You aren't beaten in this fight. We've only *begun* to fight that bitch."

"We?"

"You bet. I'm in this with you all the way."

For the first time since yesterday, I smiled. "Thanks, that helps a lot. Hey, I'm a little hungry myself."

We stayed four more days in Virginia hiking, sightseeing, making love and eating in fine local restaurants. I had forced myself to snap out of my misery for Tara's sake. She needed this little vacation as much as I did. I pushed Jeanie and Lila Milgram-Haines into a far corner of my mind.

It was time to leave the green hills of Virginia and head back to the grit and grime of the City of New York. The squad would be waiting for me, but Patrick and Kelly would not. Tara noticed the gloom descending on me the closer we got to the city. When we pulled up to our apartment late Monday night she said, "We have one more day off before we go back to work. Let's enjoy it while we can."

● ● ●

It was a several months after this crushing visit with my kids that I got a call from Frankie – long distance from California. He said he had just mustered out of the Navy and decided to start a life in the land of fruits and nuts – a term he used, and which we both had a good laugh over.

"Why California?" I asked.

"I spent some time here in the Navy and I really like it," he said.

"San Diego?" I asked.

"Mostly, but I'm going to stay in Los Angeles. More education opportunity there. I took your advice about school and I saved a lot of my pay."

"Good for you. I wish you all the best. Put the past behind you and go for it."

"I will, Detective…er, Danny."

Then I remembered something – *Los Angeles* – the last place Angela Chandler's car had turned up. Was Frankie's settling down there just a coincidence? "Okay," I said, "when you get settled in give me a call and let me now where you are living. And, of course, if you ever come back to New York, be sure to look me up."

"I sure will," he said. "Well, so long for now. And thanks for being a friend."

"Good-bye Frankie," I said wondering as I hung up the phone if I would ever see or hear from him again. A pang of guilt spread through my body as I recalled his words of thanks to me – *thanks for being a friend* – not much of a friend, I thought. I sure could have done more for him than keep his bicycle, his only possession from his past life, in my garage. That was for damn sure.

CHAPTER FIFTEEN

Danny

On occasion I think of Frankie Chandler, especially when I notice his old bike parked in a dusty area of my small garage. He never called me again from California to tell me his address and phone number and I guess he never will. The Chandlers were now all relegated to "the cases of my past," but I always wondered if Frankie had put any effort into finding his mother out in Los Angeles. And if he ever found her, I would have loved to have been a fly on the wall for *that* confrontation.

Now things have seemed to calm down for me and Spider and we handle our cases professionally and routinely. No super whodunits have come our way in a long time and things are actually a bit boring. Spider and I were catching up on paperwork and waiting for the phone to ring when he said, "Hey, partner, now that it's quiet it seems like a good time to tell me about your first homicide case here."

"Huh? You already know all there is to know about the Dragon Lady."

"No, the one before that. The one you seemed embarrassed about and said it was a story you'd tell me when you got to know me better."

"Oh," I said shaking my head and smiling. "*That* one. Yeah, I guess I can tell you now. But you'd better not laugh at me, or I'll smack you upside your head."

"Why would I laugh at you, Danny?"

"Here's why. I was brand new in the squad and it was my first night alone to catch cases and I was terrified. I was afraid I'd catch a real bad one and not know what to do. My time started at midnight and a bunch of us were having a drink in Mulvaney's on the four-to-twelve tour. I was sitting with Tara and Denny Chin and was just finishing my second beer, which was all I was going to have. I certainly didn't want to respond to my first homicide in a drunken state."

"I can understand that," Spider said. "I didn't have a drop of alcohol at all. So what happened?"

• • •

Tara said to me, "So, Danny, tonight's the night. Catching cases all alone on the midnight shift. Nervous?"

"A bit. How did yours go?"

"Nice and quiet. I left the office at one a.m., went home to bed and the phone never rang all night."

"I wasn't so lucky," Denny Chin said. "I caught a murder/suicide at 2:30 a.m., but I was done with it by noon."

MOMMY, MOMMY

"I just hope I don't catch a real complicated mystery," I said. "I don't know if I'm ready for it yet."

"Sure you are," Tara said, "you've come along very quickly. You'll be fine."

"Thanks, I'm leaving here right after this beer. I'll go keep Lana company back in the office."

I left Mulvaney's fifteen minutes later and was back in the office by eight. Lana Pearson, whose nickname was Queenie based on her resemblance to Queen Latifah, was catching cases on the four-to-twelve, and therefore not allowed to join the meeting at Mulvaney's. The two other detectives working four-to-twelve with me and Lana were Rube Wilson and Fred *Fritzi* Lange. Lana had had a quiet evening thus far, and we put on a pot of coffee and quietly caught up with our paperwork. Around 9:45 or so, Lana got up from her chair, stretched, yawned and said, "I feel it in my bones, I do."

"Oh, shit," Rube Wilson said, "here she goes."

"What's going on?" I asked.

"Detective Pearson claims she knows when bad things are happening," Rube said. "She thinks she's a voodoo lady or something."

"I can feel it Rube, and I'm feeling it now," Queenie said. "Somebody's out there shooting up a whole bunch of people. You watch, that phone's gonna ring soon."

We all involuntarily looked at the phone on her desk, but it just sat there quietly.

"I don't hear any ringing, voodoo lady," Fritzi said.

"You just wait, you'll see. I feel it and I know it."

Unbelievably, the phone rang. She smiled as she dramatically picked up the receiver saying to us, "I told you so."

She listened a few seconds then said, "It's real quiet Ray, nothing happening, but as I just told these three unbelievers, I feel it in my bones. Sure, hold on."

She handed the phone to me saying, "It's the boss just checking in. He wants to talk to you."

"Hi, Danny. I just wanted to let you know I'm leaving Mulvaney's now and heading home. If anything happens later that you feel you need help with, don't hesitate to call me, okay?"

"Okay. I just hope Lana's feelings, if they're correct, happen soon while she's still catching."

"Aw, don't listen to Queenie, although she has been right a few times before."

"Really?"

"Yeah, but don't worry. I wouldn't have put you in the duty chart if I hadn't thought you were ready for anything that can come your way."

"Thanks for the vote of confidence, but I really wouldn't mind if the phone didn't ring for me for a couple of more weeks anyway."

At midnight Lana, Fritzi and Rube said goodnight and started out of the office door.

"Well, Queenie," I said, "I guess your feelings were wrong tonight."

"Maybe, maybe not. I still feel 'em though. Maybe something's happening in another boro, not here in Nassau."

"Let's go, Queenie," Rube said. "You're getting ridiculous with this crap. Maybe you're feeling the St. Valentine's Day Massacre in Chicago eighty years ago."

"You'll see. Check the papers in the morning. Something *real* big is going down, I *know* it – believe you, me."

I finished up the supplementary reports on a couple of old routine cases and decided to head for home. It was a quarter to one and I was locking up the boss's office when the phone rang. It was very loud in the deserted office, and I hurried over and picked it up on the third ring. "Detective Boyland," I answered.

"You catching tonight, Boyland?" a bored voice asked.

"Yeah, who's this?"

"Keller, over in Central Detectives. I just received a notification from the desk officer in the Nine-Three, Lieutenant Briscoe. He just heard from a couple of his guys on patrol that they got a few dead ones at Mulvaney's. I'm sure you know where that is."

"Oh, shit. Did you say a few dead?"

"Yeah, some sort of stickup or gang war. They don't know, but since there are dead people on the floor your presence is requested."

"Who's responding?"

"So far, just you. Who do you want me to notify?"

"The deputy medical examiner on call, Crime Scene, the ADA on call – that'll be enough for now until I get there and have a look."

"Okay, Boyland. I'll make the notifications."

"Thanks, I'm on my way."

I grabbed my suit jacket and felt for my cell phone on my belt and thought of Queenie's prediction. Well, this sure as shit sounded like a big one all right, a *real* big one. Why me? On my first goddamned midnight. And who were the dead ones? Were any of our guys still there? A million things raced through my mind as I went down the stairs into the parking lot. I trotted to the response car, took a deep breath, started up and drove north on Mineola Boulevard.

Seven minutes later I pulled to the curb behind an empty marked patrol car, its flashing red lights reflecting eerily in silence off the front windows. I approached the front door of Mulvaney's and was greeted by a uniformed cop who said, "Officer Mike Peters, sir."

"Danny Boyland from Homicide, Mike. What've we got, and why is it so dark in there?"

"My partner's inside trying to get some lights on. We think the shooting may have knocked them out. A lot of bullets were sprayed around."

"How many shot?" I asked, wondering if I should call the boss right now.

"What we could tell with only our flashlights, it looks like nine or ten."

"Holy shit! Let me have your flashlight and stay right here by the door. Begin a log of persons coming to the scene."

"Sure, I'm not too keen on going back in there right now. I…er…you know…tossed my cookies, I'm ashamed to admit."

"Don't worry about it. What's your partner's name?"

"Jimmy Murrow. I see his flashlight waving around in there."

MOMMY, MOMMY

I stepped inside and moved the beam of the flashlight around the bar area. I gasped in horror at what I saw. Three bodies were slumped over the bar, their drinks spilled. Two were black females and one was a white-haired male with a huge red stain on the back of his white shirt. I involuntarily stepped back and tripped on a body. I grabbed onto the back of a chair to steady myself and I called out to Officer Murrow. "Hey, Murrow, where are you?"

"In the back room, trying to find the circuit breakers."

"I'm Danny Boyland, from Homicide. Keep looking, we need those lights."

I played the flashlight around and trembled with the vision of this ghastly scene. I said out loud, "Motherfucker, what the hell do I do now"

A voice from the bar said, "Why don't you call the Lieutenant for help, Danny Boy?" With that, the lights suddenly came on and all the corpses sprang to life shouting, *"Surprise! April fool, even if it's September! Gotcha!"*

I was at a total loss for words and in shock at what was going on. Then my eyes focused on the white-haired guy who was laughing hysterically and walking towards me. Recognition dawned – it was Willy Edwards! And the two black females were Queenie and Tara! The bodies getting up from the floor were laughing crazily and pounding each other on their backs. Gallagher! Pavlauskas! Denny Chin! Fritzi!

The door to the back room opened and Officer Murrow came out followed by five or six more members of our squad. Full realization then hit me. It was a joke! One big fucking joke at the expense of the new homicide dick – me!

Joe Pavlauskas sputtering, spitting, laughing uncontrollably handed me a tumbler of whiskey as Gallagher said, "Drink up Danny. It's Jameson's, and you look like you need it."

I gulped it down in one swallow then threw the glass across the room and said, "You drunken, sadistic motherfuckers!"

This caused even more howls of laughter from the group, causing Joe to pull a filthy handkerchief from his pocket to wipe the tears from his eyes. Manny Perez put his arm around my shoulder and said, "Looks like we got you pretty good, hey Danny?"

The Irish whiskey had worked its way quickly through my bloodstream and I nodded my head in agreement and said, "You sure did you bastards, you sure did."

I looked around the room and finally smiled, then laughed, along with them. "How long did you degenerates plan this? From the day I walked into the squad?"

"Naw," Gallagher said, "it was an impromptu thing. You were so uptight and nervous about your first night on call that we figured we'd loosen you up a little."

"Loosen me up, you big fuck? You almost gave me a heart attack!"

The laughter resumed again and I figured I'd better just shut up and stop feeding their funny bones. Lana Pearson waved her fingers in my face, laughing, and said, "Booga, booga, the big one be comin' for sure, Danny. I tol' you so."

I collapsed into a chair and Gallagher handed me another Jameson's. "I'd better not Bernie, I'm still on call you know."

"Shit, I caught a lot of murders when I was drunker than I am now. Drink up! No problem!"

I took a small sip of the whiskey and wondered how the hell Bernie could ever be drunker than he was right now as he staggered away back towards the bar. I said, "You all got me real good I must admit, but I know you wouldn't have done this if you really didn't like me, so here's to you all."

I drank the rest of my Jameson's, reached into my wallet, threw a few twenties on the bar and announced, "The next round's on me, but then I'm headed home to bed."

"Party pooper," Tara said.

"But Danny, the party's just starting," Denny Chin said.

"He's right about that," Sergeant Perski said, "but we'd better continue without our guy on call. The boss'd fry our balls if at least one of us wasn't sober enough to handle a case, so let's say our goodnights to Detective Daniel P. Boyland, now at last, a bona fide member of Nassau Homicide."

They all raised their glasses in a toast to me and drank heartily. I wondered how the hell they consumed so much and prayed that if I got a real case later this night it would be an easy one requiring no assistance. Perski must have read my mind as he accompanied me to the door. He whispered, "If you do get a big one and need help, call me or Finn."

"Thanks, Sarge."

"Good. Now when the fuck are you ever goin' to stop calling me Sarge?"

"Right now, Lenny. Good night."

The rest of the night thankfully passed without incident, although I couldn't sleep much waiting for the phone to ring, but it never did. I smiled to myself, happy to have landed in this wacky squad and to have been fully accepted into it. I couldn't wait to get back to work.

• • •

"That was a hell of a story," Spider said. "Man, I'm glad you guys didn't do something like that to me when I first got here."

"The times and personnel were different back then. It was before the Niki Wells affair. Before three-quarters of the squad got transferred out because of me."

"Oh," Spider said and we both lapsed into our own silent thoughts.

A few minutes later as I was preparing a fresh pot of coffee, Manny Perez shouted, "Line One, Danny. Sounds like you got one."

I picked up the phone and listened to a detective from my old squad, the Nine-Eight, explain that a middle-aged woman had apparently been shot to death in her second-floor apartment in Farmingdale. He told me all the usual services – Crime Scene, Medical Examiner, District Attorney – had been notified and were responding. I felt the adrenaline beginning its surge in my bloodstream. Finally, a case! I grabbed the keys to the response car and called out to my partner, "Hey, Spider! Saddle up! We got one!"

CHAPTER SIXTEEN

Frankie

I settled into a small apartment in the distant suburbs of Los Angeles and began working part-time in an electronics store that did a good part of its business in computer sales and repairs. I had deliberately chosen a neighborhood that was not too far from a branch of Los Angeles County Community College, which had a two-year offering in Computer Science, and I enrolled for twelve credits.

Between work and school I didn't have much of a social life – an occasional date with a classmate – but I was not interested in developing a long term romantic relationship. Most of my spare time was spent on my PC searching for my mother. The search was more of a database challenge for me, a puzzle to be solved, and much more interesting than spider solitaire or the current hot video games.

I had decided that to have a mathematically probable chance to locate her, I would have to somehow reduce the number of names in the database files to a manageable level. To do so I would have to make some logical assumptions, and hope that one false assumption wouldn't completely ruin my efforts.

Mommy was of Italian heritage. She looked Italian – dark-brown hair, brown eyes, slightly olive complexion – and very pretty as I remembered from my time with her and confirmed by the photo I had gotten from her job. My first assumption, and this was the big one, was that she had kept her same date of birth, and the next assumption I made was that she changed her name, but chose another Italian one to mirror the reality of her appearance. And I assumed she got a new driver's license using that new name and her original date of birth. I was now ready to begin

To see what I was up against I chose California, the state where I lived and where Mommy may have fled to, and brought up the State Motor Vehicle Data Base. There were 23 million licensed drivers out of a total population of 38 million, which was about twelve percent of the country's population. I was thus able to reduce my 4,200 nation-wide possibles to about 250 women and, since only 62 percent were licensed drivers, I was able to reduce that figure again to about 155 women born on November 17, 1967 in California and possessing a driver's license.

I entered November 17, 1967 in the "search by" box and refined it further by choosing "female." There were 148 licenses for females born on November 17, 1967, very close to my estimate. Then my elation at my success so far began to be eroded by doubts and variables I had not accounted for. Suppose she dyed her hair blonde? Suppose she had cosmetic surgery? Suppose she had not chosen an Italian surname? Suppose she had altered her date of birth by even one day? Suppose…?

I minimized the database and flopped on the couch disheartened and with a headache coming on. I thought I figured out what my next step should be, but it would have to wait awhile. I needed to eat, to sleep, to study and to go to work. The search for Mommy would have to wait a week or so.

● ● ●

When I was able to devote a few uninterrupted hours to my search I resumed the task. I once again accessed the DMV database and brought up the first license in the alphabetized list of women born on November 17, 1967. I maximized the license on the screen and stared at the photo. Barbara Aaron had long blonde hair and her listed height of 5'-8" was at least three inches taller than Mommy, and her weight was at least thirty pounds more. Not even a remote possibility.

At the rate of about one license per three minutes – I wanted to take my time and make notes – I had checked forty licenses in two hours. Three times I had seen the first name of Angela, and three times my heart had jumped. But none of the three were close. In fact only nine women made it onto my pad of paper as a "possible." They all had Italian surnames, resembled Mommy somewhat, and had a listed height plus or minus one inch of Mommy's five foot, five inches. I discounted weight as a reliable indicator for obvious reasons. I also discounted eye color although all three possibles had brown eyes. And I discounted hair color although two were listed as brown and one as auburn.

Just about the time my first semester ended I had completed my search of the California DMV database and ended up with a list which I put in two columns – strong possibilities and weak possibilities. There were thirty-two strong ones – Italian surname, good physical resemblance, brown hair, brown eyes, and height plus or minus an inch. And there were fifty-three weaker possibilities where one or two of the parameters were different. Now what was the real probability that Mommy was in that group of thirty-two? There was only one way to find out – search them out one by one and confront them. Of the thirty-two, nineteen lived in or within a hundred mile radius of Los Angeles, so I would begin here and work my way outward, and I would begin next Monday.

Well before Monday arrived my confidence in this undertaking began to seriously dissipate beginning with the biggest assumption of all – that Mommy had fled to California. What about the other forty-nine states? Yes, she could be anywhere, but I was here and I had to start somewhere. What if I was able to find and confront all the strong and weak possibles and still not find her? Do I move to Florida and start over? But I had to cross that bridge when I came to it, didn't I?

● ● ●

Monday morning found me sitting in my ten-year old Sentra about a hundred feet from the suburban home of Gloria Arcuri in Santa Monica. I was waiting for her to leave her house so I could get a good look at her. I had binoculars under my seat so I could get a real close-up of her face. If I was in doubt, I would confront her.

After two hours passed and she had not appeared, I began to get edgy. As I was debating what to do, I was startled by a firm knock on my car window. I looked up to see the stern face of a uniformed police officer. I almost peed in my pants – a basic bodily function that I then realized I had not come prepared to deal with. The cop motioned for me to roll down my window. I turned the ignition key to on and complied, my mind racing, my eyes checking around the car's interior.

"May I see your license and registration certificate, please?" the officer said.

"Sure," I said. "Is something wrong?"

He didn't answer, but just waited as I fished the documents from my wallet. He looked at what I had given him then walked around the car checking my plates and windshield stickers. I knew everything was in order. He returned to my window and said, "Mind if I ask you, Frank, what you are doing here?"

Now I had taken a few criminal justice courses and, if I remembered correctly, I didn't have to answer him. I did not even have to say a word. I decided not to take that course of action. While he was walking around the car I had concocted what I hoped was a plausible story, so I said, "I had a big fight with my girlfriend a couple of hours ago and I was just sitting here thinking things out."

"You're a long way from home – fifteen miles."

"Yes, and I'm really not sure where I am. I drove around aimlessly and ended up parking here to think things over."

"Been here long?"

"I think so, probably an hour."

"More like two. Sit tight while I check this out."

The cop walked back to his cruiser and got inside. I saw him pick up his radio mike and speak into it. About three minutes later he returned and handed me back my documents. He said, "You sitting here so long made a couple of people nervous. You can understand that, right?"

"Oh sure. My God, they probably thought I was a robber or something! Oh, officer, I'll get out of here right away."

"Good idea, Frank," he said with a smile. "And go get a cup of coffee. Don't drown your sorrows with booze while you still have to drive home."

"Thanks for the advice, Officer," I said.

"So long," he said.

I did go for a big cup of coffee – after first relieving myself in the diner's bathroom – and mulled over the situation as I drank it. I had to reformulate my plans. I would have to reason things out very carefully before I made my next move. And I would certainly have to move Gloria Arcuri to the bottom of my list right now.

• • •

It took me several days to finalize my plans and several more to move on to the next person on my list – Alicia Buonora of Ventura. Being confronted by that Santa Monica cop turned out to be a blessing in disguise; I would now choose the women to visit based on police jurisdiction. Never would I go back to the same jurisdiction until I had exhausted all the others first. I figured if a woman I visited decided to call the police to report "a strange young man asking if I was his mother," that information would not be shared among police agencies. But three or four calls like that to the *same* agency would most likely generate an inquiry.

My final plan was really simple – knock on the door, smile and ask the question, "Hello, Mrs. Buonora, I'm Frankie Chandler. I'm looking for my long lost mother, and I was wondering if you could help me."

I figured by using my name and stating the reason for my visit up front, I had a good chance of catching a guilty reaction from the woman if she were indeed my mother. In those cases of doubt I would ask to be invited inside, but would immediately leave if the woman denied knowledge and I didn't recognize her at all. And I would have to prepare another scenario if a husband or other family member opened the door.

My ace in the hole was Mommy's fingerprint card. One of the criminal justice courses I took as an elective was called criminalistics. It was fascinating and dealt with the collection and scientific analysis of physical evidence. One of the units dealt with was dactyloscopy – the science of fingerprint identification. I learned how to lift latent prints, roll human fingerprints with ink and how to determine if two fingerprints were a scientific match. I ordered a fingerprint kit from a mail order scientific supply house and read a couple of library books that dealt specifically with dactyloscopy. If a woman denied being my mother, but I was suspicious for any reason, I would ask to take her thumbprint and then compare it to the thumbprint on Angela Chandler's card. And if the woman refused to allow me to print her? Well, that would be another bridge I would have to cross when it happened.

I was about to embark on my journey to Ventura, but was still at home rehearsing the plan one more time when the question of all questions rose to the forefront of my mind as it had many times in the past. And as I had done many times in the past, I repressed it, but at this time it just wouldn't be suppressed. I knew I had to deal with it sooner or later, the question being – just what would I do if I found her? So I spent a half hour trying to answer it and the best I could do was, "The answer to that question depends on Mommy." Her reaction, her body language, her words, and her explanation – everything depended on Mommy.

The words in her note when she abandoned me were still seared in my memory, especially the last two sentences: "Maybe we will see each other again and you will then understand why I did this. Until then, I love you. Mommy." Since she had never found me – had she tried and failed? – her words seemed to imply that maybe she wanted *me* to find *her*. And at that time I would "understand" – she would explain it to me. And, she loved me.

And after she explained, then what? Do we live happily ever after or go our separate ways? The question of all questions multiplied and morphed into myriads more questions. But the answer for now was action, not thought. No more questions. Find her first. Then the questions will all finally be answered.

• • •

My simple plan had gone through many modifications and I think – I hoped – I now had a reasonable, believable approach

MOMMY, MOMMY

for success. I had anticipated that Alicia, and any other woman I would visit, would have a husband and a family, so when a man opened the door to my knock at 371 Wilson Avenue, I was not surprised. It was 7:30 in the evening, a time I had chosen figuring that no one would observe me walking to the house from my car and that dinner would be over. "Can I help you?" the man asked.

"I hope so, Mr. Buonora," I said with a smile. "Or rather I hope your wife can help me."

"How so?" he asked.

"I'm trying to locate a person who may have some information about my family and my past. May I come in?"

Mr. Buonora looked me up and down. He saw a clean-shaven, well-dressed, smiling young man carrying an attaché case. "Sure," he said.

He invited me to sit down in the den and called upstairs to his wife. "Alicia! Come down a minute!"

As I heard her steps on the staircase my heart rate increased and I felt a trickle of sweat run down my left armpit. I stood up as she entered the den and faced me, and I immediately knew this wasn't Mommy, not even close. I stood up and smiled, "I'm Roger Madsen, Mrs. Buonora, and I'm looking for my sister. I was hoping you might help me."

"I'll try," she said with a confused look on her face, "but I don't know…"

"Let me explain," I said. "My parents were killed in a car accident when I and my sister were very young. We were judged to be wards of the state, and I eventually went to a foster home. I assumed my sister had also."

"How awful, Mr. Madsen," Alicia said.

"Terrible," Mr. Buonora said.

"When I turned eighteen, I tried to find her with no success. Then recently, with the help of a private investigator, I discovered that one of my mother's sisters – my aunt – had adopted her from the state home. The problem is my mother had two sisters – Alicia and Sandra – and I don't know which one adopted her. The private eye couldn't find that out either. So, I'm on a search and my question is, Mrs. Buonora, are you my aunt Alicia Mercer and does my sister live here?"

"I'm sorry," Alicia Buonora said, "but I have to answer no to both those questions."

I sighed and said, "Unfortunately, I've heard the same answers before. Thank you for listening to me. I'll be on my way now."

"Mr. Madsen, how did you choose my wife as a possibility?"

"Based on her first name and her age."

"Then you must have a lot of women to check."

"Hundreds, Mr. Buonora, but I'm not ready to give up my search."

"Have you placed an ad in the newspaper?" Alicia asked.

"Several dozen," I responded. "No luck."

"Well, maybe your luck will change," Mr. Buonora said, shaking my hand as I prepared to leave.

"Thank you again for listening to me," I said. "Good night."

I took a deep breath of the cool March night air as I left the house. One down, thirty-one to go.

CHAPTER SEVENTEEN

Angela

Although I was now heading for fifty I still yearned for a stable, happy relationship with a man – just like I had with Tom. But as a famous author once wrote – "A Good Man is Hard to Find," and I sure had trouble finding another good one. And then, I thought, maybe I had my one good man and that would be that. So I stopped searching for a mate among the numerous businessmen who frequented Maxwell's, and became content with my life as it was.

My solitary existence was conducive to introspection and I often thought of Frankie and Jim Chandler and if I could have done things differently. Could I have toughed it out longer? Would Jim have changed when he finally got his promotion? Was it necessary to abandon my stepson? Where was Frankie now? He would be in his twenties and I hoped he was having a decent life. Had he ever tried to find me? Did he care? Did he need money? I had plenty now. I could help him…

I picked up a novel and immersed myself in it trying to suppress thoughts of my past. The cruel fact was that I could change none of it. Reflecting on it only made me gloomy and I would have to force myself to search for the bright spots of my past experiences – and there were but few – the first years with Jim Chandler and the all too brief few years with Tom O'Shea. That was about all there was. So when the handsome Sal Domenico, a regular patron of Maxwell's whispered in my ear, "Maria, would you care to go out with me sometime?" I hesitated a moment before responding, "Yes."

• • •

As I got to know Sal and our dating took a turn toward the serious side, I became troubled on occasion with something about him – his mannerisms or way of speaking – I hadn't been able to put my finger on it. Finally, it hit me. He reminded me sometimes, not always, just *sometimes*, of my father. And my father had murdered my mother.

Not that Sal physically resembled my father; it was just his actions, his laugh which at times could be a cruel one. Dad had been short and squat with a heavy jaw that always seemed to need a shave and his straight black hair was thin and receding. Sal was tall and had elegant features with a prominent Roman nose and a head covered with wavy black hair. It wasn't the differences that troubled me, it was the similarities, and I had to shortly make up my mind if this was a factor in our relationship because Sal had broached the idea of living together and then, in the near future, getting married.

Despite my misgivings I finally decided to take the plunge figuring life was passing me by and this might be my last chance at a happy marriage and a long relationship. Sal moved out of his apartment and moved into my house. He had been divorced for a few years and still paid child support for one of his two children. His ex-wife, Joanna, had gotten the house and three years alimony which had just been fulfilled. His first son, Michael, was in the Air Force and Louis, age sixteen, lived with Joanna.

Sal was open to me about his first marriage telling me that he and Joanna had just drifted apart after twenty-two years. Neither one had yet remarried although he heard she was seeing someone. "I hold no grudge," he told me. "What's past is past."

So Sal and I set up house together and after a few months things were going along just fine between us. We made love regularly, went out to dinner or a show often and enjoyed each other's company. Sal had a high paying position in the sales department of a major equipment manufacturer and told me if I wanted to quit my job at Maxwell's, he wouldn't object. He said, "That way you could be home at dinnertime all the time and be able to make your great Italian dinners for me more often."

Something about the way he said that sent a slight chill through me, but he had been smiling, so I let it slip out of my mind and thought of it no more. A few weeks later Sal's company, Manchester Machinery, held its annual Christmas holiday party at a local catering hall. It was top-shelf, with a prime rib dinner and dancing to a live orchestra, and Sal introduced me to many of his co-workers and their spouses. He would sometimes say, "This is my fiancée, Maria," or, "This is Maria, my future wife."

Then, as a couple neared us, Sal's face darkened and he said, "Crap, here comes my ex-wife. What the hell is she doing here?"

Joanna was a very nice-looking woman with upswept blond hair and high cheekbones. She was wearing an expensive dress, expensive shoes and what appeared to be a very expensive multi-jeweled necklace and matching bracelet. She said, "Hello, Sal," and her handsome escort said, "Hi, Sal. How are things going?"

The two men apparently knew each other and Sal replied, "Going okay, Matt. Oh, this is my fiancée, Maria." After the introductions were made, Matt took Sal by the arm and said, "We need to talk a few minutes of business, ladies. Please excuse us."

They walked toward the bar and I said, "Do they work together?"

"Yes," she said. "Matt's in manufacturing and I guess you know Sal is in sales."

"Yes," I said and shut my mouth not knowing what else to say.

"Awkward, isn't it?" Joanna said with a smile. "The once and future Mrs. Salvatore Domenico squaring off with drinks in our hands as weapons."

I smiled back and said, "Nothing we can do to change the past, though."

"No," she said and then turned to see where the two men were. She lowered her voice and said, "Has he hit you yet?"

"Wha-a-at? No, of course not!"

"Good," she said. "Hopefully, he's changed."

"Sal hit you?" I whispered.

"Not at first, but as the years went by it began, and then increased rapidly. Basically, that's why I asked for a divorce. I was afraid he might kill me."

"Oh my God!" I said suddenly weak in the knees. I grabbed the edge of a nearby table for support. Joanna observed my reaction and said, "Maria, I didn't mean to frighten you – and I'm not trying to screw up Sal's relationship with you. It's just that some women accept that treatment. I did for a long time."

"When did he start?" I asked. "Was alcohol involved?"

"You have previous experiences in this area?"

"My father was very abusive to my mother," I said. "I don't want that to happen to me." Of course I neglected to tell her that dear old dad killed mom and that I had killed my first husband to prevent a similar fate.

"Like I said before, hopefully he's changed, since he obviously hasn't struck you. But to answer your questions, he didn't start to hit me until we were married a few years and yes, alcohol seemed to increase the frequency and intensity of his brutality."

I decided right then and there that marriage to Sal Domenico was no longer a desired option. When the two men returned to us, Sal eyed me warily and I just smiled and took his arm. I said, "I hope business is over, gentlemen. After all this is a party. It was nice meeting you, Matt. You too, Joanna."

As I tugged Sal away he said, "You're right, let's get another drink."

If Sal had any suspicions about the conversation I just had with Joanna, I hoped I had put those suspicions to rest.

• • •

The next three months with Sal went along just fine. I was beginning to doubt Joanna's tale of brutality, but then that night at the dinner table I saw the first sign of a different Sal – and it truly frightened me. It was a Monday, my day off from Maxwell's, and I had prepared a sumptuous Italian meal for us. It was Sal's favorite – baked lasagna with meatballs on the side – all of which he would smother in my red sauce. And this main dish was accompanied with a small green salad, garlic bread and a magnum of Chianti Classico wine.

When Sal came in the front door a huge smile lit up his face as the pungent aroma of the garlic reached him. "Ah," he said. "Lasagna and meatballs?"

"Yes, indeed," I said. "And it will be ready in five minutes."

He took off his jacket and tie, grabbed a slice of garlic bread and poured the wine into our glasses. I served the meal and we both dug in. Halfway through dinner Sal said, "You know the highest compliment we old-school wops can pay to a woman's cooking is, "Yo, Maria, it's just like momma used to make."

"And I qualify?" I asked.

"Most assuredly," he said, "which makes me more certain – not that I ever had any doubts – that I want to marry you. So, when do we do it, Maria?"

He had caught me off guard and I stuttered a bit and said, "Uh, gee Sal, I don't know."

He obviously didn't care for that answer and that dark visage came over him again, now the second time I had seen it. He took a large gulp of Chianti. I noticed the magnum was almost empty and I knew I had drunk only a glass and a half myself. He said, "Whaddya mean, you don't know? Whatsa matter?"

"Uh, nothing, Sal, just that I hadn't thought about a definite date, that's all."

"Well, start thinking about it," he shouted. "Or did that bitch ex-wife of mine talk you out of it?"

He then leaped out of his chair and grabbed me around my throat hard enough that I couldn't speak. Still shouting he said, "She did, didn't she, that lyin' bitch Joanna?"

I was grasping at his hands and he finally relaxed his grip. I rubbed my neck and sobbed as he sat back down. "Well," he said. "I asked you a fucking question."

"I don't know what you are talking about," I managed to whisper and the words hurt my throat as I spoke them. "Joanna said nothing to me about you."

"Then forget about it. But you better start thinking about the date soon. Got it?"

"Sure, Sal," I said able to speak a bit more normally now that the pain was subsiding. "Tomorrow we'll check the calendar and definitely set the date."

That seemed to calm him down and he began to wolf down more food. He finished the bottle of Chianti and staggered as he got up from the table. He leered at me and said, "Joanna! Fuckin' bitch! I wish I knew the guy who's been killing those broads. I'd give him that bitch's address."

What Sal was referring to was five murders that had been committed by an unknown person over the past several months. All the victims were middle-aged women, but none of the murders was near our neighborhood. They were scattered in various locations many miles away. The police had no reason to yet believe a serial killer was responsible. All the murders were committed by different methods – shooting, stabbing, choking, bludgeoning. But law enforcement's resistance to the serial killer designation did nothing to calm the jitters and fears of Southern California women of a certain age, including me. Just last week, right after the most recent body had been discovered, Sal came home from work one day with a package. "I got a gun," he said. "I'm worried about this maniac."

"I guess my age does fit his victim's profile," I said.

"Yeah, and if he comes around here I'll blow his brains out. And if I'm not home *you'll* blow his brains out. Right?"

"I guess I could do it if I was scared enough," I said.

"I'll put this in my night-table drawer and keep it loaded. It's a .357 magnum revolver and very easy to work. Just point it at the middle of the bastard and pull the trigger. Can you do that?"

"I'm sure I could," I said.

And now I was sure of a lot of things. I was sure that we would set a wedding date tomorrow. I was sure we would *not* get married on that date, or any other date. And I was sure I had to kill Sal Domenico – soon. As I had done to Jimmy Chandler, a preemptive strike seemed once again necessary. Had Tom O'Shea been the only decent man in this world?

CHAPTER EIGHTEEN

Frankie

Although my first encounter with Alicia Buonora seemingly went well, when I later reflected on my visit I realized a couple of problems had occurred. My prepared script for a family confrontation was not comprehensive enough – I had to wing it on a lot of their questions. I had given them too much information about my search even though it was for an imaginary sister. But the biggest fault was staying there for much too long a time – they could easily describe me to the police if that occasion ever arose.

I wrote down a few alternate scenarios on paper eliminating these pitfalls and changing a few other things. When I finished there was one thing I hadn't yet been able to adequately plan for. What if I encountered someone who I really thought could be my mother, but who denied it? I would take out my trusty fingerprint kit and ask her to provide a thumbprint. That was the plan. But what if she declined? How far could I force the issue?

With my newly amended scenarios committed firmly to memory I resumed my search a few days later. The next two went well. Maxine Crisatta and Anna Caffero were home with their families and I was able to use an abbreviated version of the "missing sister" scenario with good success. And again, as was the case with Alicia Buonora, none of the woman struck me as possibly being Mommy. Although these visits were much shorter, the next one lasted much longer and happily also ended well.

Mary Donato lived alone and had the strongest resemblance to Mommy thus far. I went right to the heart of the matter after she invited me in. "Mrs. Donato, the person I am looking for is my mother. I haven't seen her in many years – since I was nine years old. Her name then was Angela Chandler, maiden name Capozzi."

I was watching her reactions as I put forth theses names, but she didn't appear to be startled at all. I continued, "Mrs. Donato, are you my mother?"

"Oh, my goodness, Mr. Wallace, I'm afraid not. Unfortunately, I never had any children. Oh, I know how you must feel. I'm so sorry."

I was pretty certain she was telling the truth and was not Mommy, but I wanted to see her reaction to the fingerprint request so I opened my attaché case and took out Angela's picture and showed it to her. "Yes," she said, "I do resemble her quite a bit."

Then I removed the fingerprint card and said, "Mrs. Donato, just to ease my mind and rule you out completely, would you let me compare your thumbprint to my mother's?"

She hesitated a bit then said, "Okay, I don't see why not." I took out the ink pad and carefully rolled her left thumb onto a white piece of cardboard. Although I was very nervous, the print came out fine. I took out a large magnifying glass and compared the two. These were huge differences in the whirls, loops and ridge endings. "Take a look," I said. "I'm somewhat experienced in this area, but even a layman can see they don't match at all."

"Yes," she said. "I certainly see that. I'm sorry."

I smiled and said, "So am I. I don't know how my mother turned out, but when I find her I hope she's half as nice as you."

"Why, thank you, Mr. Wallace. Have you been searching long?"

"No, just a few months, but I have a lot of women to go."

"Well, I hope you find her soon. I'm sure she'll be thrilled to see you after all these years. You're such a nice young man."

"Thank you," I said. "I'll be on my way now."

● ● ●

My next visit, a week later with Mrs. Joan Evacherria, did not go as smooth. She was not nearly as friendly as Mrs. Donato had been; in fact she was almost hostile to my plea. And when I asked if I could take her thumbprint she jumped out of her chair and said, "I will not! Are you some kind of pervert?"

"No, ma'am," I said, quickly packing up my stuff and closing my attaché case. "I'm sorry. I'll leave."

"Damn right you'll leave," she said as I ran for the door. I figured the faster I left the less chance that she would call the police, and even though I hadn't gotten her print there was no doubt in my mind that this cantankerous woman was not my mother.

This confrontation was the first glitch in my quest so far and I felt I had handled it as best as I could have. I was feeling pretty good and gaining confidence and had already eliminated several possibles. I figured that at the rate I was going – fitting the visits in between school and work – I would be able to complete the entire list of thirty-two in another three months. But on my very next visit things took a turn for the worse, a turn that would change my plans and drastically change me.

Nancy Griselli opened the door and glared at me. She had a cigarette in one hand and a glass containing ice and a clear liquid in the other. And from the smell of her breath the liquid contained alcohol. I had trouble speaking because I was stunned by her resemblance to my mother; it could very well be her.

'Well?" she asked, raising her eyebrows and her voice.

"My name is Sam Edwards and I'm looking for my mother," I said. "Could I ask you a few questions?"

"That's a good one," she said with a mocking laugh. "Come on in handsome, and tell me your sad story."

I followed her inside. She swayed a little as she pointed out a sofa for me to sit on. "What'll it be?" she asked as she began to walk away.

"Excuse me?" I said.

"A drink. What'll you have to drink?"

"Oh, I don't need…"

"I don't trust a man who doesn't drink, and if you want your answers…"

"Vodka on the rocks," I said.

"Good boy," she said making her way to the kitchen where I heard the clink of ice cubes and the sound of liquid gurgling out of a bottle.

MOMMY, MOMMY

She returned and sat on the sofa next to me, handing me the glass. "So, tell me honey," she said. "What can I do for you?"

I told her of my search and finished by showing her the picture of Angela. She took it, sucked down a swallow of her drink and studied it. She put her drink down and picked up her cigarette and took a deep drag on it. "I can see why you're here," she said. "It's scary. We do look a lot alike."

"So you're saying you're not Mom…my mother?"

"No way, Sammy."

"Would you mind if I fingerprinted you?" I asked.

"What for?"

"To make sure," I said, taking out the fingerprint card.

"No way," she said. "I already told you I ain't your mother. I don't have any twenty-five year old kid."

"Then why would you object to the fingerprints?"

"Tell you what, Sammy," she said moving closer to me on the sofa and placing her hand high up on my thigh. "I like you and you're a good looking guy. Make love to me, Sammy, and I'll let you fingerprint me. I'll let you do a lot of things."

"Mrs. Griselli," I said pushing her away.

"Call me Nancy," she said, grabbing me again.

"I can't do that," I said.

"Why not? Ain't I good looking enough? Am I too old for you?"

"No, not at all. You're a very attractive woman, but don't you see…?"

"See what?" she interrupted.

"If we do…if we make love and then I fingerprint you and you turned out to really be my mother that would be awful. That would be incest."

"I told you I am not you mother!"

I held out the ink pad and said, "Prove it."

"Then we'll make some hot love, Sammy boy?"

"Sure," I said.

After examining the print and determining, with a deep inward sigh of relief, that Nancy Griselli was definitely not my mother, I packed up my things and said, "Well, I guess I'd better be on my way."

"Hey!" she shouted. "We got a deal! You ain't going anywhere until after we spend some time in bed."

"Sorry," I said. "Deal's off."

I headed for the front door and she jumped off the sofa and lurched after me. She grabbed my jacket and spun me around. I tried to push her away, but she held on with surprising strength. Finally, I was able to break her tenacious grip and I threw her forcefully backwards. She stumbled over an end table and, as if in slow motion, arms flailing, trying to maintain balance, she fell face first onto the brick ledge of the fireplace with a stomach turning splat.

I rushed over to her still body and turned her over. Her forehead was split open like a ripe cantaloupe and blood and gray ooze slowly leaked out. Her glazed eyes were unmoving. I checked for her pulse and for a breath from her half-open mouth. They were not there. Nancy Griselli was dead.

Shit! Shit! Shit! How'd this happen? Tears ran down my face and I began to panic. I swallowed the rest of my vodka and forced myself to calm down a bit. Think! It was an accident. I didn't intend to kill anybody. But she was dead, and I was responsible. After all if I hadn't shown up tonight she'd be alive, wouldn't she?

I wanted to bolt out the door, but calmed myself down and took stock of things. I brought my glass into the kitchen, washed it thoroughly in hot water and soap, dried it and returned it to its cabinet. I took the dish towel and wiped my prints from every surface I remembered touching. I checked my attaché case to make sure I had everything I came with and I was set to go. Using my handkerchief I prepared to turn the doorknob on the front door when it hit me. Her thumb!

I rushed over to Nancy's body and looked at her thumb. Sure enough it still had plenty of fingerprint ink on it. I opened my case and removed a can of solvent. Pouring some on my handkerchief I wiped away all traces of the ink. My God, she was turning cold already. Glancing around once more, certain that I had removed all traces of my presence, I left the house.

• • •

The next day I bought the local papers and searched them thoroughly for any news about Mrs. Griselli. There was nothing there, and nothing on the TV news, either. The story appeared on the fourth day, on page twelve of the Times, along with a dozen other short articles considered to be of minimal interest. It was less than a hundred words and essentially said, "A neighbor found Nancy Griselli dead on the floor…medical examiner found a blood alcohol level of 0.18 percent…cause of death ruled an accidental fall from intoxication…"

Although very much relieved, I was too shook up to continue my quest any time soon and focused my efforts on my upcoming final exams at school. When they were over I would decide what to do. Maybe I should just give this whole crazy search up, but I knew I couldn't. If anything, my obsession in finding Mommy was digging deeper into my soul, and until I found out why she abandoned me it seemed I might never rest. But with the death of Nancy Griselli still in the forefront of my mind, I knew it would be a long time before I could work up the nerve to resume the search for my long lost mother.

CHAPTER NINETEEN

Angela

Sal and I set our wedding date for two months away and this seemed to mollify him, but my plans had been carefully thought out and the time was now. Being in sales Sal had to make occasional trips out of town and his next one was set for tomorrow. He was to fly to San Francisco for two days and be home late Friday night. After breakfast I helped him pack and told him I would drive him to the airport and go to work from there. He said, "No, I'll leave my car in the parking lot. When I get home Friday night you'll be working. And, by the way, after we're married I want you to quit that place."

"I was thinking the same thing," I said.

"Good, I want you home more for dinner."

He closed up his suitcase and turned to me. I was holding the Magnum. He was three feet away and the gun was steady in my hand and pointed right at the middle of his chest. He started to open his mouth and I pulled the trigger once. The noise of the gunshot was much louder than I expected and I watched Sal fall backward from the force of the large bullet. I stood next to him ready to shoot again, but I could tell by his eyes that he was already dead. I smiled ruefully thinking – one brick to the head, one shot to the body. I was getting good at this.

I put a bathroom towel over the spreading bloodstain on Sal's chest and dragged him out of the bedroom through the hallway and kitchen and into the garage where our cars sat side by side. I would have preferred to leave under the cover of darkness, but his flight was at three and the car had to be clocked into the lot well before that.

Before I put him into the trunk I removed his wallet, pinky ring and watch. I put his suitcase and business briefcase on top of his body, opened them both and rifled through their contents spreading them around before closing the trunk lid. I went back inside where I put the bloody towel into the washing machine and turned it on.

After parking his car at the airport, I walked out of the lot and took a bus halfway home and got off. Before the next bus arrived, I dropped Sal's wallet, minus the cash, down a storm drain. Then I walked around the corner, and again certain no one was watching me, threw his ring and wrist watch down another drain.

Of course, Sal didn't come home as planned on Friday night, but I waited until I awoke Saturday morning to call the police. At first they were reluctant to get involved, telling me that he probably stayed there some extra time, but I insisted saying, "He would have called me. He always does if his schedule changes."

I guess the concern in my voice convinced them, because an officer responded to my home and took down all the details of Sal's car and itinerary and asked for a photo. I acted distraught during the whole time, and I knew they bought the worried bride-to-be routine hook, line and sinker. I guess that should have been expected – after all I had previous practice.

The same officer came back later with the gruesome news that he had found Sal's car and his dead body. He told me it appeared as if Sal was a victim of a robbery. Again, I acted devastated by the news – the worried fiancée, uncontrollably weeping. They classified the case as a robbery/homicide, perpetrator unknown. I waited a month and decided it was time to leave sunny California.

Nothing really good had happened during my years there, except my brief marriage to Tom O'Shea. Although I was now financially secure, that one good thing had ended in tragedy. And there was one other troubling situation that made me flee – that killer was still on the loose. Although so far the police authorities had still not classified the murders as the work of a serial killer, it was obvious that he was only targeting middle-aged women, all of Italian descent, in a random manner throughout southern California. What was really creepy – scary actually – was that some of these women strongly resembled one another, and strongly resembled *me*. Some of the newspaper's editorials were calling for all the police jurisdictions involved to get their act together to form a Task Force, and/or involve the FBI's Behavioral Science Unit without further delay. I, for one, was leaving without further delay before I became victim number ten or eleven, or whatever this psycho was up to.

I sold my house and most of my belongings, settled up all my bills and credit cards, got into my two-year old Mercedes Benz and pointed its nose due east. Cruising along quietly on Interstate 10, my .357 Magnum tucked in my handbag on the seat next to me, I pondered my destination and my future life. I was fleeing a possible serial killer, but wasn't I also one? How many does it take before the police definitely classify you as one? Only two, like me? Or a half dozen? Or was it a person's future intent, to keep killing until finally stopped? If so, I was certainly not a serial killer for I had no desire, or intent, to ever kill anyone else in my lifetime.

• • •

Imperceptibly my Benz steered me northeast and I realized where I was headed by the time I was on Interstate 85 approaching Richmond. I was going home to Long Island, the only place I could feel comfortable. The police were no longer interested in Angela Chandler much less a woman named Maria Theresa Ferraro.

When I arrived one sunny afternoon I checked into the hotel next to the Nassau Coliseum where Jim and I had occasionally gone to a New York Islanders hockey game. I registered for five days and the next morning I began my search for an apartment. On the third day of my search the real estate agent took me to a second-floor, one-bedroom apartment in Farmingdale. Being new to the area, I had to pay the security deposit and the first two month's rent with postal money orders.

After I moved in and established myself at a local bank, I began the process of becoming a New Yorker once again. I applied for a New York driver's license and New York plates for my Benz. I booted up my laptop and changed the address for my credit cards and other online accounts. I checked my mutual funds at Vanguard investments that Tom's accountant had help me set up after my husband's death, and they were doing well. I was drawing enough money to cover my rent and other bills, and was hardly touching the principal. But I couldn't just sit here at the age of forty-nine and do nothing, so I decided to hunt for a waitress job.

• • •

"You're kidding!" exclaimed John Tomasso, the maître d' of the Wolf's Lair Restaurant when I inquired about employment.

"Pardon me?" I said. "Why would you think I would be kidding you?"

"Because one of my top waitresses gave me notice – very short notice – not five minutes ago."

"Then when can I start?"

"If you're qualified, this weekend."

I told Mr. Tomasso of my experience at Maxwell's and offered to call to get a written reference. He said, "That won't be necessary. This place is very similar to your description of Maxwell's. Come Friday night, I'll quickly know if you can handle it."

"I'll see you then," I said, thinking what a lucky break I just got – a job at a restaurant seven miles from my apartment. The move from California was already proving to be a good one.

Two days later, with Los Angeles already fading deeper into the back of my mind, I picked up a copy of the *Long Island Chronicle,* and the feature story on the front page immediately caught my attention: SERIAL KILLER STALKS SOUTHERN CALIFORNIA. The story was written by a *Los Angeles Times* reporter. The *Times* owned the *Chronicle* which explained its appearance there on page one. The body count was up to twelve and the various police jurisdictions had finally come together, formed a Task Force and requested help from the FBI. And when they had put their heads and files together they discovered the key common denominators in the murders – the women were all of Italian heritage and all the same age – the *exact* same age. They were all born on November 17, 1967 – *my* birth date. Oh, my God!

My body trembled as I read further. The FBI agent assigned, Michael Havlek, explained that the chief clue was the date of birth of the victims, and that many members of the Task Force wanted to withhold that information. However, they decided to release it as a preventive measure, so that women with that date of birth could take extra precautions to prevent becoming a victim. Havlek said that it would not be possible to assign a law enforcement presence to protect every woman in jeopardy – there were just too many with that date of birth in southern California. When he was asked how many, he declined to answer, but a check of the state DMV records by a *Times* staff researcher found 148 woman in the entire state with that date of birth and an unknown additional number who didn't possess a driver's license. However, all dozen victims thus far were licensed drivers in the state.

The bottom line was that although they knew who the future victims might be, they did not know who was committing the murders or why. Havlek said there were in the process of reviewing the cases, re-interviewing possible witnesses and they hoped to publish a composite sketch of the suspect when that review was completed. "We also hope to have his behavioral profile fully worked up very shortly," he said.

When Agent Havlek next spoke to the media, a week later, there was good news and bad news – *very* bad news for me. The good news was that no more murders had occurred, a composite sketch was now available and a definite behavioral profile of the killer was established.

That was also the bad news. The composite photo staring back at me from page one of the *Long Island Chronicle* was an exact likeness of my first husband – Jim Chandler. And the behavioral profile suggested that the killer's motive was not money, nor sexual gratification, nor mutilation of the body, but more likely revenge. Revenge against an authority figure – an *evil* authority figure in the eyes of the killer. Perhaps a former school teacher, principal, former supervisor, or even his mother or father.

I didn't have to finish the article to know that my son, Frankie, was trying to find me – and kill me, and I had to admit that I certainly understood why.

• • •

Three days passed and no more big stories came out of Los Angeles concerning the murders. The killer had not been apprehended, but no further ones had occurred. The speculation by the Task Force was now that everyone knew what he looked like, and who he was targeting, the killer was lying low, or had fled the area to parts unknown. Regardless of the reason, the stoppage of the murders brought a measure of relief to southern California, especially to forty-nine year old Italian-American women.

I now faced a moral dilemma that had been severely troubling me ever since I saw my son's picture in the paper. Should I call the Task Force and tell them my suspicions? What can of worms would I open? How much interest would they show me? Would they look again at the deaths of Sal and Jimmy? I toyed with the idea of sending an anonymous note telling them the killer's name was Frankie Chandler, but would that help them? It might if I told them his date of birth and that he was raised on Long island, but then they would come here, wouldn't they? And I was here. In the end, assuaging my conscience with the fact that the murders had stopped, I did nothing – nothing but worry what would happen if, or when, Frankie finally found me. Of course, he may never figure I went back to Long Island, but in case he did, I had come up with a plan. If he ever found me I would explain everything to him and hope that would make him understand why I abandoned him. Hopefully, he would accept my explanation, not kill me and go on his way to find his real mother. But, if that failed, I would kill him.

I located the information that had long been buried in my personal papers and put it on the coffee table, and then I tucked my .357 magnum between the armrest and seat cushion on my living room sofa.

All I could do now was go about my life and hope Frankie wouldn't find me before the Task Force in California caught him.

CHAPTER TWENTY

Frankie

A month after my exams were over, I picked up the search again and satisfactorily crossed three more look-a-likes from my list. I had now gone through half the "highly probables," and as the numbers dwindled, my anticipation increased. I became certain I would find Mommy soon, and when Maryanne Palermo opened her door and looked at me I was convinced I had found her.

"Uh, my name is Frankie Chandler," I said. "Do you remember me…Mommy?"

A scowl appeared on Maryanne's face and she said, "Mommy? I'm not your Mommy, asshole. Get off my porch."

"I just want to talk a few minutes," I said. "Please, let me come in. Please…"

"Get the hell out of here!" she screamed, "before I call the police."

I pushed my way in, kicked the door closed and grabbed her in a bear hug. I said, "I'm not a psycho and I'm not here to harm you. All I want to do is find out if you are my mother. Please, can you relax?"

"Yeah, okay, let me go," she said.

I loosened the grip of my arms from around her waist. "Let me show you a picture and you'll see why I think you may be her." I reached for my attaché case and Maryanne ran out of the living room, toward the back of her house. "I'm not going to chase you!" I yelled. "Mrs. Palermo, I'm not here to hurt you…"

Maryanne reappeared in the living room, pointing a silver automatic at me and shouted, "You're damn right you're not going to hurt me, but I'm going to hurt you, you sick psycho son-of-a-bitch!"

"Please let me show you…"

"Don't open that case another inch. What do you have in there? A gun?"

"No, no," I said. "A photo, some papers and a fingerprint kit, that's all."

"Fingerprint kit? Oh, boy, what kind of sicko are you? Sit on that chair."

She motioned me to a stuffed chair in the corner of the room. As I started toward it she turned to reach for the telephone and the gun turned with her. I took the chance and lunged for it. I grabbed the barrel, but she had a firm grip on the handle, finger still on the trigger. "Bastard!" she yelled as she pulled it.

I heard the bullet whine as it passed my ear along with the loud explosion. She was no match for my strength and I finally yanked the gun away from her and shoved her away. She picked up a lamp and rushed at me. I pulled the trigger and hit her in the shoulder. She went down in a heap. "You stupid bitch!" I yelled. "Look what you made me do!"

MOMMY, MOMMY

She was in terrible pain and crying. Blood poured from her wound. I grabbed my case and flung it open. I took Mommy's picture and shoved it in front of her face. "You see!" I shouted. "That's why I'm here! Now, answer me – are you my Mommy? Are you Angela Chandler?"

She shook her head – barely – and whispered, "No."

"Liar! Give me your hand."

She either wouldn't or couldn't comply, so I took it and pressed her thumb on the ink pad and rolled it. Her arm dropped limply from my hand as I took the magnifying glass and made the comparison. At first I thought I had something – both prints had central loops – but that was the extent of the similarities. And three other points of comparison were way off the mark. Son-of-a-bitch! I was convinced it was Mommy! Maryanne was moaning now as my anger was rising. I turned toward her and picked up the gun. I shot her through the heart, putting her out of her misery and, somewhat disturbingly, I felt no remorse at all. I put the gun in my briefcase and left.

• • •

I had now killed two women in my search for Mommy, although the first one, Nancy Griselli, was certainly unintentional. Yet that first death seemed to bother me a lot more than deliberately shooting Maryanne Palermo last night. I felt my action was justified, like when I caused the truck engine to fall on Harold Jonas many years ago. It was almost as if I had killed my mother herself instead of a look alike. And it made killing the next one easier, and with each murder my satisfaction grew almost as if I were really killing Mommy over and over again and exorcising my growing hatred of her.

Simplifying my modus operandi, I would wait until I was sure the woman was alone, and when I gained entrance to the home I went directly to the point, asking if she was Angela Chandler. As soon as I heard the word no, I pulled the trigger, or stabbed her, or choked her or bashed her over the head with a heavy object. That last method was messy, but seemed to give me the most satisfaction – and I didn't have to wonder why.

And then, after a dozen murders, I had to stop. The police were finally onto me. My likeness was in all the newspapers. Women with Mommy's birth date were on high alert. When the media referred to me as a serial killer, I was taken aback. Me? Frankie Chandler, a serial killer? No way! Serial killers were sick psychos. They tortured their victims, or mutilated them horribly usually with some sick sexual fantasy involved. They were deranged monsters. They were beasts who deserved to die. They were not *me*.

I quit my job by calling in over the telephone – I didn't want them to match my face to that in the newspapers, if they hadn't done so already. My employers, both from India, only occasionally looked at a newspaper and that was printed in their native language, so maybe I would catch a break there. I grabbed up all my belongings from my apartment, put them in my car and checked into a seedy motel on the other side of town under the name of Richard Owens. I immediately began to grow a beard and shaved my head completely. There was no doubt that I had to get out of

MOMMY, MOMMY

Los Angeles, preferably out of the whole state, very soon, but I didn't want to leave before I finished checking the few remaining names on my list. Fortunately, I hadn't been real chummy with any of my college classmates and stayed to myself while on campus, so I felt none of them would connect me with the picture in the newscasts and papers. And every day that I checked, the media still had not published or broadcast a name to go with my picture.

In a few weeks, when my beard was finally grown in and I still had not been identified, I chose the driver's license picture from the group I had remaining that looked most like Mommy and checked the house out. It appeared empty, as if no one lived there and no one answered the doorbell. I knocked on the neighbor's door and an old man answered. I said "I'm looking for my mother's friend Maria Ferraro. I promised Mom I'd say hello when I came to Los Angeles."

"Oh, Maria just moved away about a month ago. That crazy killer, you know."

"Why was she afraid?" I asked.

"Same date of birth as all the others. Wouldn't you be afraid?"

"You bet I would be if I were in her shoes. I'd run a long way away from here, that's for sure."

"So would I, and besides her husband had been killed in a robbery not long ago. No reason to stay here."

"Uh, did she say where she was going?"

"Nope, maybe the new people know, but they're not moving in for two weeks."

"Okay, thanks a lot," I said and headed for the post office.

The postal clerk took a while to find Maria's forwarding address. It seems she had telephoned the United States Postal Service and instructed them to have her local branch forward her first class mail to their main branch, general delivery, in Hicksville, Long Island, until she established a permanent address. That call had been made two days ago. So that's where Mommy had fled to! It was Mommy this time. I was certain of it. Long Island – of course! Maria Theresa Ferraro had run back home.

I went to the post office branch that serviced me the next day and had my mail forwarded to the same Hicksville branch. I checked out of the motel, packed up my car with my clothes, computer, and the Glock .40 caliber automatic I had taken from Maryanne Palermo, and set out on the long drive home.

As soon as I reached Long Island I checked into a cheap motel in Hicksville and went to the post office to inquire about my mail. The clerk had the record of forwarding, but nothing had come for me so far. I thanked him and checked out the interior of the branch. Then I went out and re-parked my car to get a good view of the front door and I waited. Closing time came and Mommy had not shown up.

I went back to the motel and unpacked and then went out shopping for food – breakfast and lunch items and bottled water. At eight o'clock the next morning, I was again parked outside the post office, in a different spot, and waited. Again, she did not show. Nor did she show the next day or the next. Finally, on Saturday morning, I saw a dark-haired woman driving a Benz come right past me into the parking lot. I had gotten a very good look at her and watched her park and walk inside. My heart beat faster. It was her for sure –Angela Chandler a/k/a Maria Ferraro – my long lost mother.

It was easy to follow her home to Farmingdale in the heavy traffic. She parked on the street and walked to a large two-family house and entered through a side door which probably led upstairs to the second floor. I waited for about a half hour but she did not reappear. Not wanting a repeat of my past experience where the cop showed up that time, I left the area.

I returned on Monday morning very early, but didn't observe her leave for work. Although I was certain that Maria was Mommy, I was not yet mentally ready to confront her. A few days of observation revealed that she worked mostly afternoons and evenings at a fancy restaurant in Woodbury about seven miles away. She usually arrived home between eleven-thirty and midnight, a perfect time to confront her.

On Wednesday night of the following week I made my move as I observed Mommy leaving her car and walking to the house. I followed her, gun drawn. She placed her key in the lock and opened the door. I stuck the gun in her back and whispered, "Don't say a word. Just go up the stairs."

She stopped, turned and smiled at me, "Hello, Frankie," she said. "It's been such a long time, and I've been waiting for you. Please come up."

I was stunned and could only say, "Mommy?"

"Yes, Frankie, but not your real one."

By the time we reached her second floor apartment I still had not yet processed her words. She turned on the lights and took off her jacket. "Please sit down," she said. "May I get you something? A drink perhaps?"

I had finally found my voice and said, "All I want is an explanation – for everything."

"And you well deserve it, Frankie. Please put the gun away. I'm sure you're not going to kill me – at least not yet."

I put the gun in my jacket pocket and said, "I'm listening, Mommy. It's taken me a long time to find you, but what did you mean when you said 'not your real one?' If you think some kind of lie will stop me from pulling this trigger, you are mistaken."

"No lies from me now, Frankie. Here's the whole lousy truth."

Mommy told me everything – her childhood, her father's abuse that killed her mother, her decision not to let a similar fate happen to her, the killing of my father and her flight to California.

"Why did you leave me?" I asked. "Couldn't you have taken me with you?"

"I knew the cops would be after me and you would have slowed me down. And, as I mentioned before, I'm not your real mother – your biological one. When I married your father you came along with him. You were eighteen months old."

"Liar!" I yelled. "You're the only mother I ever knew."

"True, Frankie, but my attachment to you wasn't that strong. That's why I abandoned you."

"Prove it," I said. "Prove you are not my mother and tell me who the real one is."

"See that envelope on the end table? Let me go get it and open it up."

MOMMY, MOMMY

"Go ahead," I said moving my gun into my waistband.

She came back and sat beside me on the sofa and opened the envelope. There were some photos of Dad, Mommy and me, but none when I was an infant. She picked up a document and handed it to me saying, "Here's the proof, Frankie, here's a copy of your Dad's wedding certificate to his first wife, Ellen Weston – your real mother."

I read it with disbelief and shook my head. She handed me another document. It was my original birth certificate listing James Chandler and Ellen Weston as my parents. I didn't want to believe it, but how could I dispute the cold hard facts in front of me. I said, "What happened to her?"

"She was very young and pregnant with you when she married your Dad. Her parents were strict Roman Catholics and disowned her. She was unable to handle motherhood, so when you were six months old she just up and left."

"You mean she abandoned me, too?"

"Yes, and also your father. And to his credit he kept you and raised you for the next year until he and I were married."

I couldn't stop the tears form pouring down my face. Abandoned twice! The tears of pity turned quickly to tears of anger. As I wiped them away I asked, "Do you know where Ellen is now?"

When Mommy –Angela – answered she was pointing a large revolver at me. "No, Frankie, I have no idea what happened to her. Now I'm going to call the police."

"Don't do that," I said. "Please."

"Why not?"

"Give me a chance to find my real mother. I understand now why you did what you did. I'm not angry anymore. I'll never bother you again."

"Why should I believe you?"

"I just want to find my real mother now."

"Are you going to leave another trail of bodies until you find her?"

"No," I said. "Here take my gun from my waist and I'll be on my way. I'd like to take these documents though, if that's okay."

Angela was debating what to do, and when she reached for the gun at my waist, I twisted away and ripped the revolver out of her hand. She gasped and got up to reach for the phone. I shot her in the side of the head with her own gun, then twice through her cold, hard heart. After carefully wiping down any items and surfaces I might have touched – I was getting proficient at this – I grabbed the papers, shoved the revolver in my waist alongside my Glock, and left the apartment closing the door as softly as I could.

CHAPTER TWENTY-ONE

Danny

"What do we have so far, partner?" Spider asked as I drove the unmarked sedan from Mineola to Farmingdale.

"The call came in about an hour ago. A waitress named Maria Ferraro failed to show up for work for the lunch trade at the Wolf's Lair restaurant in Woodbury. Although she hasn't been working there long, she had always showed up promptly for her shifts. The manager called her home, but all he got was her answering machine, so he drove over to check things out. When he knocked on the front door an elderly woman answered and said Maria was her tenant in the upstairs apartment. They knocked repeatedly and when they got no response the landlord used her key to get in. Maria was dead on the living room floor. One gunshot wound to her head was visible."

I pulled up to a two-family house in a well-kept residential street – all the lawns on the block were green and trimmed and the homes were kept in obvious good shape. I spoke first to the landlady who had returned to her living quarters downstairs. Mrs. Verna Lombardi was distraught over what had happened.

Using her hands she said, "Oh, that poor woman. Who could have done that to her? And in my home!"

I let her talk herself out for a while before I interrupted her and said, "Mrs. Lombardi, my partner is upstairs checking things out. We don't know what happened yet. This could have been an accident or a suicide. Now, if you can calm down, I would like you to answer a few questions…"

It wasn't easy getting everything there was to get from Mrs. Lombardi. Her difficulty in hearing – I had to practically shout at her – was not much help at all. Maria had only been her tenant a few weeks having told her she recently moved here from California. What she did know was that last night Maria worked the dinner shift and usually got home around midnight. However, she did not hear Maria come in the house, or hear her move around, or hear any arguments or gunshots.

"I'm usually in bed by ten o'clock," she said. "And I'm a pretty sound sleeper, so I didn't hear a thing."

Not to mention you're three-quarters deaf, I wanted to say, but I just thanked her for her cooperation and headed upstairs. Crime Scene Search people were just finishing up as was the deputy medical examiner. Doc Maguire said hello and explained that, pending the results of his post-mortem examination, Maria Ferraro died from multiple gunshot wounds, one to the head and two to the chest. "No gun anywhere around, Danny," he said. "Looks like you have a whodunit on your hands. Probably a large bore weapon – .40 caliber or a .357 magnum based on the damage."

"Any cartridge cases found?" Spider asked.

MOMMY, MOMMY

"Better ask the crime scene guys," Maguire said, "but they hadn't found any when I first got here."

"Where's the restaurant manager?" I asked.

"I let him go back to work," Spider said. "Told him we would stop over there when we finished up here to get his statement."

"Okay, let's nose around," I said walking over to Maria's body. She was lying on her side, one large gaping wound visible on her temple. I rolled her over to better see her face and when I did a flash of recognition went through my mind. Spider must have noticed a reaction from me because he said, "What's up Danny? Do you know her?"

I continued to stare at her trying to force my memory cells to connect the dots, but all I could do was shake my head and say, "No, Spider, I don't know her, but there's a familiarity to her face, maybe from the distant past."

"And the name doesn't jog your memory?"

"No, I'm sure I never knew a Maria Ferraro."

"Maybe it's her marriage name."

"Could be, we'll find out when we do the background check."

We finished up at the scene taking all of Maria's personal effects with us. We located her car parked on the street, gave it a cursory search for weapons and then posted a uniform officer on it pending the arrival of the tow truck. We drove to Woodbury, and after taking the restaurant manager's written statement, we returned to the squad room to put our heads together and go over what we had so far.

What we had was not much. Maria Ferraro was a murder victim who was apparently not sexually assaulted, or burglarized, or robbed. Her killer had taken the murder weapon and expended cartridges, if any, with him, and since there were no signs of a break-in, he may have been known by Maria. A canvas of neighbors by the responding officers and Nine-Eight squad detectives had failed to turn up anyone who saw or heard anything out the ordinary at or about the time of her death, which Doc Maguire had preliminarily determined to have occurred between 12:30 – 2:30 a.m.

It was past five o'clock and there was nothing more to do until tomorrow morning. We initiated the background check and put out a brief press release. We would attend the autopsy tomorrow, obtain Maria's fingerprints and have them run through AFIS, the national automated fingerprint database. Crime Scene would thoroughly search her car, and Spider and I would re-canvas the neighbors.

"Let's go home, Spider," I said. "Tomorrow will be a long day."

"And hopefully a productive one," he said, "because, as the saying goes, *right now we ain't got shit.*"

"Piece of cake for a couple of hot-shot dicks like us," I said smiling and poking Spider on the shoulder. Right?"

"Right," he said, "see you in the morning, Dick Tracy."

● ● ●

By the time we got back from the morgue it was 10:30 a.m. We had dropped the three slugs off at the Ballistics Section of the Police Lab where the technician, Walt Gennaro definitely identified them as .357 caliber rounds fired from a Smith and Wesson magnum revolver. "I'll run it through the national firearms database as soon as I can," he said. "If I get a hit I'll give you a shout right away."

"Thanks, Walt," I said. "We have nothing on this one yet."

We also had dropped the fingerprints off at that section and the technician there promised a quick search for us. Now back at our office our first stop was the coffee room where we found Allison Hayes, the crime reporter for the *Long Island Chronicle*, adding sugar to her mug of coffee.

"About time you two decided to come to work," she said. "This is my third cup of this crap you guys call coffee."

"Well, good morning to you, too, Lois Lane," Spider said using the nickname that had been tacked on to her for her resemblance to the actress that played that role in the *Superman* movies.

"I'll have you know, Miss Lane," I said, "that we just came back from a gruesome few hours at the morgue on our last caper."

"That's what I want to talk to you about, Danny," she said looking at her copy of the press release. "This tells me nothing. What else do you have on this woman?"

"Not much yet," Spider said and then filled her in on what we had in the works.

"Do you have her date of birth?"

"Probably," I said, "she still has a California driver's license and it would be on there. Plus I have some personal papers that we have yet to examine."

"So go examine them and get me her date of birth would you? Or do I have to wait until you both finish your damn coffee?"

"Hey," Spider said, "you're not our damn boss, you know."

"And," I said, "your snotty attitude is uncalled for."

"Okay, I'm sorry. Please just get me her DOB."

"No," I said.

"What do you mean, no?" she asked eyes flashing with anger. "I'll go to Lieutenant Veltri, I'll go to my boss…"

"Allison, calm down," I said. "What's going on with you? I'll give you the date of birth, but you have to tell me why you want it so badly."

"I don't have to tell you anything, Danny Boy."

"What the hell *is* going on with you, Allison?" Spider asked. "We always worked great with each other. You never stuck it to us in print and we always gave you all we had when we could. What's changed?"

"Nothing's changed, but I think I'm onto something big – real big. And if that date of birth is a date I'm familiar with, you'll be onto something really big, too."

"And will you tell us what this big thing is if we give you that DOB, and if we continue to give you information as it comes in?" I asked.

She seemed to calm down a bit then nodded her head and said, "Deal."

"Let me find an empty office and get Maria's papers," I said, "and we'll see what we can see."

"Here it is," Spider said holding up her driver's license and a birth certificate. "Same date on both."

"And would that date be November 17, 1967?" Allison asked.

"Bingo, Miss Lane, ace investigative reporter. Now how in the hell did you now that?" I asked

"Based on my superior investigative skills, of course," she said with a smile.

"We're listening, Lois," Spider said.

Allison told us the story of the serial killer in southern California of which Spider and I had both vaguely heard of, but not lately. When Allison had broken the story I had been on a two-week vacation down South with my wife Tara. Spider had read the feature in the *Chronicle* but paid the case no further heed; after all the maniac wasn't killing anyone in our jurisdiction. But even before Allison finished her story, we both now knew differently. "You made a great leap connecting this California killer to the murder of Maria Ferraro," I said. "Tell us how you did it."

"Two items," she said. "One, the murders had stopped over three months ago and two, Maria, according to your press release, was a new arrival from Los Angeles. So I figured he had given up killing women there and tracked Maria down to kill her here."

"This doesn't make sense," I said. "I can see why he stopped killing out there. His composite picture was in the papers and they knew who his targets would be based on physical resemblance and date of birth. But why track this particular person down all the way to Long Island? Why hadn't he killed her out there?"

"Maybe she was next on his list and he figured why not follow her to New York where there was no heat at all," Allison said.

"But now," Spider said, "he'll bring the Feds down on him. It's not a local matter anymore."

"There're already involved," Allison said. "An FBI agent from VICAP in the Behavioral Analysis Unit is on the California Task Force."

"And I'm sure he'll be winging his way here when your story hits the stands tomorrow," I said.

"You two don't have a problem with me printing the connection to the California killings and the date of birth?" she asked.

"Why should we?" Spider asked. "Do you think it will create a panic?"

"Maybe," she said.

"Wouldn't it be advisable to warn women with the same date of birth? Don't we owe that to them?" I asked.

"You know, you guys surprise me," Allison said. "I figured you'd want me to sit tight on this for a while, but you seem to be thinking the same as me."

"If we had a lead on the killer, then maybe I'd ask you to hold off," I said. "But we have absolutely nothing at this point."

We decided to get an opinion from my boss, Lieutenant Pete Veltri and from Allison's editor, Marge Bernard, when Bernie Gallagher stuck his head in the room and said, "Latent prints on line three for you, Danny."

I picked up and listened to Detective John Dennison for a few minutes and when he finished all I could say was, "Holy Shit!"

"Danny, what is it?" Spider asked. "You have no color at all left in that pink Irish face."

"I *knew* I recognized her. Her name's not Maria Ferraro, it's Angela Chandler. And I know who killed her."

"Who?" Spider and Allison asked simultaneously.

"Her son, Frankie. Frankie Chandler. This changes everything."

Allison fished around in her briefcase and came up with the first article, the one the *Chronicle* had reprinted from the *LA*

MOMMY, MOMMY

Times, the only one that showed the suspect's composite photo, the one that ran when I was away on vacation, the one where Frankie Chandler now stared right out at me. Case Closed.

CHAPTER TWENTY-TWO

Frankie

I drove straight back to my motel in Hicksville. No one had followed me and apparently no one heard the gunshots as the street in front of Mommy's home had been very quiet as I got into my car. Still in shock from Mom... my moth...*Angela Chandler's* revelation, I took stock of my situation. I was twenty-seven years old, possessed a two-year associate's degree in computer science, was a navy veteran and a so-called serial killer, my last victim being a woman I was convinced was my mother.

My basic mission in life since I was ten years old was to be re-united with my mother, and I had finally advanced to that moment when I discovered that Angela Chandler was not my mother at all. A woman named Ellen Weston was. Now the question I had to ponder was what I was going to do about it, if anything. I should really just forget about her and get on with my life. Twenty-seven years old, no job, no steady girlfriend – I guess anyone who has taken a couple of psych courses could tell you why – and the police were no doubt getting closer all the time.

After a mostly sleepless night I put the morning news on the TV. There was not yet anything about Angela's murder, probably because no one had discovered her body. I went out to get breakfast and pick up my mail which was a letter from my college congratulating me on my grades and attaining my degree. Proud of this accomplishment I carefully put it back in its envelope and walked back to the motel. I opened my laptop and spread out the documents I had taken from Angela. There was plenty of information there on my real mother, Ellen Weston, including her date of birth, date and place of marriage, and social security number.

Once again, accessing the New York State Motor Vehicle Database under the name of Ellen Weston and Ellen Chandler, and limiting the search to her date of birth of July 19, 1972, I obtained zero hits. Either Ellen had left New York or she was still here and did not have a driver's license under her maiden or original married name. And if she had re-married and took a different last name, I would be at a fast dead end.

The next morning the story of Angela's death – Maria Theresa Ferraro's death, that is – was on the morning news. The story was brief, asked for anyone with information to come forward and to contact Detective Daniel Boyland at Nassau Homicide with that information. Then I suddenly realized when Maria Ferraro's fingerprints were run in the national database and came back as belonging to Angela Chandler, the light would go off in Danny's head and he would come looking for me. It was obviously time to get out of Dodge, but to where?

• • •

I didn't run very far, just over the county line to the borough of Queens. Since community college back in California was inexpensive and I had a good paying job out there, I had managed to save quite a bit of money. I had a five-year old paid off Toyota Corolla that got great gas mileage and got me across the country without a bit of trouble, and over ten thousand dollars in cash. I checked into another inexpensive chain motel on Queens Boulevard, left my car parked in their lot and jumped on a subway to Manhattan. I had to do something that, in hindsight, I should have done a long time ago, something that Angela Chandler had the foresight to do – get a new identity.

After a few brief inquires in the Times Square area, and a twenty-dollar bill having passed from my hand into a grimy one, the unkempt, red-eyed, street person pointed to a doorway halfway down a narrow alley and said, "Knock t'ree times. Tell him Willy sent you."

I did as instructed and was welcomed into a surprisingly clean room by a smiling, unusually tall Asian man who asked how he could be of assistance. I told him what I needed and we settled on a price of six hundred dollars for a New York State Driver's license and New York state birth certificate. Mr. Li said his work was of such quality that obtaining a passport with the birth certificate would be a breeze. I gave him a down payment of three hundred dollars and he promised a two-day turnaround.

Back at the motel, the address of which I had given Mr. Li to use on my driver's license, I switched through the local news channels. There was nothing further on the death of Maria Ferraro. I was sure that in a day or two my picture would be all over the media. I could picture the newspaper headlines: *California Serial Killer Moves East – Mother Latest Victim. Frank Chandler—Mass Murderer now in New York.* But I wouldn't care one bit. By then I would be Matthew Hopkins, a resident of the state of New York, with a date of birth about three months younger. And, of course, I would look nothing like the curly-haired, clean-shaven composite photo they would display. Still totally bald, with a neatly-trimmed dark beard, I had added black horn-rimmed glasses with clear lenses. I felt certain that Boyland, and all the other cops looking for me, would never find me based on their known description.

When I paid the balance to Mr. Li he pointed out the carefulness of his work and promised complete satisfaction. He said with a grin, "Mr. Hopkins, if there is ever a problem with these, come right back and I will fix it. And send anyone who may need my services if you are happy with the products."

I thanked him and said I was going to test the documents right away as I was headed to the motor vehicle office to register my Corolla and get New York plates. The California plates would be folded up and disposed of in one of the city's myriad storm drains and I would be set to begin the search for a new job and an apartment and a whole new life back where it all began. Mommy – Angela – was dead. I had exorcised that demon and I was certain I would never kill anyone again, but I was not ready to dispose of my guns. It was time to find a girlfriend, settle down and build a new life as Matthew Hopkins. But I had to admit to myself I was more than a little curious about Ellen Weston – my real mother – but not curious enough to pursue her right now.

• • •

I had found a furnished apartment, which would shortly be available, in a private residence on a nicely tree-lined street in the

Elmhurst section of Queens within walking distance of the subway. With that taken care of I scanned the classified ads in the newspapers and the online search engines for job openings. And I checked the front pages of the newspapers for my picture. Now, seven days after I had killed Angela, there was nothing in print or on the TV. Surely the police had gotten Maria's prints back, surely they knew that Angela Chandler had the same date of birth as the dozen victims in California – so then why were they keeping the lid on?

I tried to reason it out. Danny Boyland had always impressed me as a good cop – and a smart cop. Not every cop gets to be a homicide detective, only the real good ones. And what I concluded was that major publicity would severely hinder his investigation. Danny probably figured that my photo, widely distributed, would probably cause me to do two things – flee New York in a hurry, and change my appearance. And the serial killer connection would create anxiety, if not panic, throughout the city of New York and its suburbs. And even if they stated that, with the death of Angela – the killer's mother – meant he had found his target and had no more reason to kill, the lives of women with that birth date would still be screaming for police protection.

So, I concluded, Danny was trying to find me on his own, under the radar. Fat chance! He knew everything about Frankie Chandler, but nothing about Matthew Hopkins. Maybe when he hit a dead-end, he would have to go to the media for help. And when he did, maybe I'd search out and kill another woman with the same date of birth. That would throw them for a loop. But I was done with killing, wasn't I?

When my new social security card came in the mail I started applying for the jobs on a list I had composed. Even though I would lose my previous earnings under my old social security number, it was a small price to pay for my identity protection. Besides, when I was able to collect, who knew if there would be any money left to collect from?

Another reason my confidence in not being found by the police was high, was that if I were Danny Boyland, I would figure that Frankie Chandler had left New York right after Angela's murder. He would figure I had lived in California while killing the women there, and I had fulfilled my objective with the sole murder here. He would figure I would have beat it to somewhere else, somewhere far away from both places, some place like Chicago, or St. Louis or Florida. I almost felt sorry for Danny. He had a murder on his hands and he knew *who* did it and *why* he did it, but had absolutely no clue as to *where* he was.

● ● ●

I landed a good-paying job at a large computer repair outfit in Manhattan. In addition to the salary I got an array of benefits and a 100% tuition reimbursement for pursuing a bachelor's degree in computer science. I knew that degree would enable me to command a much higher salary, money I would need to attract these beautiful Manhattan chicks I was surrounded with. But I wouldn't wait until then for some female companionship – I had already waited too long.

MOMMY, MOMMY

I began dating and working hard, and enjoying the city and all it had to offer. Life started to become very good. There was only one thing missing – my real Mommy. Although I had promised myself to purge her out of my mind, I just couldn't do it. The face of Ellen Weston – a face I had no actual conception of – intruded more and more into my dreams and then into my waking moments. One face was that of a smiling short-haired blonde, then a long-haired redhead and then one night she appeared in my dream – really a nightmare – as Angela Chandler with a bullet hole in her head.

Try as I might I couldn't get Mommy – Ellen Weston – out of my head, so I went back to the computer and began a search. Then after two days, I stopped. What was I doing? Was I gearing up for another Angela Chandler type search? No! I refuse to kill again! I would not track down women with Ellen's date of birth. No, no, no! I grabbed a bottle of beer and read through the documents I had taken from Angela once again, this time slowly, deliberately, and carefully. And by the time I took the last swallow of beer the answer – the clue – leaped off the page of Ellen's birth certificate. Father's name: George Weston. Mother's name: Eleanor Weston (nee Grady). And since Ellen had been born in a Queens hospital, and her marriage certificate showed she was married in Queens, I had to assume that the Weston's were longtime residents of the same boro in which I was now living. If I could find them – *Hi folks, I'm your grandson!* – would they know the whereabouts of their daughter Ellen? Or had they put her out of their lives even before she gave birth to me?

CHAPTER TWENTY-THREE

Danny

Case closed. Frankie Chandler had been trying to find his long lost mother for years. He figured she was in California from the car information I had given him, and he re-located there to find her. Only he had found a dozen look-alikes and killed them first. Was each murder a partial death of Angela? Was that how his mind had become – twisted, distorted, and hate-filled? Then he found the real Angela Chandler and tracked her down back to Long Island and finished his quest. He had no more reason to kill again, so as I said – case closed. All I had to do was find him and snap the cuffs on.

As I wondered where Frankie Chandler had fled – far away from here no doubt, but certainly not back to California – I also wondered if I was partly or wholly responsible for the death of twelve innocent women, and that of Angela Chandler. I believed the decision made by Wally Mason, Pam Saunders and me when Angela abandoned Frankie seventeen years ago, the decision to withhold that fact from him that Angela was not his real mother, was the correct one. But when Frankie came to see me after his tour in the Navy and inquired about her, I still kept it a secret from him. He had asked about her almost casually, certainly not with the fervor of a man who wanted to find her at all costs. If I had detected the slightest obsession in his demeanor, I would have told him immediately, and then thirteen women might still be alive.

"Danny! Partner? Hello, are you in there?" Spider asked breaking my deep thoughts and snapping me back to the present.

"Oh yeah, I was just thinking."

"Jesus," Allison said. "You tell us you know who killed Maria Ferraro and then you drift off to never-never land. Care to tell us why?"

"Sure," I said and filled them in on the Frankie Chandler story and my part in it.

"You can't blame yourself for all those deaths," Spider said. "You could not have anticipated that at all."

"Maybe I could have if I had been a little smarter and paid a bit more attention to the miserable life of young Frankie Chandler."

"Danny, what's done is done," Allison said. "Stop beating yourself up, it won't do any good. Let's concentrate on finding him. I still have the copy of his photo sketch that was printed with the original story, so I'm all set to go."

"Set to go for what?"

"For my story, that's what for. This is going to be tomorrow's page one headlines in the *Chronicle*."

"That may not be a good idea," I said.

"What do you mean? This is the biggest story of my career and you're not going to prevent me from going with it. Besides, you can't prevent me from printing it."

"I know I can't," I said, "but I can ask you to hold off for awhile."

"Why would I do that? A little while ago you thought it was a good idea to print the story. What's changed?"

"What's changed is we now have a definite suspect. And I don't think I want him to know that we know who he is."

"And," Spider said, "now that he's killed his mother – at least who he *thinks* was his mother – he has no reason to kill again."

"But you have no idea where he is," Allison said.

"True," I said, "but something's bothering me about this whole thing. Let's refresh our coffee and do some brainstorming, okay?"

After brewing a fresh pot of coffee and taking a few sips in silence I said, "Angela reads about the murders and she gets nervous – all the victims are her age and physically resemble her. Then when the Task Force discovers all the victims' dates of births are the same and decides to go public with it, Angela puts the puzzle together. Her long lost son, Frankie, is coming to get her, and he's pretty close."

"So she beats feet to Long Island," Allison said, "figuring she'd be safe three thousand miles away."

"Not really," I said, "I think she knew he would eventually track her down no matter where she ran off to."

"Then wouldn't she have prepared herself for the confrontation?" Spider asked.

"Like buy a gun?" Allison asked.

"You might think so," I said, "and I certainly would have just in case I was unsuccessful in talking him out of killing me."

"How could she have possibly talked her way out of that?" Allison asked.

"By telling him she was sorry for abandoning him, but that it was to be expected since she wasn't his real mother," Spider said.

"Obviously that didn't work," Allison said.

"No," I said. "Let me think more about this…"

• • •

The three of us had gone out to lunch and kicked some more ideas around, but we couldn't get Allison to change her mind about going with the story, so I knew another confab with our bosses would have to happen. When we got back to the squad Manny Perez said, "Hey, Lois Lane, Superman is here to see you."

"What are you talking about, Perez?"

"Superman. Looks just like him. He's in with the boss. An FBI agent interested in your murder case."

"Agent Havlek?" Allison said.

"That's what it sounded like," Manny said. "Don't fall in love now, Lois."

"Screw you, Manny," she said shaking her head, but unable to suppress a smile at the detective's antics.

We went back into the conference room to await the presence of Agent Havlek. When he came in with Lieutenant Veltri, who introduced him to us, I was startled, as I'm sure were Allison and Spider, by his appearance – Clark Kent minus the glasses. Tall, good-looking, dark hair. Too bad his attitude didn't match his looks. He said, "How come you didn't call me right away about this?"

As the lead detective on the case, I answered, "We were just about to do that. We ascertained the connection to the murders in California and figured you'd want to know."

"Brilliant!" he said. "I'm taking this case over, right now. And you, Miss Hayes, can leave right now. I'll call your editor shortly. This story stays under wraps until I say it can go. Got it?"

"Why you arrogant bastard…!" Allison said as I got up and grabbed her and escorted her out of the room to an empty office. I said, "Sit there and calm down, but don't leave. You'll be back in the mix soon, don't worry."

"What can you do about that insufferable prick?"

I just smiled and said, "Sit tight."

"Okay, Agent Havlek," I said when I returned. "You were saying that you were going to take over this case – my case – right now?"

"Correct, this is now a federal case. I am with VICAP, the Violent Criminal Apprehension Program of the Behavioral Science Unit, and I claim jurisdiction."

"Wow, that's a mouthful," I said looking at Lieutenant Veltri who had not left, but sat off in a corner with a slight smile on his face. "Now, if you come down off your high horse and play nice, I just might let you join our team and assist *me*, on *my* case."

"I guess you want to do this the hard way, Boyland," he said. "I guess I'll have to have my boss call your boss – my *big* boss in Manhattan."

"And just who is your boss?" I asked. "And just how big is he?"

"He is Edwin DeLand, the Assistant Director in charge of the New York office."

"Not high enough," I said.

"What do you mean?"

"I'm very good friends with DeLand's boss – his ultimate boss – Walter Kobak."

"Kobak? The FBI director? Give me a break, Boyland."

"Want me to call him and have him *direct* you to play the game the way I want it to be played?"

"Yeah, go right ahead, asshole. I'm calling your bluff."

I put the phone sitting on the conference room table on speaker mode and dialed a number from memory. A voice answered, "FBI Headquarters. How may I direct your call?"

"The Director's Office please," I said noticing a slight change in the smug look on Havlek's face.

"Director's Office, Miss Mays speaking."

"Hi, Wendy," I said. "It's Danny Boyland from New York."

"Oh, hello, Danny. How are you?"

"Doing great, and you?"

"Very good. Oh, I guess you want Mr. Kobak. He's got some people in his office, but I'm sure he'll pick up for you. Hold on."

The smug look was now entirely gone form Havlek's face and both Veltri and Spider sported big smiles on theirs. A voice boomed out of the speaker phone. "Danny Boy, how the hell are you?"

"I'm great, Walt," I said, "and you?"

"Never better since you and I rolled up those terrorist Romen Society bastards."

"Hey, we had a little help."

Walt laughed and said, "Yes, we did. Now what prompted this call? What can I do for you?"

I looked over at Agent Havlek whose complexion was deathly pale and said, "You know that serial murder caper out in California."

"Sure."

"We have a similar murder here. My case. Victim has the same date of birth. And the FBI case agent, Michael Havlek from VICAP, is sitting here with me, Spider Webb and Pete Veltri. He has flown all the way out here and offered his assistance and all the resources of the great FBI to help me out. I think that was terrific of him and I just wanted to convey my appreciation to you."

"You know we always serve to please. Agent Havlek?"

"Yes, sir," Havlek managed to speak.

"Do whatever you can to help them, okay? They're a great bunch of investigators."

"Yes, sir. I will."

"And hello there to Pete and Spider."

"Hi, Walt," they both said.

"Well, I have to run. Good luck on your case, Danny. Grab that psycho soon."

"We will, Walt," I said. "So long, partner."

I disconnected the call and looked over at Agent Havlek, a semblance of color returning to his face. He got up, walked out of the office and closed the door. Ten seconds later there was a knock on that door. "Come in," I said.

A smiling Michael Havlek entered, extended his hand and said, "I'm Mike Havlek from the FBI and I just flew in from L.A. to offer you whatever assistance I can in your murder investigation. Will you be so kind as to let me help?"

"Certainly," I said. "Oh, Superman, would you mind if I asked ace investigative reporter Lois Lane to join us?"

"Not at all, I would love to have Miss Lane's knowledge and input on this matter."

I was impressed. Mike Havlek had taken the heat and reacted well. If this new demeanor held up, he would be a great asset to our team. Now, where the hell was Frankie Chandler?

CHAPTER TWENTY-FOUR

Frankie

Finding the Weston's turned out to be an easy task. I accessed the Queens' white pages on my PC and found only one George Weston with a listing that was located in an apartment building on Braddock Avenue in Bellerose – Unit 4E.

The next evening I dressed in a suit and tie and placed the documents in my briefcase. Then I had a thought – suppose the Weston's were aware of the killings and the date of birth connection? But then how could they? They probably didn't even know if Jim Chandler remarried at all. But, to be on the safe side I put one of my guns in the briefcase. I chose the automatic, not the revolver I had just used to kill Mom…Angela. If I had to use it, the bullet comparison results should confuse the homicide squad a bit.

Mommy – Ellen – would be forty-five now, so I figured George and Eleanor Weston would be in their late sixties or early seventies. I had to figure out how to approach them, how to have them let me into their apartment, no easy task with suspicious elderly people, I figured. After running several scenarios through my mind, and not finding one that seemed sure to work, I decided on a ruse that might not get me inside, but might get me information.

I picked up my phone and dialed their number. A man answered and I said, "Is this Mr. Weston? George Weston?"

"Yes," he said with a trace of annoyance in his voice. "What is it?"

"I'm calling on behalf of your daughter's estate. I'm the attorney assigned to distribute her assets according to her will."

"I have no daughter," he said.

"Oh, then perhaps I have the wrong George Weston, or perhaps you are Ellen Weston's father, but decline to admit it. She mentioned that may occur in her will."

"Did she mention why?"

"Yes, but before I reveal anymore information could you tell me your wife's name?"

"No, you tell me."

"According to Ellen, it's Eleanor."

"So she's dead?"

"Yes."

"And she left us money?"

"Yes."

"How much?"

"I'd rather not go into the details on the phone," I said. "I need to ascertain your identity and have you and your wife sign some papers. Then the estate will be distributed in about two to three months."

"Okay. What was your name?"

"Hopkins. Matthew Hopkins. Are you free later this evening?"

"Yes, we are."

"How would eight o'clock be?"

"Fine. Do you know where we live?"

"Yes, on Braddock Avenue, number 224, apartment 4E. I'm happy you were listed in the phone directory."

"All right. We'll see you later."

I hung up and thought I had done a masterful job of deception in getting an appointment. George's initial comment – I have no daughter – and the coldness in his voice when he said it, led me to conclude that they had probably disowned her when she gave birth to me. Maybe even before she was ever officially married to my father. I intended to find out the answers to my questions very soon.

• • •

A nice-looking man with a full head of white hair, a lined face and piercing light-blue eyes with a distrustful look – my real biological grandfather – opened the door and let me into apartment 4E. He introduced me to his wife Eleanor – my real biological grandmother – who immediately asked me if I wanted something to drink. "Coffee, or a soda, perhaps?"

"A glass of water would be fine," I said.

Eleanor Weston was a pleasant-looking woman with short gray hair and a round face with sparkly light-brown eyes. I guessed she was about seventy years old, about two or three years younger than George. I was paying attention to their features to see if any obvious ones had passed down from them to Ellen, and then to me. The only similarity I could see so far was my brown eyes and Eleanor's.

We all sat around a coffee table in the living room and I snapped open my briefcase and withdrew Ellen's certificate of birth and her marriage certificate and handed them to George. He scanned them, nodded his head, and passed them to his wife. She read them and then took a handkerchief out of her pocket and wiped a tear from her eye. George said, "That's her all right, but I don't understand why she would want to leave us any money at all."

"Strained relationship?" I asked.

He grunted and said, "That would be an understatement. We haven't seen her nor heard from her in over twenty-five years."

"How about her husband?" I asked. "James Chandler."

"She never should have married him," Eleanor said. "Truth be told, Mr. Hopkins, we were extremely upset at her hasty marriage and her…her condition. We're strict Roman Catholics, you know."

"Oh, I understand," I said. "I'm sorry, I didn't mean to pry or re-open old wounds, but I have a sworn duty to try to locate any other kin – blood relatives of Ellen – who she did not mention in her will, before I can fully send it to probate."

"She walked out on Chandler and left him with the baby," George said. "He remarried and several years later fell down a flight of stairs and killed himself. It was in the papers. I'll tell you I didn't shed a tear over that. There was also speculation that maybe Chandler didn't fall down those steps and maybe his second wife, Angela, pushed him. She fled a week later and was never found or heard from again."

"So what happened to the baby? Your grandson?"

"We have no idea," he said. "After Angela abandoned him there was nothing further in the news."

Eleanor Weston was gushing tears now and George turned to her and said, "Stop that babbling, for Pete's sake!"

"That's pretty awful," I said.

"There was some thought that Angela fled because she figured the cops were thinking she might have pushed her dear hubby down those stairs as I just said. And she had no real attachment to the kid. It wasn't hers."

I felt the anger begin to rise in me and I said, "The *kid*, Mr. Weston, did the *kid – your biological grandson* – have a name?"

"Frankie," Eleanor blurted out. "Frankie Chandler."

"And what became of little Frankie Chandler?" I asked.

"As I said before, we don't know," George said. "I guess the state took him."

I had to bite my tongue and quell my anger for a moment, because I now had to ask the key question. I took a deep breath and said, "Okay, I'll follow up with Child Protective Services on Frankie. Now, when Ellen disappeared do you know what happened to her, or where she went? Did she remarry and have more children?"

"She went into the convent," George said. "A good place for the who…"

"George!" Eleanor snapped. "Please."

"That's good," I said. "No more people to track down. Now let me ask you something, if I may. Did you ever think to seek out your daughter and forgive her?"

"That's not your concern," George said. "Just get on with your business."

"I intend to, but first just one more question. When Angela Chandler abandoned Frankie – your biological grandson – did you ever consider taking him in and providing a loving home for him rather than have him put in an orphanage?"

Mrs. Weston started to say something, but George stopped her and said, "We didn't want the little bastard, plain and simple."

"And you didn't care about his future or what would become of him?"

"No," George said, "nor the little bastard's mother either. Now are you going to give us the papers to sign and get out of here?"

"I sure am, Grandpa," I said reaching into my briefcase and withdrawing my Glock, which I pointed directly at his face.

"What the…?"

"Shut up, George. I did not come here with any intention of killing you, but I never met anyone quite as cold and heartless as you two. And believe me I've met a lot of rotten people during my rotten life. You two call yourself Christians, strict Roman Catholics? Like hell you are! You don't have a Christian bone in your body. You disowned my mother and left me to the wolves."

"What are you talking about?" Eleanor said.

"Ellen Weston is my mother. And I'm your grandson, Frankie Chandler."

"You're a liar!" shouted George Weston as he started to rise from his seat.

I shot him right between the eyes and said, "No, I'm not, Grandpa."

MOMMY, MOMMY

I shot him twice more in the chest and turned the gun toward Grandma. She hadn't screamed when I fired the gun and killed her husband, but had clapped both her hands over her mouth. I said, "Do you want to say something to me?"

She removed her hands from her mouth and placed them in her lap. "Yes," she said in a whisper. "Yes, Frankie, I am sorry. I wanted to visit my daughter, I wanted to reconcile with her so many times, but George would not hear of it. And when I heard what happened to you – when Angela left you – I took it as a sign from God. I would take you in and find my daughter and bring us all together as a family."

"Why didn't you?"

"Again, George wouldn't hear any of it. 'My sentimental bullshit,' he called it."

"Grandma, there comes a time in just about everyone's life, when they have to find the courage to stand up to whoever is restraining them and do the right thing. You didn't do that, though. You blew it."

"No, I…I didn't, but you seem to have turned out to be a nice young man, Frankie. Are you really a lawyer?"

"No, Grandma, I'm not a lawyer. I'm not much of anything. Let me tell you what became of your ten-year old grandson when you didn't do the right thing."

I told her everything and ended with, "…so your grandson ended up as a serial killer. Thanks, Grandma and thanks Grandpa," I said looking down at his body.

Eleanor was crying again and said, "What are you going to do now, Frankie?"

"I just want to find my mother. I want to have a chance at some happiness. Can you help me, Grandma?"

"Like I said, she went into the convent. It's the one way out east on Long Island, on the south fork."

"Do you know if she is still there?"

"No, I don't know anything else, or what happened to her, or where she may have gone if she left there."

I looked at my grandmother and suddenly felt a pang of sympathy as my anger drained out of me. I thought about sparing her life, but realized I had already gone too far and couldn't allow her to live. I shot her quickly three times in the chest avoiding looking into her eyes. I left the apartment after wiping my fingerprints from the glass of water I had used and collecting the six expended cartridge cases. Stepping over grandma's body, I looked down at her, shook my head, and wiped a few tears from my eyes.

When I arrived back home I first cleaned and reloaded the automatic and then booted up my PC and began the search for Roman Catholic convents on Long Island. There was just one on the south fork – St. John of the Cross –and their website was chock full of information. St. John's school, taught by both nuns and lay faculty, was the main function of the convent, and since a healthy tuition was charged to the rich east-end Catholics, the school was the chief support of the entire facility, including the church.

There were about thirty faculty and administrators and each had half a page devoted to them including a color picture, short biography and academic credentials. It took me less than two minutes to find Ellen Weston, although that name was not mentioned. She was Sister Audrey LaSalle a member since January

MOMMY, MOMMY

1991, when I was ten months old. Her date of birth was not listed, but her beautiful brown eyes, Grandma Eleanor's eyes, my eyes, stared out at me. And no other woman entered within a year of her. This was her. Mommy. I had finally found her. Well, not yet, but that would be soon – very soon.

CHAPTER TWENTY-FIVE

Danny

The four of us – Allison, Mike Havlek, Spider and me – sat around drinking coffee and going over the California murders and the murder here on the Island with one goal in mind – how do we find and arrest Frankie Chandler? It got to be past five o'clock and we were all tired and out of ideas. I said, "Why don't we wrap it up for now and mull it over in our dreams?"

"Yeah, I'm beat and still on West coast time," Havlek said.

"Where are you staying?" Spider asked. "Do you need a lift?"

"No, thanks. I have a rental and I'm going to stop first at the Long Island FBI office. They're getting a hotel room for me."

We decided to meet back at the squad by eight the next morning and, as we walked to our cars, Havlek grabbed my arm and said, "Thanks again, Danny, for the way you handled this with the Director. I know you could have really stuck it to me."

I smiled and said, "I saw through your arrogant FBI exterior and visualized the good guy underneath."

"X-ray vision," he said with a laugh.

"That's *your* thing, Superman. Not mine."

"What's with the reporter, Allison?"

"Good reporter and she knows when to keep her mouth shut. She has yet to violate any confidence over the years she's worked with us."

"Not bad looking, either," Havlek said.

"Is Superman interested in Lois Lane?"

"Is she married?"

"Nope, unless you consider married to her job as being married. Probably very much like you."

"You're very perceptive, Danny Boy."

"That's why I'm a detective, Superman."

• • •

I had taken Wally Mason's original case file home with me, the one of Jim Chandler's murder seventeen years ago. I vaguely remembered him and the social worker, Pam Saunders, trying to locate relatives who could have possibly taken Frankie in. As usual, I discussed the case with my wife, Tara, a former homicide detective and still on the Job working in the District Attorney's Squad. After relating the happenings of the day she said, "So Manny Perez is still at it sticking nicknames on people, I see."

"Yeah," I said, "and it's amazing how accurate he is with them, ax-lady."

"Well, when you catch three ax-murders in one year what else would he call me?" she asked poking me in the ribs.

"He could have called you Halle Berry like I did."

"You're so sweet, Danny. You still do know the right words."

"Help me go over this case of Wally's and then we'll turn those sweet words into some sweet lovin'," I said.

"Sounds good. Let's have a look."

We both read the entire case, twice, making notes and sipping a little red wine. When we agreed we were done Tara said, "If Angela told Frankie that she was not his real mother, would she have known who his real mother was?"

"I don't know," I said. "She married Jim Chandler when Frankie was a year and a half old. His first wife walked out on him and who knows if he ever knew – or cared – where she went."

"I'm sure Angela would have known her name, at least. Jim would have mentioned it."

"So, we assume Frankie also knows his real mother's name and is now searching for her?"

"Yes, and we may have a new string of murders beginning soon, depending on how much information he has on her."

"What could he possibly have besides her name? How would he know her physical description, or date of birth, or where she might live?"

"You just read the same case I did, Danny Boy. You tell me."

I looked at my notes and then it hit me. "The Chandlers!" I exclaimed. "Jim's parents."

"Correct," Tara said. "Angela's parents are dead and wouldn't know anything anyway. But the Chandlers..."

"Yeah, the world travelers form Colorado who wanted no part of their grandson."

"Suppose Angela told Frankie of the existence and whereabouts of his grandparents?"

"He could be tracking them down in an effort to get information on the whereabouts of his real mother," I said.

"And?"

"And they might be his next two victims."

"And?"

"And their number is here in the file. So let's call them – right now."

"Great police work, lover boy."

The message on the Chandler's answering machine said, "Hello, we're off traveling again. Please leave a message." I found the number of the local police department in Wally's notes and called their detective squad and filled them in on my concerns. One of them went through the patrol force's vacant home list and said the Chandlers were due back in two weeks. That gave us a breather and I asked them to call me immediately when they got home and to put a watch on them for protection from a possible visit by Frankie Chandler. They were very cooperative and wished me success in nabbing our serial killer before he got out their way.

"A good night's work," I said to Tara. "Thanks a lot for your input. How about a nightcap?"

"Sure, lover boy, and then I'd like a little *input* from you, if you get my drift."

"I sure do, lover girl. Drink up."

• • •

There was a message on my desk when I got into the office at eight the next morning. It said, "Call Detective Gennaro in Ballistics."

And when I did he informed me that the bullets recovered from Angela's body came from a .357 S&W Magnum revolver and they matched with the bullets taken from a recent robbery victim in Los Angeles. "What was the victim's name, Walt?"

"Salvatore Domenico, and I have something real interesting for you, Danny Boy."

"I'm all ears," I said my curiosity now fully engaged.

"I called the case detective out there and he told me the case is still unsolved. He also told me the name of the deceased's fiancée – Maria Ferraro."

"Holy crap! Angela killed another one!"

"Don't be so hasty," Walt said. "Frankie Chandler could have done it."

"Yeah, you're right. We'll have to mull this one over."

After I thanked him and got the Los Angeles detective's contact information, I filled in the rest of my team who had all arrived in the office while I was on the phone. I also told them of my attempts to contact Frankie's grandparents the night before.

"I think that Angela killed Sal, for whatever reason, and fled from the area taking the gun with her for protection from Frankie when he showed up," Allison Hayes said.

"Sounds plausible," Spider said. "What reason would Frankie have to kill this guy, Domenico, anyway?"

"Maybe something we don't know,' Danny said. "But all the other murders committed out there with a firearm were done with a .40 caliber automatic. I'll call the LA detective later and see what else he knows. Who did Sal in is not that important right now anyway."

"I guess all we can do is wait for the Chandlers to get home," Agent Havlek said. "As soon as they do I'll send a couple of agents up to babysit them until I can fly out there – with you Danny, of course."

"Of course," I smiled.

"Can I go with any of the story now?" Allison asked.

"I would say no," Havlek said. "We still don't want to alert Chandler."

Allison looked as if she were about to object, so I said, "Miss Lane, I'll give you Wally's case to read. Put the whole thing together so far. All you'll have to write is the ending when it happens. The Pulitzer Prize will be all yours."

She smiled and said, "Okay, Danny, I'll start writing. It looks like we are at a dead-end right now."

"Yeah," Spider said. "It's that time in the investigation when all we can do is hurry up and wait."

"For the Chandlers to come home," I said.

"Or the next body to turn up," Havlek said.

"Or several bodies," Allison said, "as the psycho Frankie Chandler hunts for mommy number two."

We sat in silence for a while and then got up to disperse. Allison was first up and said, "Back to the world of mundane journalism."

Mike Havlek said he was going out to the FBI Office in Melville to check in on what other serial murders might need his attention. He said, "Uh, Miss Hayes, uh, Allison?"

"Yes, Mike?"

"Would you care to have dinner with me tonight?"

"Oh, is the out-of-town FBI agent lonely?"

MOMMY, MOMMY

"Well, yeah."

"Sure," she said, taking her card and a pen out of her purse. "Here's my number and home address. Pick me up at six-thirty. I'll make a reservation for seven at a nice place."

She smiled and walked out the door. Havlek stood there with his mouth open and Allison's card in his hand. "Wow!" he said.

"Whaddya know," Spider said. "Superman and Lois Lane have a date."

When Mike Havlek left I said to Spider, "Here we go again – cops and reporters. Dangerous combination."

Spider just looked at me and nodded. He knew I was referring to his *almost affair* with the late reporter, the beautiful Tiffany Adams-Kim, of a major New York newspaper – an event that we had both agreed to keep buried in the past. That was the first slight reference I had made to it since it occurred a few years ago, and I let it go now without a further word.

● ● ●

We waited. Mike Havlek flew back down to Washington to assist on a couple of other possible serial murder cases and Allison went back to her regular police beat. Three days later, Detective Gennaro called me once more and said, "Danny, I may have something more for you. This is real interesting."

I came immediately to mental attention wondering what Walt Gennaro might have now, and how it pertained to the Chandler case. "Go," I said.

"Yesterday morning Queens Homicide was called to the scene of a double murder in Bellerose. An elderly couple – George and Eleanor Weston – were found murdered in their apartment. The bullets recovered from their bodies, three in each…"

"…were from a .357 S & W Magnum," I interrupted.

"Wrong. They were from a .40 caliber automatic. I'll give you one guess as to which *particular* .40 caliber auto it could be."

"You gotta be kidding, Walt. The one used in the California murders?"

"Bingo! Danny Boy. I knew you were a great detective."

After I hung up with Gennaro I yelled for Spider and shared the information with him. He said, "So the same gun used to murder several women in California is used to murder a couple in Queens. What's the connection? If Frankie Chandler did this, what were the Weston's to him? And if it was Frankie, why didn't he use the revolver he killed Angela with?"

"Don't know the answers, Spider, but we'll sure find out. I'm a bit confused, though. Do we have two different perps out there? Or do you think Frankie Chandler is twisting our tails by switching guns?"

"Who knows? Think we should call Superman?"

"Yes," I said, "but let's not call Lois Lane until we can figure this puzzle out. Let's go with the assumption that Angela did use that .357 magnum to kill her intended husband and took it with her when she drove cross-country. That would explain how it got out here. And then Frankie finds it in her apartment – maybe she tried to pull it on him – and now he has it."

"But he uses the automatic to kill those two old folks."

"Yeah," I said. "And he still may have the revolver, too."

"And he killed the Weston's because…?"

"Who the fuck knows, Spider? We're homicide detectives. Let's figure it out."

"Sure," Spider said shaking his head. "A piece of cake."

And then a dim bulb turned on somewhere in the back of my mind – way back to when I was a rookie cop called to the scene of Jim Chandler's *accidental* fall down the cellar stairs. The bulb grew brighter as I remember Social Worker Pam Saunders relating to me and Wally Mason her conversation with Jim Chandler's parents and them telling her of Jim's first wife. The bulb now blasted into white brilliance as the name jumped into the forefront of my mind – Ellen it was, *Ellen Weston*. "Spider," I said. "The Weston's are Frankie Chandler's biological grandparents, the parents of his *real* mother, Ellen Weston."

Spider smiled and said, "See, just like I said – a piece of cake. Now would you care to tell me how the hell you just figured that out, Sherlock?"

"Elementary, my dear Watson. I'll tell you all about it on the way to Queens tomorrow."

CHAPTER TWENTY-SIX

Ellen

After I had made my decision to abandon my son for the second time, I tried to put him out of my mind. I couldn't do it. If anything, I thought of him more now than before the news story of the death of his father. I knew Jim Chandler had been a good man and this was confirmed when the story said he had kept Frankie after his first wife left him and then eventually remarried. My guilt was assuaged by the fact that my son was in what appeared to be a loving two-parent home.

Now that home was shattered – the father dead – the mother gone – and the son was alone in the world. This was now my chance at true redemption for my original sin. I could have reclaimed my son and given him a loving home with a loving mother. But I hadn't done so, and now as the years passed, the consequences of that decision weighed increasingly heavy on my conscience. Oh, I went to mass every day and confession every week, and led a good Christian life keeping my vows of poverty and celibacy. But deep inside my core, my one great sin – now compounded – ate at my soul much like a cancer eats at one's body. If there was indeed a hell, I knew I would burn there forever. True redemption for me was now unattainable.

And then, one fine early summer day, everything changed and my redemption became a possibility. I had dismissed my second-grade class and was walking through the park-like grounds of the campus, trees and bushes now almost in full bloom, when a young man approached me and said, "Sister Audrey?"

"Yes," I said realizing that maybe I had known him in the distant past.

"Do you know who I am?" he asked.

I studied his face which was mostly covered in a trim black beard. His scalp was bald, but it was obvious that was intentional as it was thickly covered with tiny dots of black. It was his eyes that drew my attention. "No," I said, "but you do look a bit familiar. Were you one of my former students?"

"No," he said and pointed at a nearby garden bench. "May we sit down?"

He guided me to the bench and we both sat. He took my hand – for some reason I did not protest – and he said, "Mommy, I'm your son. I'm Frankie Chandler."

I was shocked. I could not utter a word. I stared at him and had no doubts that he was who he just said he was – my long lost son.

"Are you all right?" he asked, deep concern on his face.

My response was to throw my arms around him and burst into tears. He held me tight for several minutes until my sobs tailed off. He said, "I finally found you, Mommy. After all these years, I finally found you."

All my guilt crashed down upon my shoulders at the sound of his words. Without looking up at him I murmured, "Have you

MOMMY, MOMMY

come to kill me, Frankie, for what I did to you all those years ago?"

"What? Kill you? No, Mommy, I have come to love you."

"Love me? I am undeserving of your love. I abandoned you as a baby. I..."

"Mommy," he said, "I know all that. That's in the past. We are here together, right now, in the present. All our misdeeds don't matter. Our only direction is forward."

I looked up at him and smiled, "Oh, Frankie," I said, "if only it were that easy – to forget how bad my past sins are."

"I have my share of past sins, too," he said. "Some very bad ones."

"What bad things could you – my son – have done?"

He smiled at me and said, "And what sins could you – my mother – have committed. You are a nun."

"Even nuns and priests commit sins, Frankie. Have you confessed your sins to your priest?"

"No, Mommy. Have you confessed yours?"

Things seemed to be getting too serious, so I said, "Why don't we shelve our sins, be they real or imagined, for some other time, Frankie?"

"Great idea," he said with a big smile. "Let's get to know each other a bit and fill in the gaps, the long gaps, in our lives."

I smiled back at him and took his hand and said, "Let's take a walk and we'll have a long, long talk."

We stood up and began to walk when Frankie said, "You never questioned me when I told you I was your son. How do you know I am Frankie Chandler?"

"I know," I said. "What mother doesn't know her own child?"

He smiled and then dropped my hand which he had been holding. He said, "It may not be a good idea to stroll around hand in hand with a nun."

I laughed and said, "Oh, yes, they'll think I'm a cougar in disguise trying to seduce a handsome young man!"

We talked for about an hour and Frankie told me about his past life in foster homes and his time in the Navy and his jobs. I sensed he glossed over things quite a bit, that things were a lot tougher in his past than what he was really telling me, but I did not question him. I told him my rather boring but peaceful life as a teaching nun, but I did not tell him that I chose not to act when Angela deserted him. As we had agreed, we put the telling of our past sins on hold for awhile. When it became obvious that both of us were not going to open up further to each other at this time – a decision seemingly reached by some type of telepathy between us – I said, "So, my son, where do we go from here?"

"I want to be part of your life, Mommy," he said. "A big part. That is, if that's okay with you?"

"Of course it is," I said.

"I'm between jobs right now," he said, "but I have quite a bit of cash stashed away. I could get a room out here to be closer to you."

"That would be fine," I said. "The school year is over in a few weeks; maybe we can go away on a little vacation and really get to know each other."

"I like that idea," he said, "we can figure out our future."

"I like teaching," I said. "But I can do that anyplace."

"You mean you'd leave the church?"

"Well, maybe. Who knows? You may be the force in my life that could make me make a real change – a brand new beginning."

After exchanging telephone numbers – my room and his cell – we agreed to meet often and continue to get to know each other better. The next night he took me to a nice steak dinner in Southampton, and the days he didn't come over to the school, we chatted on the phone. Everything was going fine until one day Frankie said, "Mommy, have you noticed any suspicious people around the area?"

"Whatever do you mean?" I asked.

"I've gotten a few threatening calls on my cell phone from bill collectors," he said. "I think they have me confused with some other Chandler, but I had the feeling I was being followed the other night."

"I don't recall seeing any strange people around, but I'll keep a sharp eye out."

"Thanks, Mommy. I'll try to clear up this misunderstanding as soon as I can."

Now when someone plants a thought like that in your head it causes you to become extra alert and suspicious. And what do you know, over the next few days I *did* see some strange men around – two to be exact. I never saw them together – one was white, one black – but I swear that when I did see them they were looking right at me. And when I looked back at them, they averted their eyes and walked the other way. Then I wondered if I was just suspicious or getting paranoid?

I didn't see them again, but I did see other strangers from time to time over the next few days. I had the feeling, although

I didn't know why, that these men, and a woman as well, were law enforcement officers and they were observing me. But why? Then I thought of Frankie and his unmentioned "past sins" and I wondered if somehow they were looking for *him* and knew of our new found relationship. Then I dismissed this whole paranoid scenario and looked forward to seeing my son again in two days. He was going to meet me here at school and treat me to a Friday night seafood dinner at a fancy restaurant on the water. Then I changed my mind again and figured maybe I'd mention these strangers to him during our phone call tonight. Better to be safe than sorry, right?

CHAPTER TWENTY-SEVEN

Danny

The next morning Spider and I drove into the Queens Homicide office in Forest Hills and met with Detective Sam Hervell who had handled the murder cases of George and Eleanor Weston. "Gennaro in Ballistics tells me you might have a connection between one of your cases and the Weston's." he said.

"Maybe we do, Sam," I said. "We think the gun used to kill the Weston's, which as you now know was used in the L.A. murders, may be in possession of the perpetrator of our murder case in Farmingdale."

"Although," Spider said, "he used a .357 magnum in that case."

"And your perp is?" Sam asked.

"A guy by the name of Frankie Chandler," I said.

"What's the connection?"

"We were hoping you could confirm something I recently remembered from a long time ago." I said. "I believe the Weston's had a daughter named Ellen and she is Frankie Chandler's real mother. Can you dig out your case file and then we'll put our heads together?"

"Let's put some coffee on and we'll do just that," Sam said.

After reading Sam's case and giving him all the info we had on Chandler so far, the three of us came to the same conclusion, albeit a shaky unsubstantiated one, that Frankie discovered the Weston's were his real mother's parents – his grandparents – and he had killed them after finding out – or *not* finding out – the whereabouts of his mother.

"Sam," Spider said, "was there anything in the Weston's apartment that indicated they had a daughter? An album? A picture on the dresser?"

"Not a damn thing," Sam said. "No photos of children at all. Just one of George and Eleanor, when they were maybe fifteen years younger, posing with another couple in their same age range."

"Any idea who that couple was?" I asked.

"Maybe George's brother. Hold on a sec."

Sam flipped through his case file and said, "His brother's name is Edward. I'm pretty sure he handled the funeral details. Lives in Jersey."

"Is anyone in the Weston's apartment now?" Spider asked.

"I don't think so," Sam said. "It was on a long-term lease and I don't know if Edward removed anything yet."

"So you released the scene?" Spider asked.

"Yeah, so you can go poke around there all you want," Sam replied.

"We'll do that now and then we'll go see Edward Weston tomorrow," Danny said. "Maybe he knows of a daughter his brother may have fathered."

MOMMY, MOMMY

"Good luck, guys," Sam said. "Go solve your case – and solve mine, too, while you're at it."

"Don't we all wish," Spider said laughing as we headed out the door.

• • •

The building super, Vladis Kauskas, obligingly opened the door to apartment 4E and left us alone saying, "Let me know venn you done, pliz."

We searched for over an hour, under carpets, in the drawers, between the clothes, behind the radiator covers, in the freezer, but got the same results as Sam had gotten – nothing. Nothing in the way of showing that the Weston's ever had a daughter or any other children. I looked at my notes and found Edward Weston's New Jersey phone number and dialed it from the apartment's phone which had not yet been disconnected. He answered on the third ring and I identified myself and told him where I was and got right to the point. I said, "Mr. Weston, did your brother and his wife have any children?"

"Yes," he said. "One daughter."

I took a deep breath and nodded at Spider also giving him a thumbs up signal. "Mr. Weston, can my partner and I drive over to your place tomorrow? I need to know everything I can about your niece...."

"Ellen is her name," he said. "And I can save you the trip. I'm coming to the apartment tomorrow to clean it out. Most everything I'm going to donate to the Salvation Army. I'll only keep any pertinent memorabilia."

"There may not be much of that," I said. "There are no indications here that a daughter ever existed."

"That does not surprise me," he said. "My brother was a stubborn fool. For a professed person of Christian faith there was not a forgiving bone in his body."

"When do you plan to arrive?" I asked.

"Around eleven, after the rush hour, and I'll bring what I have of Ellen."

"Do you have any photos?"

"Several, and I have her wedding invitation, too."

"Of her marriage to Jim Chandler?"

"Yes."

"We'll see you tomorrow, Mr. Weston, Thank you."

I hung up the phone and told Spider what I had found out. He said, "Finally a break. Maybe we can track her down before Frankie finds her. Maybe we can save her life before he kills her, too."

"Do you think he means to kill her?" I asked.

My question seemed to surprise Spider and he said, "Well, he killed Angela."

"But she wasn't his mother, was she?"

"No, but...but Danny, who knows how a psycho's mind works? He's killed a lot of people so far."

"I wonder how much of a psycho Frankie Chandler really is," I said. "I sometimes think he may have been involuntarily turned by society and circumstances from an innocent kid into a cold-blooded murderer."

"Are you feeling sorry for him?"

"Yeah, maybe I am. He's had nothing but bad breaks his whole young life."

"But don't forget, Danny, right now he is fucking scary – and very dangerous – no matter how, or why, he got that way."

• • •

We met Edward and Agatha Weston late the following morning as scheduled. The Salvation Army pickup had not yet arrived, so we had time to talk uninterrupted. After identifying the group photo of the foursome we found in the apartment, Edward said, "My brother was a hard man."

Agatha rolled her eyes and said, "No, Ed, he was a lot worse than that – he was a rotten, unforgiving bastard."

Edward looked from the photo to his wife and nodded his head in affirmation. "Agatha's right, but it pains me to admit it. He was my brother, you know."

"You wouldn't know they were brothers if you compared their inner beings," Agatha said. "My husband is a loving, God-fearing, honest man, thank God."

Before I could ask, Edward placed a paper shopping bag on the table and took out a cardboard box. He opened its flaps and pulled out a handful of photos and papers. After putting on his glasses he searched through them for a minute or so selecting three photos and an envelope. The photos were of his niece, Ellen Weston, and the envelope contained the original wedding invitation they had received from James and Ellen.

"Did you attend the wedding?" Spider asked.

"Shamefully, no," Edward said. "My brother said he would disown us both if we dared to show up."

"I wanted to go regardless," Agatha said. "That poor lovely girl didn't deserve the treatment he gave her. I didn't care if he disowned me. That would have been fine with me, but I'm ashamed to say, I stayed away, too."

"We sent them a nice check, though," Edward said.

"With a note never to mention it to her father," Agatha said.

I scrutinized the wedding invitation and was disappointed to discover they were not married in a church – of course not stupid, I thought – but had a civil ceremony at the place of their reception, a catering hall in Queens. It was time to ask the big question, "Mr. and Mrs. Weston," I said, "do you know where Ellen is now?"

Agatha opened her mouth, but Edward put his hand up and stopped her. "Before we answer that," he said, "can you answer a few of our questions and let us know what's going on here?"

"Sure, go ahead," I said.

"Do you think Ellen killed my brother and his wife?"

"No."

"Do you know who killed them and why?"

"I think so, but I have no proof yet."

"Is Ellen possibly now in danger?"

"That's a strong possibility, and that's why we have to find her right away."

"Who would want to kill a nun?" Agatha asked.

"Pardon me?" Spider said.

"She went into the convent after giving up the baby," she said.

"Do you know where she is?" I asked again.

"I want my answer first," Edward said.

"Frankie Chandler is our suspect," Mr. Weston. "Ellen's son. Your brother's grandson."

That shocked both of them speechless and I gave them some more information, but left out the serial killer part. When I finished Edward said, "So Frankie searches out who he thinks is his mother and kills her. And you think she probably told him who his real mother was before she was murdered."

"And based on her name," Agatha said, "Frankie locates her parents and comes here to find out from them where his long, lost real mother is."

"Correct," I said. "Did they know where she is, and do you two also know?"

"She's out on Long Island," Edward said. "At St. John of the Cross convent. At least that's where she went all those years ago."

"And Frankie's grandparents knew that?"

"Yes," Edward said. "I had kept contact with Ellen for a while and I whispered her whereabouts to my sister-in-law, Eleanor. I'm not sure if she told my brother."

"Do you know her religious name?" Spider asked.

"Sister Audrey LaSalle," Agatha replied. "She teaches second grade."

"Thank you very much," I said. "As you can surmise, my partner and I have to move quickly on this. And I'd like to keep one of these photos of Ellen if I may."

"Sure," Edward said handing me the three photos.

I selected the best one and Spider and I started to leave. Agatha Weston grabbed my arm and said, "Detective Boyland, what kind of person kills his mother, biological or not, and his grandparents?"

"I don't know," I said. "I suppose one answer is deranged maniac. Or a stealthy psychopath. Or maybe a grown-up boy who was tossed around cruelly his whole life and just wants his mother – his real mother – to comfort him."

"You'll keep us up-to-date?" Edward asked.

"Yes," I said. "Thank you both again for your help."

On the drive back to Mineola I called down to Agent Havlek in Washington and said, "We caught a break. Try to get up here as soon as you can."

• • •

I stayed true to my word and brought Lois Lane into the meeting I had set up for seven that evening. Havlek and I decided on a team of six to do the surveillance out at St. John's. We had assumed Frankie would be making contact with his mother soon – one way or the other – where else would he go, except the one place where he might be able to fulfill his life's goal?

We decided on Spider, Manny Perez, Havlek and another FBI Agent from the local office, and Sam Hervell and his partner from Queens Homicide. We would begin surveillance the next day with Spider and Mike Havlek. I would not be a part of the up-close surveillance at any time as my face was well known to Frankie Chandler, but I would be one of us to always be in the immediate area should the surveillance team spot him. Allison Hayes agreed to stay a few blocks away from the immediate location, but we promised to call her as soon as the surveillance paid off and we decided to make our move to bring Frankie into custody.

On the first day of surveillance both Spider and Havlek observed Sister Audrey at various times and at various locations on the campus. On the second day both reported that Sister Audrey looked at them suspiciously on separate occasions. We switched teams for the next day using Sam Hervell and his female partner with the caveat to be extra careful and observe the nun from as far away as possible We supplied them with high powered binoculars and waited.

Since I couldn't be seen, I sat off campus in a car and began to prepare an affidavit for a wiretap on Sister Audrey's phone. That would take a couple of days, at least, for approval. We hoped the case would break before that, but so far there were absolutely no signs of Frankie Chandler.

CHAPTER TWENTY-EIGHT

Frankie

When Mommy called me tonight and told me of her suspicions regarding seeing an unusual number of strangers around the school and grounds, I calmed her fears as best I could. I told her that any past sins I had committed were not of such a nature as to attract law enforcement's attention. That seemed to satisfy her, but I had to find out one important thing. I said, "Mommy, can you remember what they looked like?"

"Frankie, there were several of them, both men and women, black and white."

"Concentrate on the white man," I said. "I think I'm being followed by a guy, maybe a bill collector that looks like this..." I then gave her as detailed a description of Detective Danny Boyland as I could, and waited, holding my breath.

"No, Frankie, none of them looked like that at all."

"Thanks," I said my red warning flag changing to yellow. "Let's forget about it. I'll call you tomorrow and see you Friday for dinner."

After I closed my cell phone, I thought about this situation some more and decided to take the bull by the horns. Danny *had* to be looking for me since he had the murder case on Angela. I'm sure he suspected me – I mean, come on, he damn well *knew* it was me – but his suspicions still had not been voiced on the television news or in the papers. I decided to call him the next morning using my cell phone which still had a 562 California area code. Won't he be surprised when he hears my voice, the voice of the killer he was no doubt desperate to catch?

• • •

"Homicide Squad, Detective Boyland."

"Hello, Danny. It's been awhile. Frankie Chandler here."

Danny was good, I give him that. He didn't miss a beat and sounded genuinely happy when he said," Frankie! Good to hear from you. How are you?"

I could visualize him waving madly at someone and writing my cell number down off his caller ID, but he betrayed no trace of anxiety in his voice.

"I'm doing okay," I said.

"Still out in sunny California?" he asked.

"Yeah, got my Associate's degree now."

"Good for you. Uh…are you planning on coming back East anytime soon?"

"No, no reason to."

"Well, I may give you one. I'm glad you called because I had no way of finding you."

"You were looking for me?"

"Yeah, Frank. Listen, I have some bad news I have to tell you."

MOMMY, MOMMY

"What is it?"

"Frankie, this is a hard one to say. You were always interested in locating your mother, ever since you were a young boy..."

"Well, I'm still looking, but this doesn't sound good."

"I caught a murder case a couple of weeks ago in Farmingdale. Woman's name was Maria Ferraro. When we ran her prints they came back to Angela Chandler. Frankie, I'm sorry. We're pretty certain she's your mother."

"Holy shit!" I said. "Are you sure?"

"Yeah, and I wanted to notify you right away in case you wanted to claim her body and provide a burial."

"Is she still in the morgue?"

"Yes, she is."

"I'll have to think this whole thing over," I said. "This news is a tremendous surprise – and a shock."

"Give me a call when you digest it all," Danny said. "I'm here on days all week. And once more, Frankie, let me tell you how sorry I am. I knew you had a lot of bad breaks in this life. You didn't need this."

"Any idea who did it?"

"Unfortunately, no," he said. "She was shot at close range with a .357 caliber weapon. No bullet matches so far."

"Who the hell would want to kill my mother?" I asked.

"No clues yet. No motive yet. It's still a mystery. Hey, when you come back I still have your bicycle sitting in my garage waiting for you."

My bike! Danny was pulling out all the stops to lure me back. I disconnected the call after promising him to get in touch again soon and I mulled over the conversation. Danny *seemed* to be totally on the up and up. But was he so good that he was able to conceal his true knowledge about me and all the other murders? Was he just trying to get me to return to New York under the pretext of burying my mother, just to slap the cuffs on me? Or was he really concerned about me as he had always been ever since I met him when I was nine years old?

That evening I called Mommy and asked her about any more sightings of strangers. She told me she hadn't been out and about much today as she had a ton of papers to grade. She said, "During my walks from the convent to the school, I didn't notice anyone I didn't know."

"That's good news," I said. "Maybe those strangers were there for a purpose entirely unrelated to me and you."

"Probably," she said. "I feel better about it now."

"Good. I'll meet you tomorrow when you leave school."

"That's a good idea, Frankie. We can take a walk and then I can change into street clothes for our dinner date."

"Okay, Mommy. I'll be there around three."

I was pretty much convinced that the suspicious people Mommy observed had nothing at all to do with me, especially after my conversation with Danny Boyland. I breathed easier and smiled in anticipation of dinner tomorrow with my new found real mother and the planning we would do for our new life together.

• • •

Friday afternoon arrived and I had shaved my head, trimmed my beard and dressed in navy blue slacks, white dress shirt and light-blue checked blazer. My black penny loafers sported a bright shine as I left my rented room and got into my car for the short drive over to St. John of the Cross.

I arrived a half hour early and sat unobserved in my car from a vantage point where I could observe the entire grounds. Using binoculars I scanned the school, the church, the convent, the maintenance sheds and all the grounds in-between them. I noticed no suspicious persons or anything else out of the ordinary. When I observed activity at the school – the first students were beginning to leave the building – I got out of my car, settled my .40 caliber automatic firmly into my belt at the rear of my slacks, and headed toward the school.

CHAPTER TWENTY-NINE

Danny

On Friday afternoon just when we were all beginning to feel that this would be another day that Frankie wouldn't show, the radio in the car in which I was sitting with Spider crackled and Mike Havlek said, "All units, I'm watching a gray Chevy near the front of the parking lot. It's been there about ten minutes and the driver has not left, but seems to be doing what I'm doing – observing with binoculars."

"Ten-four, Mike," I said. "Let's all sit tight until he makes a move – and Mike, any description of him?"

"No, Danny, I can just make out the back of his head. He seems bald. Was Frankie bald?"

"Not the last time I saw him," I said. "And he has a head of hair that looked as if it would never leave him."

Fifteen minutes later Havlek was back on the radio and said, "Subject now leaving his car. He is bald, but has a full black beard. Height and weight appear to be in line with those of Chandler."

"Okay, guys, this could be it," I said, "everyone out of their cars and begin to converge on the campus. Make sure you switch to walkie-talkie mode."

They all acknowledged me. Spider and I, along with six others, came slowly toward the campus from the four points of the compass. Sam Hervell was the next to break the silence saying, "I got him. He's walking directly across the campus toward the school."

Manny Perez chimed in and said, "Shit, there's a bunch of kids piling out of there."

"Everyone lay back," I said. "Let's see where he goes, and let's hope those kids get out of there fast."

"They will," Sam said. "It's Friday afternoon."

Sam was right about that and five minutes later, with all the kids gone, we watched as Frankie greeted a nun with a big hug, no doubt Sister Audrey LaSalle, his long lost mother. They began strolling toward the middle of the park-like grounds, arm in arm, happy smiles on their faces. Jesus, I thought, how many times has this poor kid ever been happy in his tragic life? I got on the radio and said, "Okay guys, this is it. Let's take him. Who's directly in front of him?"

"Me and my partner," Mike Havlek said.

"Go right at him," I said, "and the rest of us will close fast from the other three compass directions. No matter which way he runs we'll have him. And remember, he is no doubt armed. All acknowledge."

When all four ten-fours came in, I said, "Okay, move!"

Frankie spotted Havlek's team coming right at him, and despite Mike's shouted warning of "Freeze!" he disengaged his arm from his mother, shoved her to the ground, turned around and ran toward the school – right into the approaching team of Manny Perez and Queenie Pearson. He pulled a gun out and exchanged a few shots with Manny and Queenie and made it to the school when they were forced to dive for cover. It seemed no one got hit during the exchange. We all caught up to Manny and Queenie and verified they were okay. From a previous study of the campus layout we knew the buildings were all connected via underground tunnels. But did Frankie know that? Or would he shortly discover that?

The tunnels connected five buildings – the school, the church, the convent, the priest's residence and the largest maintenance building. I'm sure everyone thought of the potential hostage situations as we split up to cover the buildings. Spider and I further split to cover the two buildings that we figured were occupied by the least number of people. Spider took the maintenance building and I headed for the church.

Gun down, I slipped into the church through a side door and closed it behind me. The afternoon sun, slanting through the stained-glass windows, provided adequate lighting as I peeked from behind a marble pillar at the gloomy interior of the church. All the pews were empty. I heard no sounds or movement. There were two confessionals, one on each side of the aisle. I moved up the right side and checked that one. Empty. I moved toward the back of the church and checked the two restrooms in the vestibule. Both empty. Back down the left aisle toward the other confessional. Empty. I was moving fast. I didn't figure Frankie to be here at all. Most likely he had a nun hostage in the convent and my presence would be better served there. But I had to finish the search, just in case. I would check the offices adjacent to the altar, then the choir loft and finally the basement. Then I'd move through the tunnel to join the others.

The first office door I opened was the priest's changing room. Unoccupied. A door to a small kitchen stood ajar and I pushed it fully open and peered in. A hand grabbed my arm and whirled me around. Frankie Chandler stood there pointing a gun at my face. My gun was pointed directly at his belly. "Danny," he said.

"Hello, Frankie," I said.

"Are you going to shoot me, Danny?"

"No, Frankie. Are you going to shoot me?"

"No, but I should. How else am I going to get away?"

"Let's talk about it," I said. "Let's sit at the table and talk about it."

We groped our way over to the table, eyes locked, neither one of us lowering our guns. I sat with my back to the door and he sat directly across from me. We were no more than thirty inches apart. "I don't like to talk with a gun pointed at me," I said.

"Neither do I," he said. "Put yours down."

"You first, Frankie," I said with a smile.

"You first," he responded.

I thought for a moment and then said, "Sure, Frankie." I laid the gun down near the center of the table. He looked surprised and laid down his Glock next to my Glock.

"What now, Detective Boyland?"

"You surrender to me. Nobody gets shot."

"And exactly what am I surrendering for?"

"Murders. A lot of murders in California. And my murder case – your mother, Angela Chandler."

"So, you knew all along. You knew everything while we spoke on the phone. And you acted so cool, as if you knew none of it. Great acting job."

"Experience, Frankie."

"Okay, I surrender and I die anyway by lethal injection. You don't have to shoot me and your conscience is clear."

"You won't die at all. New York and California have both abolished the death penalty once again. And as far as my conscience concerning you, Frankie, it will never be clear. I'm sorry, Frankie, I'm sorry for what I did to you."

"What do you mean?"

"Society failed you, Frankie, and I personally failed you. I thought seriously of taking you in – adopting you – when Angela took off. But I chickened out. I had a baby on the way and I didn't want the responsibility of raising a ten year old, too."

"Jesus," Frankie whispered wiping a tear form his eye.

"It gets worse," I said. "I knew from day one that Angela Chandler was not your real mother, and I chose not to tell you for what I then thought were good reasons."

Frankie stared at me, anger flashing through his eyes, as he absorbed my revelations. He said, "If you had told me…"

"If I had told you maybe you wouldn't have killed all those women. Maybe you wouldn't be a wanted serial killer – a serial killer created by my stupidity. Go ahead, pick up your gun and blast away. I deserve it."

"Danny, I would never kill you. No matter what you just told me, you're one of the only people in my lousy life who ever showed me any decency. You cared for me. You saved my bicycle for me. You still have it you told me."

"Yeah, Frankie, I do, and I always keep it clean and shiny. I guess that lessens my guilt a little bit."

"Tell me again why you didn't tell me about Angela."

"You were nine years old and I didn't want to crush your hopes that your mother would someday return."

"I can understand that."

"Okay, but when you came out of the Navy, that's when I should have told you."

"I know I asked about her, but I remember it was casually and it was before my search for her became an obsession. How could you have known what would happen?"

"I'm a goddamn Detective, that's how I should have known. I'm supposed to understand human nature better than the average Joe."

"What's done is done," Frankie said. "The question on the table is still what do we do now?"

Before I could answer that – not that I had an answer – Mike Havlek's voice came over my earpiece. I pointed to it and put my finger to my lips. Havlek said, "How about a status update? Spider first."

Spider said he was halfway through his building and should be completed in about fifteen minutes."

"Danny?" Havlek said.

"Same here," I said looking at Frankie and pushing the talk button on my lapel radio. "Almost halfway done. Probably another ten minutes."

After getting everyone's status, Mike said that when we were done, assuming Frankie wasn't located, we should all gravitate to the convent the search of which was only fractionally completed due to its many rooms and potential hostage situations. He also said that he requested assistance from the Southampton Town and Village Police Forces who we had previously notified to standby, and they were sending twenty officers to assist us.

"So, Danny, as I said, what now?"

"Same answer. Surrender to me."

"I can't do that. For the first time in my life I have a chance at real happiness. I want that chance. Goddammit! I deserve that chance!"

"You know," I said with a smile, "when I saw you and your mother walking arm in arm across the grass I had an urge to get on the radio and call the whole thing off. 'Guys,' I wanted to say, 'let's leave these two people alone. They have surely suffered enough.'"

"But you didn't, did you?"

"No. I'm a cop, and you are a serial killer."

"Which may have been caused by you as you recently told me."

"Okay, you won't surrender to me. What's your plan?"

"Wait the twenty minutes and leave. I'll sneak out after dark."

"Won't work," I said.

"Why not?"

I told him what Havlek said about all the extra cops. "Frankie, none of us are leaving until you are found. This church will get searched again and again."

"You mentioned you were concerned about hostages. Suppose I take a hostage?"

"A nun?"

"No, Danny. You."

"I'm listening," I said.

"We walk out of here together, my gun pointed at your head. Your buddies produce my mother to join us. We get in my car, and with you driving, leave the scene. After we're a safe distance away I let you out and disappear with Mommy to parts unknown."

"Then what?" I asked.

"What do you mean? We're gone. Free. Escaped."

"What happens when Mommy finds out you, her darling long lost son, is a multiple murderer? This is going to be all over the TV and the papers. And now she'll be wanted too for aiding and abetting a felon. How long do you think you'll last out there before you're both hunted down and shot to shit like Bonny and Clyde?"

"Even a few days of happiness will be worth it," he said.

"Okay, then," I said. "I'm game. Let's do it."

"Wait a minute," he said. "Let me think this over a bit more."

About ten seconds later the lights went out – *my* lights. I felt a brief pain in the back of my head and a fleeting sense of déjà vu – then nothing.

• • •

I woke up with a pounding headache. My face was on the table. When I opened my eyes I saw a puddle of blood spreading out beneath my face. I blinked a few times and began to raise my head, fighting the pain. I lightly touched the back of my head and my fingers came away sticky with blood. Frankie's gun was gone, my gun was gone – and so was Frankie. What the hell had happened?

MOMMY, MOMMY

I staggered over to the sink and washed the blood from my nose which felt as if it were broken. I splashed cold water all over my face and then turned to try to see the back of my head in the small mirror. I couldn't see the wound but my suit jacket collar and shoulders were heavily soaked with blood. I reached for my radio when my earpiece came to life with the sound of Sam Hervell's voice screaming, "There he is! Now!"

The radio went dead and I heard several gun shots from outside the church, but at some distance away. I staggered out the front door of the church shielding my eyes from the brilliant sunshine. A lot of people were running in the direction of the convent including a few uniformed police officers. I followed the crowd and when they stopped I elbowed my way to the front and saw the rest of my team. They all stared, guns still drawn, at a wooden bench in front of them. Sister Audrey LaSalle sat there weeping. In her arms she held her son, Frankie Chandler, several bullet holes apparent in his head and body. There was no doubt he was dead. Suddenly Audrey cried out with a long, howling wail and then she screamed out, "You murderers! Look what you have done! You killed my only son! My baby! O, My God!

The heat, the pounding in my head, the pitiful sight in front of me assaulted my brain and I fell to the ground, almost unconscious. Noticing me for the first time, Spider rushed to my aid and sat me up. The police began dispersing the crowd and I noticed Allison Hayes snapping pictures. After Spider looked me over he said, "Jesus, you're a mess. What the hell happened to you anyway?"

"Damned if I know, partner," I said.

CHAPTER THIRTY

Allison

When I saw the appearance of twenty uniformed Southampton police officers double-timing it onto the grounds, I dialed Mike Havlek's cell phone and asked what was going on. He told me he was busy and to continue sitting tight where I was. He said he'd call me when he had something to report. Give me a break! I wasn't *sitting* anymore. I grabbed my Minolta and pocket recorder and double-timed myself right into the middle of the action.

I got the scoop and my pictures. They took Frankie Chandler to the morgue. They took Danny Boyland to the hospital. They took Sister Audrey away in handcuffs. I was invited to the meeting at the Nassau Homicide squad set for ten o'clock the following morning. I headed back to my office to print my pictures and finish the story I had been working on for weeks. But I couldn't really finish it until after the wrap-up. There were still a few unanswered questions, the main one being what the heck happened to Danny Boyland?

• • •

A tired-looking Danny Boyland, with fresh bandages on his broken nose and the rear of his shaved scalp sporting ten ugly stitches, listened with the rest of us as Agent Mike Havlek related his interview with Sister Audrey LaSalle at the Suffolk County Jail the previous afternoon and evening. "When the first shots were fired and everyone scattered for cover," he said, "Sister Audrey saw Frankie head for the school after he pushed her to the ground. She immediately went to another entrance, found him and showed him the way down to the connecting tunnels. Before she came back upstairs she saw him head in the direction of the church and priest's residence. She made her way to the convent and locked herself in her room, expecting us to come crashing through it at any minute.

"When nothing happened in the next few minutes she slipped out of her room and started looking for Frankie following his path through the tunnel into the church. When she got in the vicinity of the altar she heard voices coming from the back of it. She snuck up to the kitchen and saw you, Danny, talking with Frankie. Without hesitation she picked up one of those huge brass candlesticks that were standing in her vicinity and whacked you over the head."

"She's got a mean swing," Danny said.

"After you went down," Havlek continued, "she grabbed your Glock and she and Frankie ran through the tunnel and exited from the maintenance building which was nearest to Frankie's car. However, they were observed by your partner, Spider Webb, and a couple of uniformed cops. The foot pursuit began and Frankie, using your gun as well as his own, decided to shoot it out with us near the west end of the campus. Of course he was overmatched and went down as several slugs hit him."

"And just as he was falling into his mother's arms I arrived on the scene," I said. "Sister Audrey collapsed onto a bench cradling Frankie in her arms. And I got the picture."

I produced a full-color 8 x 10 snapshot and held it up for all to see and they all immediately saw what I had captured – a modern *Pieta*. A woman in full clerical garb bent over her dead son, weeping. The resemblance to the famed sculpture by Michelangelo of Mary and her dead son, Jesus, was startling. There were a few moments of silence as everyone stared at my picture then Danny said, "There's no way I can follow through on the assault charge against this poor woman."

"Mike, how did she react when you told her the true story of Frankie Chandler?" Lieutenant Veltri asked.

"At first she refused to believe it, but we finally showed her enough evidence to convince her. The poor woman is suffering a tremendous amount of guilt, as you can well imagine."

"I'm heading back to the office to prepare my first article for tomorrow's paper," I said. "And this picture will be on page one."

"We're having a press conference at headquarters at four this afternoon," Veltri said. "We have to keep your competitors informed, too."

"Allison," Mike Havlek said, "After the press conference will you have some time to have a drink and maybe dinner with me?"

"I'd love to, Mike," I said and then realized the squad pervert, that bastard Detective Bernie Gallagher, was leering at us with his patented lewd grin. "Does Lois Lane have a thing going with Superman? Be careful Lois, the Man of Steel might have a dick of steel. Could hurt."

"Up yours, Bernie," I said, "with a steel baseball bat."

At least Bernie had reduced the gloomy mood in the squad room with his comment, but not by much.

My photo of Sister Audrey and Frankie did appear on page one the next day along with the first installment of a planned seven to eight part series titled, "The Short, Tragic Life of Frankie Chandler," and it would be nationally syndicated.

True to his word, Danny Boyland did not press assault charges against Sister Audrey. Unfortunately, this proved to be a mistake – she hanged herself the next day in her room at St. John's. Tragedy upon tragedy, but I now had another installment to add to the series and my editor assured me a Pulitzer Prize was "in the bag."

Although I consider myself a tough reporter, this whole Frankie Chandler case had gotten me depressed. Why should my success depend on someone else's downfall? But I guess that's the way of the world and my mood lightened a bit as I stepped into the shower. Things would be better in a couple of hours. They had to be – I had another date with Superman.

• • •

The phones rang off the hook at the *Chronicle* right after the morning edition hit the stands with its half-page picture of the dead Frankie Chandler in his mother's arms. I was inundated with requests for interviews from all the major networks, major news weekly magazines and cable news channels, all of which I politely declined until the series was over. I still had a lot of background work to research – I had to get the facts to detail the *tragic* part of Frankie's short life.

I flew to Los Angeles with Mike Havlek and he introduced me to the members of the Task Force out there, and I interviewed them about their search for the serial killer. I also interviewed Frankie's employers at the computer shop where he worked and took photos of the store and the outside of the apartment where Frankie had lived. I was able to talk with many of the women who Frankie had visited during his search for Angela. They had come forward when they read the story of his death in the *Los Angeles Times*. And I got the same story from everyone who had met and interacted with him – a bright, handsome young man surely destined for a successful life. A serial killer? No way. Never in a million years.

When we were finished in L.A., Mike flew back to his home base in Quantico and I flew back to New York. After putting the finishing touches on another two installments of my series to run in the next few days, I drove upstate to the State School for Boys and interviewed the headmaster, Mr. Eglund, who was now approaching retirement age. Eglund told me nothing I had not already known, and when I pressed him on the sodomy issue, either at his school or at the various foster homes Frankie had been in, he claimed total ignorance of such *awful* occurrences, acting horrified that I would even bring up such a *terrible* subject.

At the Hammond's farm I fared no better. Jethro Hammond refused to let me speak with his current crop of four foster children claiming "they aren't even the same ones who lived here when the Chandler boy was here." He also refused to give me the names of the children who *were* there at that time citing privacy concerns. "Maybe Eglund will give the names to you," he said, "and if there's nothing else you want to ask, we'll say good-bye."

The entire interview took place at their front door which he now closed in my face. Mrs. Hammond, who had stood behind her husband, never said a word, and all Jethro had told me was that Frankie was there only a short time and he returned him to the Home after the fire in the barn. He would elaborate no further.

My next stop at the Jonas farm proved to be a waste of time also. Vicky Jonas had remarried not too long after the untimely death of her husband. She told me she had to return Frankie to the Home after Harold's death because she needed an older man to help her run the farm. She said, "I really hated to lose him, he was such a nice, handsome boy, but I really had no choice." The way she said it with a wistful, sultry voice made my reporter's instincts wonder what had on gone on when Frankie was here, but no more information was forthcoming from the glamorous Vicky Jonas.

I located Margaret Ryan, now Mrs. Margaret Anderson, happily married with a two-year old child and another on the way. And of all of Frankie's trials and tribulations his brief time with the Ryan's was the most heart rending. It was his only real chance at happiness during his entire childhood, and it was crushed by the untimely and unexpected death of Mike Ryan, Margaret's father. Margaret related the story of her all too brief time with Frankie, and she finished saying, "I almost had another brother once again." She then burst into tears – and so did this hardened crime reporter.

I called Wally Mason and Pam Saunders, but they could add little to what I already knew from Danny and their case files. Navy personnel could give me no more pertinent information other than Frankie had an unblemished record during his four years of service and received an honorable discharge. I finished typing the next to the last installment of my series and looked up to see a messenger drop a big bouquet of red and white roses on my desk. I inhaled their sweet fragrance as I read the card – *Hey, Lois, I miss you. When can I get to see the ace investigative reporter again? Love you, Superman.* Two dozen roses plus those last two important words – *Love you*. Wow!

I called Mike right away and thanked him for the flowers and promised I would fly down to D.C. to be with him as soon as I finished the last of the series in a couple of days. "Terrific," he said. "Let me know exactly when you're coming in and I'll pick you up at Reagan airport and I'll reserve a good restaurant for dinner."

"Sounds great," I said. "Oh, could you reserve a motel for me for a couple of nights, too?"

"I was thinking you might like to stay with me at my place? It will save you a few bucks."

"Only if you plan to treat me real super, Superman."

"Yes, indeed, Miss Lane. That's exactly what I plan to do."

• • •

I finished up the series as planned and it was a tremendous success and syndicated in hundreds of newspapers including all the biggest ones. I did all the TV and magazine interviews I could stand and leafed through the dozens of job offers I had received since the story first hit. I selected the one from the *Washington Post* to pursue, of course, because that was where my future husband lived and worked. I was at the peak of my professional career and personal life, but one thing kept bothering me – Danny Boyland. The Chandler case had affected him deeply and I couldn't get him out of my mind as I winged my way to Washington. Frankie's blue bike, which featured prominently throughout my series, still rested in Danny's garage, a constant reminder of the guilt he felt over Frankie's life and death. I promised myself to call him, and have Mike call him, regularly to see how he was doing. And we would invite him and several other Homicide Squad detectives to our wedding, excluding the lecherous Bernie Gallagher. Bernie's last words to me when he found out Mike and I were to be married were, "Hey, Lois, you should get a big horseshoe magnet and place it around your snapper. That way the Man of Steel with the dick of steel can't possibly miss the entrance to the promised land."

Some things just never change.

CHAPTER THIRTY-ONE

Danny

Although I managed to attend the wrap-up session the morning after the death of Frankie Chandler, I then took the next few days off to allow my wounds to heal – and I don't just mean the broken nose and split head. I mean the psychological wounds, some of which were self-inflicted, that I sustained over the course of the investigation. Allison Hayes had certainly titled her series appropriately, with *tragedy* being the key word. Tragedy heaped upon tragedy in this whole lousy case from the moment Frankie was born, to his death at our hands, and right through to Ellen Weston's suicide.

My wife, Tara, was a great help during this time helping me assuage my guilt, showing me the futility of second-guessing myself about my actions during the case and, of course, being there and loving me. Occasionally, I would go into our garage and remove the tarp from Frankie's bike and stare at it awhile, or oil it or wipe it down. It was still in pristine condition – after all, it hadn't had much use, had it? I figured I'd give it away to a charity for some needy kid – but just not now.

A week later I was back in the office and told the boss I was ready to get back in the action and catch cases again. I called Allison and she answered her cell phone informing me she was down in D.C. "Are you with Superman," I asked.

"You bet," she said. "We were in Los Angeles a few days to wrap things up and get a few interviews for my series."

"It's great so far," I said. "I hope it gets you the Big Prize."

"Thanks, Danny, and how are you doing?"

"Okay, I guess. I'm back to work, but it's going to be a long time before I get over Frankie Chandler."

"I know. It was a real tough one."

"At least one good thing came out of this though - you and Superman. I hope things really last with you two."

"Thank you, Danny. I do, too."

"Well, say hello to Mike Havlek for me."

"Sure, I'll be seeing him later."

"Tell him, despite being a lousy Fed, he's a good investigator and a good guy."

Allison laughed and said, "I'm sure he'll appreciate that, Danny Boy. Good-bye."

• • •

Two weeks later my physical wounds were all nicely healed up and I was relaxing in the office waiting for a good case to come my way. The phone rang on Spider's desk, and after a few seconds of conversation, I heard him say, "Who are you again?"

Spider had raised his voice a bit which caused me to look across at him. His eyes were wide and he said, "Hold on, I think

MOMMY, MOMMY

he's still in the office." He then put the call on hold and looked at me shaking his head.

"What's up, partner?" I asked.

"Guy on the phone wants to talk to you, but I'm not sure you want to talk to him."

"Why not? Who is he?"

"Says his name is Patrick. Patrick Boyland. Says he's your son."

I was stunned, to say the least. I took a deep breath and punched the blinking light on my phone. "Detective Boyland here," I said.

"Dad?"

"Patrick?"

"Yes, it's me."

"I guess you can understand I'm really surprised hearing your voice," I said.

"Yeah, I guess so."

"Is something wrong, Pat? Can I help you with something – anything?"

"Something's very wrong, but I don't think you can help. Mom's dying. She has cancer."

"Oh, my God. Is it very bad?"

"What they call Stage Four. It's her pancreas. I figured it was the right thing to let you know."

"Thanks, Pat. I gather you're doing this on your own?"

"Yeah, Mom didn't want you to know. I overheard her discuss it with Grandma and Grandpa and they agreed."

"I understand," I said. "I guess you all still hate me for what I did, but I appreciate the call."

"Uh, Dad?"

"Yes?"

"I'd like to see you. I want to talk with you. No one else has to know."

"Sure, Pat. When can I come down there?"

"How about this weekend?"

"I'll drive down Friday afternoon and meet you Saturday morning. You pick the place and send me an e-mail with directions, okay?"

"Okay, let me have your address."

I gave Pat my e-mail address and we hung up. I said, "Goodbye, I love you." He said, "So long."

What a turn of events! I had a lot to think about in the next few days.

• • •

When I had last attempted to visit Patrick and Kelly they were both under ten years old and refused to go with me when I got there. Their mother had successfully turned them against me. I guess I couldn't blame her, but then again I *was* their father.

Although Jean cashed my support and alimony checks she "returned to sender" all my correspondence to Patrick and Kelly. On their birthdays and for Christmas I sent them a card with a check in it. I wrote that I loved them and to buy whatever they wanted. But of course they never got them, and I'm sure Jean never told them of their arrival before she sent them back to me. So to say I was surprised – shocked was a better word – when Patrick called me was the understatement of the century.

When Patrick sent me the directions to a park near his home where we would meet, I decided to press him on why he wanted to see me. I detected something in his tone of voice when we had spoken on the phone, something troubling him other than just his mother's illness. "Okay, Pat," I typed. "I'll be there. Is there anything you'd like to know, or ask, before I get there?"

He responded right away and he was obviously more comfortable with a keyboard than with a telephone. He said, "I have a situation in my life that your past experience with Niki Wells may help me understand. Oh, by the way, I read the whole series about your case with Frankie Chandler. It was in the main Roanoke newspaper which we get delivered. Very sad."

I responded, tapping away with two fingers. "Yes, it was a sad and tragic case. Pat, I kept a lengthy journal about the Niki Wells affair. How about I send it to you and you can read it before I get there? It may help with your situation. Or will someone intercept it to prevent you from getting it?"

"School's out. I'll be home when it comes. Grandma and grandpa are here with us most of the time and they wouldn't take anything – I hope – that was addressed to me. Not like Mom did."

So he knew what Jean had done! I told Pat I would send the journal out this afternoon with guaranteed over-night delivery. He responded, "Thanks, Dad. See you Saturday."

I had talked this whole thing over with Tara. She agreed that she not accompany me to Virginia. "It's best you keep this first meeting with him strictly one on one."

"My kids have to find out sooner or later I married again," I said.

"Patrick already knows. He probably told Kelly, too."

"Huh?"

"You said Patrick read Allison's series, right?"

"Yeah."

"She mentioned in there somewhere, maybe the fourth installment, that Detective Boyland was married to Detective Brown."

"You're right! I remember that."

"How old is Patrick now?" she asked.

"Fourteen, close to fifteen."

"When you drive down, take the Highlander and put Frankie's bike in the back. It would make a great gift for your son."

I suspected Tara had another motive for getting rid of that bike, but I wisely kept my mouth shut saying only, "Great idea. Thanks."

• • •

Patrick and I met as scheduled at ten o'clock Saturday in a small park smelling of new-mown grass on a warm late spring morning. I noticed he had my journal tucked under his arm, and as he approached closer, I was struck by how tall he had grown and how much he resembled me. "Hello, Pat," I said extending my hand.

He did not hesitate to reach out and take it giving me a firm grip and saying, "Hi, Dad."

We sat on a bench in the shade with about three feet between us. I said, "How's your mom doing?"

"Not good," he said. "Maybe only a few weeks left."

"I truly feel bad for her, and you and Kelly, too. Unfortunately, sometimes life is not fair."

He just nodded and then said, "I read your journal. It was some story and it helped me understand you much better, and why you did what you did."

"Did it also help with your, uh… situation?"

"Yes, because I did an awful thing, too. And now I'm paying for it just like you."

"Pat, what awful thing could you have done that was as bad as my actions?"

"I had a great girlfriend, Jamie Cunningham was her name. She had long, dark brown hair, deep blue eyes, and a great smile. Dad, we were in love ever since the fifth grade and then this year, sophomore year, I ruined everything."

I saw a tear form in Patrick's left eye and start down his cheek. I said nothing and waited for him to gain his composure. He wiped the tear away and said, "One day in the hallway I locked eyes with a girl I had never seen before. She was beautiful – a tall redhead with green eyes. It was like I was hit with a hammer. I was instantly in love with her and nothing else mattered until I could get her to love me."

"Oh, boy," I said.

"Yeah, Barbara Corwin became my Niki Wells. I dumped Jamie and pursued Barbara until I caught her. We went out for most of this semester and then, three weeks ago, right before the big Sophomore Smash end-of-year dance, she dumped me for some junior jock on the football team. I was devastated. Still am."

I moved closer to Pat and tentatively put my arm around his shoulder. I said, "Maybe you got a bad gene from me. If so, I am truly sorry."

"That's about what Mom and Grandpa and Grandma said when they found out what I had done to Jamie, who has not spoken a word to me since. Mom said, 'You're turning out just like your lousy father. You disgust me.' What made it worse was that we were on the way to the hospital when she said it."

I hugged him tighter and said, "Patrick, what you did was a bad thing, but certainly not uncommon in high school love affairs. Unlike me, you didn't break any marriage vows or destroy a family. You have to try to put your broken heart, and Jamie's broken heart, into that perspective."

"I understand, Dad, but I don't know if I will ever get over this."

"Time will tell, but I believe in the future you will look back on this period with sadness, but not with tragedy."

"Thanks, Dad," he said. "I hope you're right. What I did was not as bad as what you did…"

He stopped speaking obviously realizing what he had just said. "Ouch," I said with a smile. "The truth still hurts."

"Dad, I didn't mean…"

I stopped him and said, "I don't think we have to talk about this anymore. I think we both understand our situations very well now."

"Right," he said. "Can you tell me some more about Frankie Chandler?"

"Sure," I said, and when I finished the story it was approaching lunch time. "Hungry?" I asked.

"Starved," he said as do most growing teenagers.

As we walked to my car I said, "Do you ride a bike?"

"Yeah, but it's in bad shape. It needs a new tire and the brakes are shot. That's why I had to walk here."

I popped the lift gate and motioned for Pat to look inside. "Would you like to have this one? It's in great shape."

"Is that the one in the story in the papers – Frankie Chandler's bike?"

"That it is."

"I'd love to have it, Dad. Thanks."

"What do you think your grandparents will say when they find out I was here and gave you that bike?"

"Oh, boy," he said. "They won't be happy with this. They're still piss…uh, upset over the girl thing."

"Maybe it's about time your grandparents and I had a talk about a few things. Are they home?"

"Uh, yeah. Are you sure about this?"

"Yes."

Patrick shook his head and said, "They can be grumpy and mean, you know. I hope you brought your gun. You may need it."

● ● ●

After devouring our cheeseburgers at the diner, plus two slices of pepperoni pizza for Patrick, I drove him home. When we pulled up I noticed a blond-haired girl on a swing in the side yard. And just as Patrick resembled me, Kelly was the image of her mother. So much so, that my heart skipped a beat in remembrance of the youthful beauty of my ex-wife.

When we got out of the car she came over to us and said, "Dad?"

"Hi, Kelly," I said kneeling down to her level. "How are you?"

"Not good. Mom is very sick."

"I know, Pat told me. Can you tell your grandma and grandpa that I'm here, and would like to speak with them?"

"Sure," she said and skipped up the porch steps and into the front door.

Patrick and I went up onto the porch and waited. A minute later my former father-in-law, Bill Schneider, appeared on his side of the screen door. He glared at me and said, "What the hell are you doing here?"

"Good afternoon to you, too, Bill," I said. "I'd like to talk to you and Doris."

"There's nothing to talk about," he said. "And you're not welcome inside this house – my daughter's house."

"I'd like to talk about the future of my children."

"As I said, there's nothing to discuss. You aren't getting them when Jean passes. We already discussed it with our lawyer, and we decided we will fight you in court if it takes every cent we have."

"I don't think that will be necessary," I said. "I agree it would be best for the children to remain here, with you and Doris, and with their friends, in their home and neighborhood for as long as they want."

"You do?" he said seeming to soften just a bit.

"Yes, can we talk some more?"

He considered this request for a few moments and then said, "Meet me and Doris in the backyard. Pat and Kelly, you stay in the house while we talk. It won't be long."

The kids went into the house. I walked through the side yard into the back and joined Bill and Doris sitting around a patio table. "Okay, say your piece," Bill said.

"Hello, Doris," I said. She just nodded and I did say my piece re-stating the fact that I agreed the kids would be better off remaining with them, but that I would visit more often and expected no resistance to my visits. I concluded by saying, "When Jean passes I'm coming down to pay my respects to you, and to be there for my children."

"We don't want you there," Bill said. "Jean wouldn't want you there. You ruined all our lives, you know."

"I know, and I've apologized over and over for my actions. That won't change things, but regardless I'm coming down, so get used to seeing me."

"I guess we're finished then," Bill said, getting up from the table.

"Please send Patrick and Kelly out front so I can say good-bye to them," I said.

I got the bike out of the back of the Highlander and handed it over to Pat. "I didn't have a chance to buy something for you, Kelly, so please take this," I said handing her three crisp twenty-dollar bills. "Buy something nice for yourself."

"Oh, thank you, Daddy," she said throwing her arms around me.

The three of us hugged and kissed and when I drove away from the curb I saw Patrick jump on his new bike and take off down the street with a huge smile on his face. For one brief moment he looked like a young Frankie Chandler pedaling his brand new blue bike toward happiness.

And for the first time in a long time, I smiled, too.

Acknowledgments

Thanks once more to my readers, family, friends and supporters for their continued encouragement in this sometimes discouraging adventure.

Many thanks to Vicki Rutkowsky, publisher of the Country Pointe Newsletter, and to Stephanie Bracco, President of the Country Pointe Book Club, and to all the members of the Club, for their reading time and helpful comments on my two previous *Danny Boyland* novels.

A special thanks to my daughter, Allison Arend, who did a magnificent job deciphering my longhand scratching and turning it into a beautifully typed manuscript, while also pointing out defects in the storyline which had escaped my scrutiny.

And to my wife, Lorraine, my final reader, nonsense detector and copy editor, all my thanks and love for continuing to believe in my work – you made me a believer, too.

CPSIA information can be obtained
at www.ICGtesting.com
Printed in the USA
BVOW03s1154310817
493658BV00001B/1/P